GATHERING
of the
REALM

Also by Sheryl McCorry

AUTOBIOGRAPHIES

Diamonds and Dust
(Pan Macmillan)
Stars over Shiralee
(Pan Macmillan)
Love on Forrest Downs
(Pan Macmillan)

GATHERING
of the
REALM

Naughty Sexy and Outback

SHERYL McCORRY

Shiralee Enterprises Pty Ltd

NATIONAL
LIBRARY
OF AUSTRALIA

A catalogue record for this
book is available from the
National Library of Australia

ISBN: 9780648268604 (Paperback)
ISBN: 9780648268611 (Hard Cover)
ISBN: 9780648268628 (Ebook)

Interior and cover layout: Pickawoowoo Publishing Group
Book cover concept: Tara Hatton
Cover photograph:
Kirsten Sivyer - Stockman (foreground)
Eilysh Evans - Cattle (background)

Publisher: Shiralee Enterprises Pty Ltd

Printed & Channel Distribution
Lightning Source | Ingram (USA/UK/EUROPE/AUS)

Dedicated to
The memory of my dear mother
Little Eva

Character cannot be developed in ease & quiet.
Only through experience of trial & suffering
can the soul be strengthened,
ambition inspired, & success achieved.

— Helen Keller

CHAPTER 1

A Little Bit Naughty

It was common knowledge that the gathering of the realm at Rosengarten Castle meant the start of another extremely competitive hunt season for all blue-blooded males. But there was always a little more to it than simply hunting with the hounds. For it was well known that as long as hot 'red blood' ran in the veins of the current Lord Wentworth, he and his many friends of good fortune could be guaranteed another seasonal round of evenings filled with attractive women and overflowing booze parties that came with a closeted offer of a narcotic which added more than a little spice to the orgies of the well-heeled gentlemen and their colourful mistresses.

Once again the ageing Lord Alexander Wentworth II had indulged heavily on his family's excellent whiskey supply. He and his cronies had caused havoc in the gentlemen's smoking room, and the beautifully detailed walnut whiskey cabinet, which had always held pride of place in the smoking room, was now wrecked beyond repair due to their antics. This was the one room in the Rosengarten Castle that Grand-mama, Lady Elizabeth, had once boldly and rather blazingly said to any persons who cared to listen, 'The smoking room at Rosengarten Castle was a room that no respectable lady would ever consider to enter.'

The plush red and gold autumn leaf carpet that covered the cold polished floorboards of the gentlemen's room had helped cushion a scattering of partly clad, deliriously happy and fornicating couples. The young performed as animals in the wild, and mated as though they would never experience another tomorrow – a tomorrow where many horny individuals knew that all opportunities of exploring any new faces in the district would be sadly missed as the hunt season came to a climactic end.

It was the wild 1930s, and once again the gravelled circular driveway of Rosengarten Castle of Hamfordshire England became an arena full of anticipated excitement. Ageing head butler Muldoon, it seemed, had even more power at Rosengarten Castle than his lordship, Alexander Wentworth II. It was Muldoon who had meticulously planned each nobleman's arrival so as not to allow another to infringe on one's grand entrance. The head butler took his position seriously and had worked for Lord Alexander Wentworth II of Rosengarten Castle for the past forty years – he understood intimately the intrinsic ties of many a nobleman's family.

Arriving at the castle were elegant pairs of fine thoroughbred horses, each pair pulling a buggy that carried the owner and his excited family. These buggies were followed by the more speedy and arrogant rich showing off in their modern and shiny new Bentleys. But of course the competition had begun long before the actual event with the beginning of the hunt season bringing with it a battle of male egos. These well-suited aristocratic gentlemen boldly flashed their wealth, exposing many carats of solid gold chain attached to their expensive pocket watches. Their haughty wives, daughters and over-the-top mistresses competed silently in the background, all dressed especially for the occasion by some of England's finest couture houses.

And as always, most of the people who attended the hunt on the Rosengarten Estate were the progeny of the country's finest equestrian families. Many had exceptional horsemanship, and today they would prepare to hunt with the hounds.

These annual events were looked upon as 'show time', and were always eagerly anticipated by the village folk. 'Show time' brought with it the prospect of employment for the young, who would line up in droves to willingly accept any work offered to them. Over the years Lord Alexander Wentworth II of Rosengarten had taken it upon himself to personally oversee the hiring of the many attractive young kitchen maids and groomsmen needed from the village at this special time of the year. He wanted them to be smart and attentive, although good looks were the real criteria. It was common knowledge in the local pubs and the village that many persons used this three-day event to showcase their hidden, although some would say misplaced, talent in one of England's most prestigious sporting events.

While other competitors weren't ignored for favouring a slower pace, the anticipation of skirting around the moors, or the slow stalk in the undergrowth on the pheasant shoot, was the real attraction. But for some unknown reason it was always 'the hunt and chase' of the wayward little red foxes that stirred the gentlemen farmers' testosterone levels to all-time highs. For at the end of a hectic day's hunt, with energy levels escalating, there seemed even more need for them to parade their masculinity.

Accompanying these gentlemen to the equestrian events at Rosengarten were their extremely elegant wives and far too young daughters who found this type of entertainment all rather dull and quite boring, although it did have its benefits. These fine cultured ladies passed their time away gathered in Grand-mama's elegant sun-room. It was here between their neat embroidery stitches that they often shared a titbit of colourful or sordid gossip while consuming rosehip tea and orange tea cake on some of England's finest china. The gentlemen's inconspicuous mistresses preferred the privacy of the gentlemen's library where it was possible to share an early goblet of champagne whilst they inhaled the exotic aroma of finely cut tobacco through elaborate ivory cigarette holders.

It was quite evident during this three-day event that equal numbers of the visiting male progeny looked at the hunt season from a very different perspective. Was it due to the fact that many of the evenings at Rosengarten Castle were filled with wild entertainment and the most outrageous festivities in the county? Is this why many of the seasonal contenders and their male offspring were happy to hunt out the evening's entertainment with glee? Of course this entertainment wasn't for the faint-hearted, or indeed for the eyes and ears of the participants' own womenfolk.

On this final evening of the hunt, the older and more distinguished gentlemen, the lords and lads of their own county realms, had left the tending of their wives and younger children to the ladies' personal maids and the children's devoted nannies.

Once the family frivolities were out of the way, a handful of these older gentlemen – with their dyed white hair, immaculately trimmed beards and ponderous mating rituals – would prowl the perimeter of the smoking room to winkle out any willing prey. Others, with their ageing and perspiring bodies and droopy penises, battled to achieve an orgasm as they performed their own sexual acrobatics among the empty whiskey bottles left scattered about the smoking room floor.

Disgusting creatures, flashed through an extremely shocked and shaken young James. "They're doing terrible, terrible things," the youngest grandson of Lord Wentworth II blurted out. Older brother Morgan had boasted lurid information on the so-called 'adult parties' held for men only in Grandfather's smoking room. Twelve-year-old Morgan had boasted openly to younger brother James, "When I turn fourteen, father said I will be old enough to attend the parties for 'men only'. I must learn how to entertain myself. You must remember James, it is I who will be the future heir. I will be the Lord Morgan Alexander Wentworth IV of Rosengarten Castle one day. You must not forget that, James."

Over time the constant taunts from older brother Morgan, blended with a large dose of youthful curiosity, got the better of ten-year-old James. Blond and of slight build for his age, it took all the young lad's strength to push a heavy Victorian dining chair smack-up against the smoking room door. James climbed up onto the red velvet seat and stood on tiptoe to peek through the looking glass, which gave him a bird's-eye view of the smoking room antics. What he saw bothered young James Wentworth well into his own adulthood, although at the time James was very sure in his own mind that his beloved Grandfather was not in that awful room. Therefore, James never allowed any of the scandalous gossip overheard from whispering staff to ever enter his mind, or change the depth of love he felt for Lord Alexander Wentworth II of Rosengarten Castle.

Grandfather, Lord Alexander II, was a tall, distinguished and extremely well-dressed gentleman, who always insisted his valet put extra care into his attire during the family's annual hunt with the hounds. Many of the upper-crust guests had prepared themselves well in advance before arriving from all over England to join in the festivities. Others had travelled to the property from as far away as Paris and other parts of Europe and even Africa. It was well known throughout England that the privileged Wentworth males truly followed in the footsteps of their forebears as they too were known for entertaining with the wildest and most controversial parties during any annual hunt season – something Grandfather was proud of, although the same couldn't be said of Grand-mama.

Grandfather's closet of bright paisley dinner vests, offset with gold clasps and pearl inlayed buttons, exemplified his flashy sense of style. Oozing more than his fair share of charisma, accompanied by dashingly good looks topped with a generous smattering of grey in his once jet-black hair, he had always attracted the opposite sex in droves. Yet on that night Grandfather's mind was again believed to be muddled and full of wild dreams after consuming far too much whiskey. His breathing had become hoarse and heavy, and while his ageing body had enjoyed the pounding of the ride, his wanton lust hungered for even more of the enjoyment on that last evening.

"Ride him my beautiful filly, ride the devil out of him like you've never ridden this old stallion before," Lord Alexander Wentworth II offered between frantically gulping for more oxygen to fill his fast depleting lung capacity. "Ride him extra hard my beauty," begged Lord Alexander II in a low gravelly voice. His ageing body had begun to perspire heavily as he struggled to keep his airways clear. Lord Alexander rose up from the day bed in the smoking room, and with both hands clasped firmly about the silken skin of the big bosomed, auburn-haired beauty's tiny waist, he expertly and ever so smoothly rolled his companion over and under his slowly fading manhood, then with a vengeance and as if his entire life depended on consummating this lustful act, he forcibly pushed his manhood between the extremely wet lips of his lover's pussy.

CHAPTER 2

Strength behind the Man

'Yes, it is truly wild, remote and pristine,' were the words Lord Wentworth II had used to describe the Australian Outback to his youngest grandson James. Lord Wentworth II and young James were extremely close – well, as close as a well-seasoned, and sometimes pickled old aristocrat and his youngest grandson could possibly be. But James admired and loved his Grandfather dearly, and this extreme closeness possibly contributed to young James's loneliness when his Grandfather disappeared for months on end to visit the Australian Outback. By ten years old James could just about calculate the weeks before his Grandfather's return to England.

"Grandfather has had three months away in Australia," young James had volunteered to his Grand-mama one day. It wasn't that James was complaining loudly of his Grandfather's many extensive holidays away, it was simply that he became lonely and pined terribly for his Grandfather's gruff companionship in his absence.

Days before Lord Wentworth's return to Rosengarten Castle, the excitement and anticipation would begin to build within the young James, who always looked forward to the warm summer days they shared resting together on the stone bench under the aged oak tree. The gnarly oak's enormous reach gave cool shade in the summer months to the Wentworth family ancestors buried below its roots. Now centuries later, many of the early monumental headstones were cloaked in varying shades of cool green moss, others had weathered, some were pitted by age, while the odd fifteenth-century headstone had begun to crumble over the past few years. Some still stood proudly upright in the fields of striking blue cornflowers. Each headstone was another history lesson for the young James, and he did enjoy the tales told by Grandfather who was extremely proud of his family's heritage.

On Grandfather's return to England, his stories were mainly of a far and distant continent. His amazing tales would paint vivid pictures of jagged limestone ranges and spectacular gorges fashioned by wild wind and torrential rains. He would frequently describe how these remarkable monuments often shared their evening colour with the earth and sea around them. As always in young James's mind's eye he could picture these amazing formations for himself and wished for the day to arrive when he would visit them.

The quiet peacefulness Lord Wentworth described of a billabong on his beloved 'Lonesome Downs' in the West Kimberley would be broken by the high-pitched deep-throated call of an Australian native bird. Grandfather said the Australians called the bird a brolga, a tall and elegant species with long thin legs that supported a wide wing-span. Often this magnificent creature would perform a graceful and theatrical presentation of a dance, or a corroboree, to its own concerto in the golden spinifex.

But young James Wentworth was more interested and truly fascinated by the story of the staunch and silent 'old man goanna'. Grandfather said this was a very large lizard which stood tall on its tail as it eyeballed him at waist height through the wild thick buffalo grass at Bullocka's Billabong. At the time, Grandfather said, it had never entered his mind to think that this over-freckled giant Australian lizard was about to destroy his good English tweed trousers and jacket when it took fright of him. The frightened goanna mistook Grandfather for a tree, he said. The goanna used its long toenails as claws to pull itself up the excellent tweed cloth of his trousers and jacket to where it felt safe at the top of Grandfather's thinning thatch of greying hair. How the young James loved that story and laughed out loud as he mimicked what he thought were his Grandfather's antics among the family gravestones. At times Grandfather would play-act with James and pretend to be quite indignant about it all. But it never stopped young James mimicking what he thought were Grandfather's terrified cries and reckless moves as he danced about the Australian bush trying to remove the wild reptile from his bleeding head by frantically pulling the frightened goanna by its long tail, willing it to let go of his thinning locks. James appreciated that every single hair Grandfather had left on his head at that time was very precious to him.

Then James remembered how his Grandfather's voice dropped ever so low, as if whispering a secret. "Dear me, young James," he said, "didn't your Grand-mama give me a terrible roasting when I showed her how this giant lizard had torn up my very best tweed suit." The young James laughed out loud; he had never seen his grandparents have cross words. "Yes James, your Grand-mama told me she had especially selected the very finest of the season's tweed fabric for my suits this last year. This tongue lashing reminded me of what a wonderful strong woman your Grand-mama is." For a while they both remained seated on the cold stone bench in the shade of the great oaks, with young and old travelling back to times long ago while enjoying the other's company.

The stories and the intricacies of the Australian Outback had always held a fascination for the young blue blood James Wentworth, the youngest grandson of Lord Wentworth of Rosengarten Castle. He treasured the many wild and vivid stories of the Kimberley long after Grandfather had gone. Yes, he was dead now, and that meant some things had changed. Although Grand-mama, Lady Elizabeth, was well enough and still resided with the family, much of the time since Grandfather's sudden death she spent sailing around the world on her namesake, the splendid cruise ship *Lady Elizabeth*.

Grand-mama said, 'It was unfortunate the way Grandfather had to die, but he did love hunting with the hounds, and he especially loved the steady flow of young and pretty women who came tripping through the huge wrought-iron gates of our Rosengarten Castle during the hunt season, and all eager to attend the many festivities that the annual hunt season brought with it.'

Each year the castle gates were opened to all in the Wentworth's circle of friends to attend the many cocktail parties and the grand evening ball which was known to be the most outrageous of all parties in the district. As Grand-mama grew older she couldn't wait for the morning of the Champagne Breakfast, when the disheveled guests would rise from their beds to nibble at their breakfast food before saying their final goodbyes to everyone, for the hunt season had come to an end. Only then would Grand-mama truly be able to rest peacefully.

James was rather young at the time of Grandfather's death and yet old enough to remember the day vividly. James loved his Grandfather dearly. He could never forget that particular morning when the guests were saying their final goodbyes to family and friends when suddenly a frightful and rather grey looking Muldoon came and stood solemnly under the great arch of the green and gold lounge room. Muldoon had hesitated as he slowly pulled out a huge white handkerchief from his trouser pocket, excused himself, turned his back slightly to the crowded room to clear his gravelly throat of his nervousness and then spoke softly to dear Grand-mama.

"Lady Elizabeth, may I speak to you in private, please. The matter is extremely important, madam." Muldoon seemed breathless, his rather grey complexion began to pale considerably, and his deadpan face gave nothing away as he stood in silence under the lounge room arch, hoping Lady Elizabeth would allow him to accompany her to the privacy of her sitting room before she demanded he volunteer any information at all.

"My dear Muldoon," said Grand-mama as she unknowingly arched her back while immediately holding her head higher than usual, as only a prominent matriarch could do so naturally, "you have been with the family long enough now to know that whatever has to be said can be spoken in the presence of my family." Grand-mama punctuated each point with just a few seconds of silence. Grand-mama felt in her arthritic bones there was a problem, but had no idea how it would affect her personally or the immediate family members. Was there trouble with a servant or the new cook? She hoped not, as it was terribly difficult to find an honest servant or a reasonably good cook these days.

After addressing Muldoon, Grand-mama opened her small beaded handbag and produced her rose gold lorgnette, its handle embedded with pearls and two carats of diamonds. She felt there was a serious matter to attend to here and she needed to see Muldoon's face clearly.

Grand-mama's eyes spoke volumes as she looked directly at head butler Muldoon through her lorgnette, prompting him to hurry up and get on with it. Muldoon understood Grand-mama only too well, and she wasn't one to beat about the bush, although he still felt it only right to break this terrible news to Grand-mama privately.

Then with an obvious straightening of his back, Muldoon cleared his throat again and raised his sad brown eyes as he turned to the anxious and many blank faces of Lady Elizabeth and the waiting family in front of him before delivering the news of Grandfather's sudden and unexpected death that morning.

The extended family had gathered together in the green and gold lounge room to say their final goodbyes before leaving Rosengarten Castle after another successful hunt season. Some slumbered on lounges and others sat in rather uncomfortable high-backed winged chairs. Not a word was spoken, just deathly silence as each member absorbed Muldoon's devastating news in their own way. Lady Elizabeth beckoned Muldoon to her side and demanded some answers. The manservant felt extremely uncomfortable for being put on the spot, and Muldoon asked Lady Elizabeth one more time if he could please speak with her in the privacy of her sitting room. But the family understood that dear Grand-mama was more than a cyclonic force to be reckoned with, leaving Muldoon no other choice than to get down on bended knee and whisper something in Grand-mama's right ear.

Young James remembered Grand-mama's sudden jerky movement as she squared her shoulders and sat upright and perfectly still in her winged chair, a million miles away. Then a sudden dry choking cough wracked her body as she attempted to straighten her already tidy jacket. Grand-mama began to gather herself and brushed away an imaginary wisp of silver-grey hair from her forehead, and yet, in her pale blue eyes, there were no tears.

James had seen his Grand-mama cry only once before, and that was when her favourite dressage mare, Lady Love, had to be put down due to her agonising and severe arthritis. Now after receiving the devastating news of her husband, Lord Alexander Wentworth's II death, there seemed only a distant sadness in Grand-mama's eyes.

"Yes, what a terrible, terrible shame that your Grandfather had to pass away in the middle of an unspeakable act with a nobody, or was she an unknown model, I believe," she said after some hesitation, her head bowed slightly as her voice softly faded away. There was no other way to say it but to tell the truth, she told herself. Grand-mama never minced her words, although her mixed bag of emotions was held deep within her heart. She suddenly looked pale and very tired – Lady Elizabeth had spent her entire life holding her head high while loving and living with a husband who never understood the boundaries of a real marriage. There seemed no point in hiding the facts as Lord Alexander II was well known throughout the family and district villages for his infidelities that ran a close second to his love of horses. As for Lady Elizabeth, he needed her love, her strength, and he never let her go.

Grand-mama took her time to produce a fine, crisp white handkerchief from the confines of her beaded handbag, then snapped the clasp shut rather loudly, as if shutting the door on her heart and securing for herself a little time to think over the terrible news just delivered. Raising the handkerchief, she gently patted around her eyes and along her prominent cheekbones. There were no tears, only deathly silence filled the room as Grand-mama continued to speak.

"I always felt his lordship's unfaithfulness would eventually destroy Alexander II." Grand-mama's words drifted quietly away, as did her enormous sigh.

Lady Elizabeth looked slowly across to the mass of family faces although none of their features were really registering through her haze when she spoke. Then as if grasping for an excuse of some kind, or was it possibly a muddled afterthought, she whispered more to herself than any other, "Our family doctor did mention that Alexander had a weak heart, you know."

Her voice usually strong, now trailed softly away while her mind was trying to accept the shocking news recently whispered in her ear. Grand-mama then gathered herself, and young James couldn't help but overhear the slight agitation in her voice as she spoke, as if there were no other person in the room.

"Out of all the young women who flocked to the Rosengarten Castle for the parties and events held during the hunt season, most were born with titles and position in our circle of society. Why did his lordship have to die going down on an unknown woman?"

It was obvious that Grand-mama was beginning to feel a little emotional, although it was well known 'her backbone was a rod of steel'. But now she fought to hold back her anger over the matter, or was it the sheer humiliation and shame that she understood what

Alexander's death would mean to the Wentworth family and its future heirs. Mind you, Grand-mama was outspoken at the best of times and it was widely agreed that she was the real strength behind the Wentworth men.

On day three after Grandfather's sudden death he was buried alongside his forebears. In the shadow of the old oak tree that marked the family's graveyard on the distant rise, the stone bench often used by Grandfather and James was close by. Lady Elizabeth was a stickler for correctness, and insisted the right protocol be used for all occasions – the family, including the two grandsons, would dress accordingly in black mourning attire. The family would hold their heads high and show their respect for the deceased, the once head of their noble family, Lord Wentworth II. Lady Elizabeth never let it enter her head again that Grandfather's sudden death occurred on the top of his young mistress. It didn't matter really as he was dead now anyway. Grand-mama fully understood that Grandfather was no saint, and there was certainly no chance of him rising from his coffin to sit holding her hand late at night in their bedroom, as he did when apologising profusely and begging her forgiveness for his misdemeanors one more time. Mind you, Grand-mama had since heard via Molly, her lady's maid and confidante in the castle, that 'Lord Wentworth's mistress very nearly met her maker at the same time as he.' While the lord's death was by heart attack caused from over-exertion, according to his doctor, his young mistress was also close to death from suffocation brought on by the weight of his lordship's dead body atop the model's waif-like one. But when this terrible image floated across Grand-mama's mind for the second time she allowed herself a slight smile. As strong as Grand-mama was, she also had a mischievous mind, and with her thoughts muddled and all over place, she always returned to the circumstances of Grandfather's death, only this time she felt very ashamed as she tried not to choke with laughter on her own wicked thoughts.

On the morning of Grandfather's burial, James remembered how sombre the event was for family members and friends, and how magnificent and stately his Grand-mama appeared dressed in her black morning coat. Around her neck hung three long strands of magnificent pearls, all of which were gifts from Grandfather after some extreme misdemeanor. James had never seen Grand-mama wear such a large quantity of pearls before, and he wondered, was this a celebration? He had overheard Lady Elizabeth whisper in rather strong tones to his father, the now Lord Wentworth III, as she glanced across the families surrounding the grave site: "Shame, not one of these family members was a faithful man you know, none had risen from the dead." At such a young and tender age, James wondered if this was a gentle warning to his father's errant ways? Could Grand-mama be suggesting that father begin to tidy up his own house of infidelities – and promptly. If not, was it possible he would go the same way as Grandfather? James noticed there were still no tears in Grand-mama's eyes and wished he was as strong as her. James then turned towards Rosengarten Castle, filled his lungs with the crisp morning air and thought just how majestic their family home looked bathed in the morning's glorious sunshine. Grandfather had always remarked on the excellent stonework of their home, he was proud to be the owner of Rosengarten Castle. But for now James had to fight back tears of sadness as he knew he would miss his Grandfather and their time together terribly.

It really didn't matter much to young James at that time what she-nanigans his Grandfather had got up to – no one had sat him down and quietly explained anything bad to him anyway, and in some ways he was too young to care. James decided to walk the short distance across the green undulating countryside to the castle, allowing him time away from family and friends. Time to remind himself of the stories of the Australian Outback his Grandfather had shared with him and time to reminisce. The morning's sunshine and its warmth on his back would make him feel good and bring life back to the neat stone forecourt of Rosengarten Castle once again. There, James sat quietly and let his own mind drift back over the many precious stories he and Grandfather had shared together. For twelve-year-old James this was his way of communicating with his much loved grandparent.

It was after Grandfather's death that Grand-mama began to travel, staying away from Rosengarten for longer and longer periods of time and journeying to distant places across the ocean. She said it helped to heal her painful and rather sad loss of a wonderful and sometime shameful rascal of a husband, as Grandfather had been the only true love in her Victorian life.

CHAPTER 3

Grandfather's Stories

It was Grandfather's stories that remained with James long after he was gone. Stories of vast open plains covered in a sea of wild grasses, with huge red ant mounds mimicking world famous statues, and magnificent timeworn ranges slashed in colour as if by a paint brush dipped into the depths of a rainbow. And of the great gorges, nature's way of slowing down rivers, with their spectacular high waterfalls forming deep crystal-clear water holes shielded by tall spiky livistona palms and surrounded by verdant wild ferns growing from every crevice. These water holes, or billabongs as Grandfather had referred to them, made wonderful drinking and bathing places for humans and animals. How the young and sometimes lonely James Wentworth wished he was there.

There were many stories of the million-acre cattle stations sparsely populated by man and wild beast. Also, the many large and extended families of black and white – full blood, half-caste and quarter-caste Aboriginal stock men and women, and their happy children. The beautiful little black piccaninnies were forever smiling or hanging in a dilly bag while suckling from a mother's breast as she sat astride a gentle old stock horse on the tail of a mob of quiet cattle to help her man, a stockman, drive the herd along the dry stock route to try to prevent the beasts dying from starvation in times of drought. Everyone who owned a humpy or camped on the cattle station wanted to be a part of the survival plan, he said, although it was the much younger generation who loved the action and often wagged school to help muster these great Outback properties. How young James wished he could have been there too with the Aboriginal children. The stockmen and their families formed part of one big happy station family, Grandfather had said. And when evening came around, Grandfather said, he felt he could simply push a button and the Kimberley sky opened its massive rooftop and became this huge opera. The night sky would be filled with millions of bright twinkling stars, more stars than he had ever seen before, while the muted sounds from nightfall would fade and blend into a gentle distant melody. Once Grandfather had told James that 'When you become a young man James, you must visit the Australian Outback. It will open your eyes to the rest of the world.' James never needed any prompting to visit the colonies, these were his own future plans.

When in Australia Grandfather often visited his long-standing friend Doctor Nicholls, a Heart specialist from Adelaide, South Australia. Dr Nicholls was also half owner of Lonesome Downs with Grandfather, a cattle station in the West Kimberley region of Western Australia and one of the Outback's most isolated cattle stations. Grandfather had said that he had originally met Dr Nicholls at a worldwide botanical gathering in the Adelaide Hills. It was at that time when Grandfather had first been invited to spend a holiday with the Nicholls family at their Adelaide Hills farm, 'Koowonga'. That was when Grandfather had been introduced to Mrs Nicholls, the doctor's wife. Her constant ill health had been callously brushed off by her doctor husband because he believed it was self-inflicted by her dependence on alcohol. There was also a gangly teenager who arrived home from an up-market boarding school as Grandfather was leaving for England, a rather pale quiet and tall boy called David. He was introduced to Grandfather by Dr Nicholls as 'My only son and heir, who has no interest at all in the land.'

Ever since James was a child he had always looked forward to his Grandfather's return from his Australian trips, and any news he may have on Dr Nicholl's son David, as they were the same age. James found the yarns from Grandfather's Australian trips even more interesting than the stories he brought home after the long trips he took periodically to South Africa. James knew that when his Grandfather returned to Rosengarten Castle he brought with him a Pandora's box of more fascinating stories to tell him in the evenings before his bed-time. And at twelve years old, James could hardly contain himself as he waited for Grandfather to tilt his head back and let the last drop from his one-hundred-year-old crystal glass of aged whiskey trickle down his throat and warm his larynx. Only then would the box be opened and the more interesting bedtime stories begin.

James was the younger of the two sons, and Lord Alexander Wentworth II of Rosengarten Castle realised that this young grand-son would never inherit his family title and that he would never become Lord Wentworth IV of Rosengarten Castle, unless there was some terrible illness or unexpected accident to Morgan. In some small way this thought pleased Lord Alexander II as he saw young James as the gentler of his two grandsons, and frequently asked himself, 'Did this boy really need the worry of Rosengarten and a pompous title to carry for the rest of his life?' In Grandfather's mind he blamed the family title for playing a helping hand in exposing his own infidelities in earlier times, and for the many nights he'd spent sleeping alone in the freezing cold of the Rosengarten stables.

James's brother Morgan was the elder son by eighteen months. He was born with a head of shocking black hair, looking more Spanish than English, while James was the blond Norwegian version. Both sons were born in the 1920s to Lord Alexander III and Lady Gabrielle Wentworth of Rosengarten.

Their home was the very beautiful hand-chiselled stone man-sion of Rosengarten Castle. It was built by skilled stonemasons of European descent with the help of the local folk who fashioned every facet of stone by hand until each piece was shaped and perfected to be set and rendered into the mansion's huge walls. The stone exte-rior had weathered gradually over the centuries to a delicate soft grey colour, as did the majestic granite lions mounted on either side of the grand entrance. The interior of the house had stood the test of time rather well with its muted tones and tasteful drapes. The window and doorframes of dark timber gave the boy's bedrooms a boarding school look, but the main ballroom and entrance hall were nothing short of magnificent with five crystal chandeliers hanging from soaring ceil-ings down the centre of the main ballroom. Here was a touch of class that still carried fine memories of the past, memories that stood taller than the aged oak trees that surrounded and protected Rosengarten Castle, two hours on a partly cobbled road south of London in the middle of evergreen rolling moors.

Lord Alexander Wentworth and his grandsons' lineage was one of rather noble gentle men and women who local historians could trace as far back as the fifteenth century. But that pedigree wasn't to say they were free of scandal. Whispers of their many wives, murders, mistresses and the attractive housemaids who bore a child or two out of wedlock to several of these aristocratic gentlemen over the years still circulated throughout the surrounding villages and marketplaces. It was still as if these happenings had come about only yesterday.

In the later years and for the first few years after Alexander II had passed, the castle became more commonly known for Lord Wentworth III's annual pheasant shoot and fox hunt after-parties. At these times his wife, Lady Gabrielle, would put as much distance as possible between herself and the hunting season. A refined lady with a kind and gentle soul, Lady Gabrielle, even as a child in Europe, could never bring herself to join the gentlemen as they hunted with the hounds, or attend the evening's events with her own family at the annual Hunt Ball. It was during the hunt season on the estate that she would make excuses to visit her friends in the south of France or to shop for clothing for herself around Paris – she loved Europe.

Her mother-in-law, Lady Elizabeth, Lord Alexander III's mother, would remain at Rosengarten Castle for the entire hunt season for her son's benefit, and then, when she believed her duty was fulfilled towards her son and Rosengarten, she would take her leave and her freedom to sail the high seas. She would use the excuse that 'The holiday was to indulge her arthritic body with a glorious warm summer rest somewhere in the wilds of Australia.'

Lady Gabrielle's feelings on the annual fox hunt never changed over the years, and she still felt that hunting with the hounds on the distant moors of England was nothing more than an outrageous act of cruelty. Therefore, Lady Gabrielle tried to ensure she was unavailable at Rosengarten to entertain her husband's guests during their hunting season, and it was at this particular time of the year they really did live separate lives – Lady Gabrielle refused to bow to society for society's sake.

Of course, Lord Alexander Wentworth III had a reputation from a very early age for concluding the hunting season at Rosengarten with wild after-shoot parties, parties the locals believed bordered on bohemian at times, while also labelling him a 'true chip off the old block'. A smattering of the locals had served as housemaids, butlers and stable hands, and talked of Lord Alexander as if he were a bit of a cad. The staff often gossiped and giggled in the hallways, others whispered among themselves that these parties were really more like wild orgies, and they didn't like the fact that they were always held at the time of the year when Lord Alexander's wife, Lady Gabrielle, accompanied by her lady-in-waiting, took her annual holiday to France, or to the other side of the continent. Little did they know these trips away from Rosengarten were planned by Lady Gabrielle herself.

Of course it wasn't long after one of these outrageous parties that rather lewd stories began to circulate throughout the district. Late one evening the staff couldn't help but overhear the loud moaning and breathless grunting, wild laughter and female squeals of delight which reverberated from the stables throughout the boozy night. Once, young Preston, a new employee – a proud but retarded sty boy – reported that the pigs had broken out of their sty that evening and he believed they were rooting up the new stable complex. Much to the dismay and embarrassment of the livery staff, who raced into the dark stables with lanterns in hand to check the situation out, they were met by the sight of a gravitating and sweating threesome of fashionable people hard at it.

"My lord," whispered one young stable boy who found it hard to contain his excitement at such a scene of partially naked and writhing sweating bodies caught in a tangled mass of arms and protruding legs. "Is this what they call an orgy...or a fornicating mess?" The stable boy, whose eyes were bulging and who daren't turn his head in case he missed something, was shocked to notice two fine feet still encased in elegant silver evening slippers. Even the light of the stable's lamp wasn't enough to alert these busy folk that they had company.

"Quiet please," commanded the older livery foremen in a deep authoritarian tone. "I don't need a running commentary, just shhhh and be quiet lad. We must get out of here before we're caught and accused of spying in places where staff members are not invited. Dear me...dear me, dear lord forgive me for walking in on such a mess," the old foreman kept mumbling to himself. Now he too was in need of a very stiff drink.

With that the senior livery hand gave the young lad a rough push on the shoulder to help break the trance-like grip the scene before them had on the young fellow, "And please do hurry up and do not ever speak of this incident again."

"Yes Sir…I mean no Sir…I will never speak of this again Sir," stuttered the young stable hand as he felt his way back out of the stable complex in the dark, followed closely by his stumbling and floundering livery foreman who was even more shook up than his much younger staff member. And now the young lad was feeling somewhat embarrassed as he battled to hide a huge first erection of his own.

The lords and ladies of high society, while making good use of the fresh straw in the stables, thought nothing of destroying their beautiful and extremely expensive gowns and suits, or even gave a thought to the livery's expensive saddle blankets that were frequently used to protect their delicate and pearly white bottoms from becoming pin cushions from the sharp straw needles at these raunchy times.

Lord Alexander's friends, seemingly all cut from the one cloth, would devour an enormous amount of expensive champagne, aged whiskey and gin, as he himself did. Quite often at these events Alexander's old uncle would be present. A well-suited and balding aristocrat – who used his pure silk ruby cravat as a sweat band and handkerchief while trying in vain to prop himself up in a chair – he would try to show there was still some respectability left in him even as he made lecherous advances towards several of society's well-to-do and overly endowed young ladies. That was until he snorted far too much cocaine from the whiskey tray and was found dead under the table. It seemed Lord Wentworth's parties at that time frequently made newspaper headlines, usually for all the wrong reasons. It was while Lady Gabrielle was holidaying in Paris that the staff of Rosengarten Castle made sure that these local gossip papers were used for lighting the kitchen stove and the mansion's many elaborate fireplaces, and staff had all the fires blazing. Muldoon, Lord Alexander's personal butler, believed, her ladyship didn't need to be bothered by the shenanigans of her often wayward husband for there was very little one could do for him anyway.

CHAPTER 4

Gabrielle the French Beauty

Lady Gabrielle was certainly not blind to her husband's foolish-ness, as she called his unfaithfulness to her. He wasn't always as dishonorable, she would muse to herself, while remembering the early days of their marriage filled with laughter and passion and afternoon cocktail parties, and yes, they were the good times. But sadly, that all seemed to have changed after her second son, James, was born. Complications in the latter part of her pregnancy with high blood pressure and further complications from a massive haemorrhage led to near-death experiences during the home birth for both James and herself. This left Lady Gabrielle traumatised, lifeless and terribly unwell for many a long month after James's birth at Rosengarten. It was during this time Gabrielle made a silent pledge to herself that she would never again carry another child. As much as she loved her children, Gabrielle firmly believed it was really all too much, and took too heavy a toll on her health.

Of course it didn't help matters that while still suffering ill health, Lady Gabrielle, on deciding to walk the huge corridors of Rosengarten for a little exercise on a wet and dreary day, overheard a couple of young and rather inexperienced housemaids gossiping about Lord Alexander's escapades in the livery with one of their colleagues.

This terrible incident had happened while she had been near death and in bed resting after battling to give birth to their second son. Immediately on hearing this gossip, her frail body became engulfed in panic, her breathing became shallow, followed by a burning sensation, then unbearable pain. Her appearance a ghostly white, and with her head down in shame, she turned around and fumbled her way back down the long cold and dimly lit corridor to find her own suite of rooms again. This was the only place where Gabrielle felt she could hide herself from the shame and humiliation of what her husband had brought upon her once again. To hear this terrible gossip of her husband 'having it off with a new servant' was about all Gabrielle could handle at that time, and the thought of 'doing away' with herself was very much on her mind. It was during her healing period that her doctor had recommended that it would probably be wise for Gabrielle to remain in her own suite of rooms and not sleep with her husband just yet, as she and baby James needed peace and quiet and some time to rest and convalesce. Her doctor's parting words as he stood at her bedroom door that day had been, 'My dear lady, we must try to build up your health again to what it was before James was born, and please try not to let the servants' gossip get to you, as they are probably misplaced and the gossip untrue anyway. We must not allow all this worry to bring on the depression sickness, following the terrible trauma of the birth.'

Back in her own suite of rooms, alone with baby James still sleeping peacefully in the family heirloom bassinet, Lady Gabrielle let out a long drawn-out sigh. She really did feel extremely weak and tired, and for a moment felt as if the room had begun to cloud over while it circled around her. Now with her body burning and the frightening feeling of her consciousness evading her, she reached out towards her favourite soft blue feeding chair. She needed a moment, she told herself, to recover and think over what her doctor had said to her earlier in the day. "No," whispering softly to herself, "no, I do not want the 'mad' sickness again," while thinking she had never felt so alone, lost or ostracised from people after Morgan's birth. I cannot go there again, Gabrielle promised herself.

As the circling cloud in her head began to clear, Lady Gabrielle moved from her feeding chair to the comfort of her bed where she lay and rested her head, allowing her tangled mass of rich chestnut curls to spill onto the crisp white pillow case. Now back in the security and darkness of her own suite of rooms, where hung a delicate waft of lavender, she would try to sleep away that awful gossip overheard earlier in the cold distant corridors of Rosengarten.

CHAPTER 5

Not the Favourite

James realised from a tender age that he was not the favourite child in this huge household. He had felt special to his grandparents, Lord Alexander II and Lady Elizabeth, extra special because Grandfather spent so much time telling him stories of the Australian Outback. Lord Alexander II had said he wanted James to visit Australia when he completed his schooling and turned the mature age of twenty-one, for he had land and family connections there. Of course Grandfather never did elaborate on this family matter while he was still alive, and young James never asked, believing when Grandfather's time came – he being the second son – the family heritage would not involve him anyway. James understood it was his older brother Morgan who had been meticulously groomed from birth to become the next Lord Wentworth of Rosengarten Castle.

Even the Rosengarten staff had made it obvious that it was older brother Morgan who had to be groomed and attended to first each morning before younger brother James, who always came second. What had always stuck in James's mind was that his shoes were never cleaned or shined as well as Morgan's were, nor were his clothes hung or pressed as crisply. It was that noticeable that Grand-mama thought it was about time this matter was brought to the attention of James's mother, Lady Gabrielle. The following morning at the breakfast table Lady Elizabeth waited patiently for the last of the staff members to leave the breakfast room before she leaned across the breakfast table towards young James and tapped him on the wrist. "James, do please stand up dear and face your mother." James pushed his chair out slowly and did as he was told, and then nervously began to pull at his tie. "Don't do that, James," came the weary and slightly agitated voice from his mother. She looked sleepy and tired, and it looked as if she was ill again, he thought. While standing looking at his mother he wondered what was going to happen next. Then in a tone that bordered on disgust Grand-mama spoke to her daughter-in-law.

"Please Gabrielle dear, please take a good hard look at James's suit and shoes. His shoes are not cleaned to a high standard nor is his suit pressed properly. I am ashamed of the way you are letting the staff drop our standards here at Rosengarten dear." Grand-mama looked towards James and with a much softer tone to her voice said, "You may sit down now dear boy."

As young James took his seat again at the breakfast table, his older brother Morgan's facial expression hardened as his brown eyes flashed with more than a hint of anger. "But Grand-mama, I'm to be the next Lord Wentworth of Rosengarten Castle and not James, please do remember that I am the eldest sibling, so really Grand-mama, why does it matter if his shoes and suits are not presented as well as mine?"

Grand-mama looked directly at her daughter-in-law, hoping as the child's mother she would give Morgan the right answer. But Lady Gabrielle seemed to be drifting away from them, day dreaming, or if not her mind was in some faraway place and certainly not at this morning's breakfast table. It seemed as if Gabrielle had not heard a word at all this morning. My goodness, thought Lady Elizabeth, my daughter-in-law is slipping back into 'the depression sickness', how sad for her and the children…how sad for us all.

Lady Elizabeth turned her gaze towards her eldest grandson. "Tut-tut Morgan, where are your nice manners this morning? You are not Lord Wentworth IV just yet my dear."

"But Grand-mama," a defiant Morgan protested as he stood up from his breakfast chair. He was not to be beaten down. It crossed Lady Elizabeth's mind just how much Morgan was like his own father and his Grandfather before him, and she silently prayed that somehow he would turn out to be a better person. But she realised at this early age that Morgan knew of his destiny, that one day sometime in the future it was he who would reign as Lord Wentworth IV of Rosengarten Castle, and not his younger brother James. Yes, it was a certainty thought Grand-mama.

Both Morgan and James had spent most of their lives being groomed and raised by a nanny. But as the first-born and heir, Morgan had been shown more love and tender care by Lady Gabrielle as she would rest in her feeding chair in the nursery breast-feeding her son while gently placing tiny kisses on his forehead. This was the daily ritual for mother and son until Lady Gabrielle began to doze off or forget to feed her precious baby at all. She had begun to sleep through baby Morgan's feed times. It was then Lord Alexander III decided to hire a full-time wet nurse from the nearby village to live in and assist his wife with rearing their first child at Rosengarten.

Alexander was rather calculating because he also believed that with a nanny by Gabrielle's side day and night, he would not have to be there as often to help prop her up, or to remind her to wash and feed their son, and therefore he would have an alibi when his mother, Lady Elizabeth, constantly reminded him that his and Gabrielle's life would be much rosier if he was more of a loving and attentive husband to her.

Realising she was not well, Lady Gabrielle took her trusted doctor's advice to get outside the musky walls and corridors of Rosengarten – they too could be adding to her illness – and to absorb as much clean air and sunshine as she could.

'Morning and evenings if the weather allowed,' the doctor said. With that prompting Lady Gabrielle decided to try to help herself. It helped that she liked and trusted her doctor. Lady Gabrielle immediately began to take long walks across the green fields to try to get away from the stories of her husband's unfaithfulness that circulated throughout Rosengarten. Of course this gossip should not bother me, she would tell herself, but in all truth it certainly does. Gabrielle would think to herself, if only I could get rid of all the gossiping staff, but then who would attend to the house? She really didn't want to and wasn't trained for house duties, and was certainly not at all capable of handling such an enormous task by herself. She had been attended to all her life by servants and a lady's maid.

CHAPTER 6

Arousing Sensations

While out in the fields Lady Gabrielle would let her mane of long thick chestnut hair fly free in the breeze. Gabrielle also left all her undergarments and the many layers of unnecessary petticoats and her corset behind in her wardrobe. How free and beautiful it felt, she thought to herself. To run through the tall swaying grasses with arms outstretched, allowing her still young and supple body to feel the arousing sensations in her awaken as the field grasses brushed against it. Just to be free to accept the cool caressing breezes while drawing in deep breaths of crystal clean air, this was her way of allowing the wind to blow that ugly gossip and thoughts of the other women in her husband's arms clean out of her mind and soul.

Gabrielle was an extremely good looking woman, sexy and sensual to be around – she had been told this by her husband's male friends. But she was afraid to say she ever felt lonely. As a family friend and well-off London banker, Lord Oliver, had whispered in her ear at a mutual friend's luncheon: "Gabrielle…your huge brown eyes tell me you are sad and lonely at times dear…you only have to click your long and delicate fingers together and I'll be by your side…I promise you…I can make you happy and make you laugh and love again."

On hearing these few words Gabrielle immediately turned a bright red that rose up from her firm breasts to the very roots of her shiny chestnut hair. Her blushing gave away her immediate fear, or maybe it was a tingle of the excitement that had been long gone from her life of late. But Lord Oliver's extreme closeness as he brushed against her body with his overly cologned one, combined with the warmth of his breath in her ear as he audaciously followed her throughout the room crammed with their many close society friends, created in him a hope that he would find that crack in her veneer that would expose her vulnerability to his persuasion and let him into her life.

Lord Oliver was not oblivious to Lady Gabrielle's good looks. He also knew of her well-to-do family, the Duprees, from the European continent. As the younger generation of England's well-to-do society, both Gabrielle and Lord Oliver had circulated within the same circle of friends when visiting Europe, although they had never courted. Now that Lord Oliver's marriage of three years to a well-heeled viscount's daughter was over he was on the prowl again for a companion of sorts, and with rumours swirling that Lord Alexander III was womanising about in the circles of society, Lord Oliver hoped that Lady Gabrielle had heard the gossip in the halls and corridors of Rosengarten Castle and that she may have had enough of her husband's infidelities and would be ready to play Alexander's own game herself. Gabrielle felt a touch of both fear and the unknown from Lord Oliver's rather ambitious offer, but no, mused Gabrielle to herself, I couldn't go there… Alexander had been the only man in my life, remembering that she had been a virgin when she married him.

Lady Gabrielle could never forget how vigorously her husband had pursued her, telling her how her beauty outshone all others, how deeply he loved her and how he had to have her to himself. Because his love was so deep for Lady Gabrielle he would allow her to keep her pureness and virginity until their wedding night. Of course, the young and gallant Lord Wentworth did wait to sow his wild oats with his wife on their wedding night, but in the meantime he saw that his time between visiting the very formal Lady Gabrielle Dupree was well spent by seeing the mistresses that he was supposedly leaving behind.

Sadly, once Lord Alexander III had caught his virgin maiden and made his conquest, all the excitement and fun had gone for Alexander and married life. And so as Gabrielle twirled and laughed aloud in the wheat fields, the fresh air brushing against her near naked body and with her mind clearer, she could see that her marriage was really a sham. In all reality and in her wavering depression, she thought their marriage was no different to that of certain breeds of wild animals he used. Yes, he consummated our marriage for future heirs whilst attending to the lust of another...now wasn't that what their prize Angus bull did to their herd of cows? Only Alexander and Gabrielle were still living together under the one roof because that's what was expected of them. What hurt Gabrielle most of all was that she felt she was the only one putting up a rosy front – her and Alexander were very happily married and their life was as wonderful as could be. Meanwhile, her husband never had the decency to even try to hide his foolish passion for a certain type of woman, sadly it was always the freelancing whores who never minded sharing their favours around freely. This continuing false display played out at the many family gatherings and functions they attended and was starting to make Gabrielle extremely ill again.

CHAPTER 7

Distant Dream

James had not felt the divide between himself and Morgan as a very young child, but he did remember spending more time playing and laughing with his favourite nanny Gemma from Australia. She too had many wonderful stories about koalas, white cockatoos and red dingoes, and on several occasions when she thought James was being openly left out of talks on the future of Rosengarten Castle, she would take him gently by the hand and they would wander through the many pathways in the rose garden. While walking with young James, Gemma remembered a story that had been told to her by an old Aboriginal woman who had lived with her family on Coolamun Downs, her grandparents' cattle station in Outback Australia. Suddenly, James became more alert and his questions on Outback Australia began to tumble freely and swiftly to Gemma. "Gemma, did you go to school on the station or did you have to go away to boarding school like Morgan and I?" James asked before continuing. "Were you ever sad and homesick when you had to return to the city and leave behind your animal friends?" After answering all of James's questions as best as she could, and without wanting to paint her beloved Outback as too glossy or an overly romantic place, Gemma decided to tell James a story that the Aboriginal woman from Coolamun Downs had told her. It was the story of a little black cockatoo that had been cast out of its nest as a skinny hatchling. It had survived and grown up to produce a proud strong colony of its very own. When Gemma thought young James had heard enough of her story, they both investigated all the nooks and crannies and the old stone wishing well hidden among the neatly trimmed hedges and circular rose beds in Rosengarten's manicured grounds before turning towards the stairs at the lions entrance and home. But just as James reached the top step, he stopped, turned and reached his pale hand out to Gemma.

"Thank you Gemma, for telling me the story of the little black cockatoo, because one day when I am older, I will fly away on my own too."

"Oh no, James," said a now worried Gemma. "I never ever meant to put such ideas in your head. I never meant for you to think about leaving. You must not leave Rosengarten. This is your home too James. You must always remember that, dear boy." Gemma emphasised this last point even though it was not her place to inform the young James of his family heritage.

But Young James was adamant that when he was older, but not that much older, he would leave Rosengarten Castle for Australia and visit the Kimberley and the Outback and Adelaide where he intended to visit Dr Nicholls' son David, and to see all the places Grandfather had talked about from his Australian adventures.

"Yes, Gemma, that is what I will do. Please don't speak of this to Grand-mama or mother, it would only worry them." Suddenly young James felt truly confident, happier and even stronger, and he promised himself, I *will* go to Australia one day.

CHAPTER 8

Ten Years later

Ten years later, at twenty-one years of age, James felt that Australia had begun its call to him to pack his bags and all his precious belongings. The time felt right for James to break away from Rosengarten, the family and England. Plus there really was no need for him to be at Rosengarten with the family now. Father was the current Lord Wentworth III, older brother Morgan had turned twenty-three and was next in line for the family heritage and title, while mother Gabrielle, a little delicate at times from her battle with the depression sickness and her husband's infidelities, currently seemed well enough. And of course Grand-mama, Lady Elizabeth, was always at Rosengarten to help father manage the annual hunt season festivities. Besides, James thought life at Rosengarten was becoming a little monotonous for him as he had only minimal interest in the family party and social scenes and preferred to spend as much time as he could alone training the estate's well-bred horses. It was during this time that James had made quite a name for himself within the circles of society as a very strong, capable and extremely good-looking horseman who had caught the eye of numerous eligible young women at the many grand society equestrian events. But sadly, even James's training of the estate's horses was becoming a thorn in older brother

Morgan's side, for he constantly picked and pulled and found fault with the younger James's horse breaking and polo training methods, and yet it was the estate's horses Morgan had shown the least interest in previously.

One fine crisp morning while in the middle of a training session with a new spirited chestnut colt, James's attention was drawn to the far side of the paddock by the wild strawberry blonde locks of his friend Lady Catherine.

"Is it true what they say James, you are talking of leaving for Australia someday soon?" asked an inquisitive Catherine.

While slowly dismounting from his chestnut colt, James sensed Catherine's agitation, she seemed quite upset or was it ruffled, he thought, not like her at all. Their friendship had been just that, purely platonic. James's mind raced with thoughts like, I haven't kissed Catherine, and certainly haven't taken her chastity from her, I haven't behaved like father or Morgan would have with a lady of Catherine's attractiveness, or even led her on.

But James wasn't at all blind. His friend Lady Catherine was certainly an attractive woman if not a flirtatious one, with her wild tangled mass of strawberry curls piled high atop her head, offset by fine porcelain skin that resembled the finest china. But on this particular morning James thought it glowed with delicate golden tones, showing her more beautiful and desirable than ever in the soft sunshine.

Lady Catherine knew of the desire many men in society felt towards her, but why didn't James Wentworth feel the same way? She had wanted him for over twelve months now, why didn't he feel the same way about her, why was he holding her at arm's length? As these thoughts and questions flashed through Catherine's mind she unknowingly began flicking her exquisitely engraved silver-handled horsewhip about the air in anger, until she realised this sort of behaviour wouldn't help her need for James at all, and James wasn't the type of man who would bend easily to her frustrations for him. No, he seemed distant, proud and too proper, thought Lady Catherine as she attempted to gather herself. Does he prefer gentlemen to me? That's not possible, I must be tired, murmured Lady Catherine to herself now realising her own mind was rambling. James, on the other hand was thinking how Lady Catherine reminded him of a proud if rather spoiled unbroken filly he once had to work on in the Rosengarten horse yards. A filly that older brother Morgan suggested, "James, you will need to break that filly's spirit first before attempting to break her into rein and saddle." Not James's method at all.

Now that Catherine had realised her whipping display of anger was foolish, if not stupid, she let the whip fall to the ground and stood with her hands on her curvaceous hips. The fire in her green smolder-ing eyes exposed her wanton desire, her firm breasts rising and falling in a gentle rhythm to her shallow breathing. James took his time to answer her.

"Why, yes Lady Catherine, but there are no definite plans as yet, but I feel Australia holds my destiny," James replied, feeling that hon-esty was the only way to go in this situation.

With this, Catherine again lost control of her inner self. She bent down and grabbed her whip, turned her back to James, tossed her mane of wild blonde hair into the air and stomped off to her own shiny black mare, Beauty, her ruffled petticoats becoming exposed with her hurried movement and temper. Catherine stopped short, turned to look straight at James and said, "Do not expect me to wait for your return from Australia James." Catherine turned back towards her patiently waiting mare, lifted the bridle from the staging post, swung herself high up into the saddle and away she madly galloped, taking her frustrations out on her mare by slapping the animal across the offside shoulder and rump with her whip, leaving behind only the panicked pounding of a horse's hooves under pressure.

Australia had always been the one country that had kept James intrigued from a very early age, and Grandfather's stories had played a huge part in this. Yes, Australia, then maybe Africa, he thought to himself. I'll see how my visit goes after testing the waters.

That evening at the family dinner James made the announcement that he intended to leave for Australia by the end of the month. From the age of eighteen both James and Morgan had been receiving a small inheritance from Grandfather's estate. James had saved and banked his share for the day he intended to venture forth to Australia, where he planned to support himself with his own saved funds, and if he was lucky enough, to find a paying position on a cattle station knowing the extra money would help him along the way.

Lord Wentworth asked Muldoon for all wine glasses to be topped up, then on raising his crystal glass of fine wine towards James, he proceeded: "I wish to announce a special toast to our second son James who is leaving for Australia at the end of the month, may God travel with you, James, in that great Australian Outback your Grandfather forever talked of."

Lord Wentworth then said he thought the trip would be tougher on James without the connections Grandfather had. Lady Gabrielle wondered if travelling so far to a place like Australia was such a good idea after all. She did love James dearly and worried for him at times because he wasn't as outgoing as his older brother Morgan or his father Lord Wentworth. But Gabrielle felt that young James had inherited the inner strength of his Grand-mama, and that was just as well since he was leaving the family nest for the ruggedness of the Australian Outback.

"It's the distance James," she said, "but I suppose it's what you dreamed of doing for so long, and of course you will return to England dear."

Grand-mama piped up and said, "I still have the address of Doctor Nicholls in the Adelaide Hills and Lonesome Downs in the West Kimberley from Grandfather's trips to Australia, even if it was many years ago when Grandfather visited the country. They may still be of some help, James." James thanked his Grand-mama and said he would collect them from her the following morning. He was excited that his plans were out in the open now and felt so much happier that his family were accepting of his wish to visit Australia. Now all he really wanted was to have everything in order and fly to Australia and begin this great adventure as soon as possible.

CHAPTER 9

Australia

After an extremely long and trying trip via Europe and India and a rough and bumpy landing on the small airstrip in Darwin, James was pleased to have his feet planted safely on the tarmac in the 'Top End' of Australia at long last. He was met by a blast of intense heat and humidity on the opening of the aircraft door. The heat was soon accompanied by many annoying flies, and the sky was smeared with varying shades of red from billowing dust storms.

But none of the Territory's 'Wet Season' build-up of heat, dust or flies was about to deter James in any way from enjoying his Australian adventure, in fact he couldn't get going fast enough and hailed a cab to take him into Darwin town where he hoped to find accommodation at a pub somewhere in the main street, and also somewhere to dine. Tomorrow was the beginning of his first full day on Australian soil in the Outback.

"Where to mate?" asked the shrivelled and bent Chinese taxi driver.

"A hotel in the centre of Darwin, Sir," answered James.

"Lucky I stopped for you mate, only three taxis left in town now." The cab driver held up three buckled looking fingers just in case James didn't really understand.

The taxi driver's mind must have been bubbling over with curiosity, as James's pale skin, blond hair and broad shoulders didn't really fit the norm of men who would arrive regularly and alone in the Northern Territory looking for work. Most were rugged and tough in appearance, some were even hardened criminals running from the law, and most had hard, chiselled facial features tanned to match their well-worn leather boots.

"What's your name? This ...this first time to Darwin for you?" asked the taxi driver in broken English.

"James Sir, and your name?" James responded.

"China is my name, not my real name, but everybody calls me China in Darwin." After a slight hesitation he added he was born in Darwin. The taxi driver skillfully changed gears in his Plymouth while manoeuvring it steadily along Darwin's very narrow roads. After finding out China's name, James's attention was drawn to the destruction of buildings and infrastructure that was still clearly visible as a result of the Japanese bombing of Darwin in 1942. There's not a lot here, James thought as he gazed beyond the destruction – a little store called Delaney's and a lot of bush.

A group or family of Indigenous people carrying what looked like their belongings on poles strung between them walked along the side of the road. Soon, the odd house began to pop up in the countryside followed by many more as they drove closer to the town of Darwin. Then suddenly China slammed his foot down hard on the brake pedal directly in front of a sign that read Victoria Hotel Darwin.

James looked out of his passenger seat window noting a couple of tanned and rough looking types lounging about the footpath, with one using the gutter as a seat, and the other using the solid pub wall as a backrest. James noted how protective each man was of the tin mug or jam tin he used for a drinking vessel, which was topped up from a large brown bottle they passed between them with extreme care. Then China asked for "one pound fare Sir." China then dropped James's expensive suitcase on the cement pavement for him to collect. James paid the taxi fare, not knowing whether the fare was fair or not, then China quickly found his way into the hotel and out again in no time carrying a large brown bottle of beer. China waved it at James and said, "King brown mate," and then jumped into his taxi and sped off, leaving behind a waft of petrol fumes while on the lookout for another fare.

Back then in the Northern Territory anyone with a vehicle could use it as a local taxi. All they had to do was go around to the local police station and register it as a taxi cab. They would be given a number to sit on the dashboard of the vehicle and away they went into the taxi business.

James stood for a moment out the front of the Victoria Hotel to get his bearings. He glanced up and down the main street thinking there really wasn't very much here. But then this was Outback Australia and it was one of the towns James had set his heart on visiting, and now here he was with his feet planted firmly on the pavement out the front of the Victoria Hotel Darwin, a tropical metropolis and the only pub in the centre of town. James picked up his suitcase and walked through the entrance doorway looking for a reception desk where he could make enquiries about accommodation.

"Looking for a room...bookings up the end of the bar mate," was the advice given to him from the perspiring barman in a blue singlet. Immediately a neat older woman dressed in a flowery, heavily starched and well-pressed dress, and seemingly full of authority, arrived to take control of his booking, promptly asking James how long he wished to stay.

"A week to start," answered James. "Is there much work around Darwin...I mean on the cattle stations, madam?"

The woman was seemingly giving James's question some thought as she hurriedly flicked through the brown dog-eared ledger on the counter in front of her, before saying, "There's been plenty of work in and around Darwin since the war...in the bar there's a bunch of half drunken ringers on a break from a cattle station south of here, don't know if they'd be of any help or not, but the boss fellow is there. Bandit's his name, he might know of any station work available.

"By the way, my name's Molly. Don't get caught up with the local drunks and call me the 'old Moll'...I'm just warning you, there's a pound penalty across the bar if you do."

Goodness me, thought James, as he began to fumble with his fob watch and made a clumsy attempt to straighten his waistcoat before eventually gathering himself again in Molly's presence. Molly leaned across the bar and pointed at James's waistcoat and said "You won't be wearing that for long around here."

Molly remained leaning towards James, whose eyes and ears were wide open as she handed him his room keys and added, "No boozing, fighting or wild women in the room, and by that I mean drunken lubras. If there is, I'll find 'em and I'll throw yah out quick smart with 'em." She went on mumbling and grumbling to herself, saying someone went clean through a wall last night and now we're a room short. Well, thought James, boozing, fighting and wild women won't be a problem, well, not tonight anyway unless my ideals change terribly quickly.

As James bent to pick up his suitcase, he couldn't help but let a gentle smile brush across his slightly reddened face while pondering how Grand-mama would have handled the good advice given by the hotel's receptionist. Well, thought James, England and Australia are certainly many thousands of miles apart, but the Australians are right up-front with their advice. This is probably a good thing – at least they don't beat about the bush, James thought as he began his walk around the side verandah until he found his room. It was towards the front of the building and James noted there was a much-appreciated light sea breeze which felt wonderful against his perspiring pale English body. After several attempts of trying to open his hotel room door with the damaged key, James took the advice of a stockman lounging on a cane chair close by. "If yah can't get in mate, yah twist the key and boot the bottom of the door at the same time, it always works," the stranger suggested. James found it did for him too. The room was clean but well used, emitting a strong smell of tobacco smoke, while the carpet was worn and sported several cigarette burns. It had simple furnishings and he had the use of a communal bathroom. That's all I need, thought James. It would do just fine. Of course James wasn't expecting to find luxury accommodation in the Outback after hearing Grandfather's many stories. He would unpack and make himself a much-needed cup of tea.

James left the hotel to walk about the tropical town, finding parklands covered in brilliant green manicured lawns, many palm trees and ferns, while brightly coloured crotons filled other areas. James realised he was perspiring profusely and took his suit jacket off to find some relief from the sapping heat, and yet he thought how great it was to be perspiring for once, compared to being rugged up for protection from the cold and snow of England. James spotted a little corner café advertising freshly caught barramundi on the menu, and he wasn't about to walk past it as Grandfather had talked of the many extremely tasty meals of barramundi he had enjoyed while visiting Australia. Now, thought James, it is my turn to sample this fine fish, and wondered if the barramundi was as tasty as Grandfather had described. James savoured every mouthful and he knew instantly that this wouldn't be his last meal of the saltwater fish. During his walk James had spotted what looked like a bulging haberdashery shop not that far from his café. He planned to return and purchase a set of work clothes and an Akubra wide-brimmed hat to shade the sun from his pale face and to blend in with the locals.

On James's return to the hotel, no sooner had he walked through the bar's bat-winged doors than he was greeted by a rowdy intoxicated bunch of stockmen he had seen earlier at the bar.

"Have a drink mate. Where yah from," asked one, while another larger cleaner looking stockman pushed through the group of inquisitive men to offer James a tin mug half-full of dark liquid that smelt like straight rum. James wondered if he would end up on his ear, or worse still in the gutter with several others out the front of the hotel if he drank too much of this foul smelling brew. The light-hearted bunch gathered around James, then the big fella stuck his hand out and introduced himself. "I'm known as Bandit around here, what's your name young fella?" James met Bandit's handshake halfway with, "I'm James Wentworth Sir." His reply bought forth a roar of laughter accompanied by much back-slapping from the wild unrefined bunch of rough diamonds that surrounded them.

"Well young fella, we'll call yah Jim for now, that's it," yelled Bandit. "Jim it'll be, and who's turn to shout. Make it rum all round, and we'll drink to Jim's arrival in the Territory." So James sat and talked and drank with the stockmen, and as the evening wore on the stockmen became more jovial and intoxicated. Then a fight broke out between two men who had been mates earlier in the evening. From what James could gather, it was over who would be the lucky person to escort the attractive blonde barmaid to the Star Picture Theatre, directly across the road from the hotel.

It was just after the war, and Darwin was extremely short on womenfolk, and of course the competition to escort a lady anywhere about the town brought on nothing short of fierce aggression among the plentiful menfolk. So as word travelled down the bar numerous suitors were lining up. The stockmen decided to fight it out among themselves. The winner would have the honour of escorting the classy looking lady to the Star Picture later that evening.

Immediately a punch was thrown, just missing James. James stepped back out of the way as another wild and woolly fist went flying through the group of men. James could see it wasn't meant for him. Then another couple of stockmen, still with their wide-brim felt hats attached firmly to their heads, got into it, swinging their fists left, right and centre, each trying to land a blow on the other. While the stockmen's fists were missing their target, it didn't help much that their bowed legs, with feet clad in worn Cuban-heeled riding boots made one hell of a racket on the pub's wooden floorboards as they staggered about.

James was beginning to find it all quite entertaining, and believed a mob of stampeding buffaloes wouldn't have entertained as much, when another two half-cut stockmen joined the fight and began 'the soft-boot' shuffle about the bar, which brought Bandit to his feet in no time. Bandit stood all of six foot seven, all sinew and muscle it seemed as he stretched himself to his full height. "Yep, now the young'uns are punch drunk," he muttered to himself as he yanked his jeans up around his waist, rolled his shirt sleeves even higher and pulled the brim of his own badly stained and dust covered felt hat down hard on his forehead while leaving just enough room for his piercing dark eyes to stare out under the brim, as if meaning business, before leaning towards James, saying: "It's time to call it a night mate, I'll sort these young blokes out before Molly kicks the whole bloody lot of us out of the pub for good." Bandit extended his hand to James with, "I'll see yah around," and was gone to sort his rowdy bunch of stockmen and ringers out.

Within minutes Bandit had a routine going, and it looked as if he had done this sort of thing many times before, thought James as he stood quietly by the arched doorway and watched fascinated as Bandit interacted with the men. Bandit grabbed each one of the intoxicated stockmen, one after the other, by their shirt collars and the seat of their pants, giving each an almighty swing which sent the young wild stockmen flying through the pub doorway like human missiles to land on the hard footpath beyond, where the intoxicated bodies had begun to pile up one on top of the other, just like sardines in a can. Interesting folk, James thought to himself as he found his way around the hotel's dimly lit verandah, which meant stepping over several sleeping bodies curled up in swags as he went in search of his own hotel room.

James rose early the following morning after an uncomfortable night's sleep that had him tossing and turning in bed as he tried in vain to find some relief from the unwavering heat and humidity, which was accompanied by the biting and high-pitched buzzing of insects. What had been left of the night had made it an extremely long one for James, as it was filled with intermittent conversations and bursts of loud uneven snoring. And just as exhaustion from the night's disturbances threatened sleep, the harsh banging on the hotel room doors would begin as the last of the drunken stockmen from the bar went in search of their own hotel rooms and swags to crash in.

CHAPTER 10

Back of the Bedford

After James had taken a cool shower, dressed in his newly purchased and much lighter attire – much more suited to the climate he thought – he pulled his Akubra felt hat with light corded edging around the brim firmly down on his forehead, just like his friend Bandit did the evening before. Feeling good, James decided he would go to the café he had frequented the previous evening for breakfast. After an extremely hearty Australian breakfast of steak and eggs, James left the café and set off down the street towards the hotel where he spotted a red Bedford truck surrounded by a rowdy group of what looked to be the stockmen he had met the night before in the hotel bar.

"Hey, it's young Jim. You're up nice and early," yelled one of the blokes.

"Good morning chaps," James replied, which immediately had the mob of men in fits of laughter. "Chaps, chaps, we're not bloody chaps, we're bloody blokes mate," came a gruff reply. Then James was told to 'forget the highfalutin talk young Jim, we'll educate ya ourselves the Aussie way mate.' As James shook hands with the blokes he couldn't help but notice the odd black and swollen eye accompanied by cuts and bruises on some faces, but on the whole the stockmen were extremely cheerful this morning considering the events of the night before. James noticed that Bandit was several paces away from the men, leaning against a lamppost and seemingly in deep thought while rolling a cigarette. Beside him on the ground was a well-used brown leather duffle bag and on the bag in large gold lettering was the name Brock Anderson. James would have liked to ask Bandit about the name on his duffel bag, but thought better of it this morning, plus he had only just met the man the night before.

James moved towards Bandit and asked, "Are all of you leaving town this morning?" while still thinking just how entertaining the men were the previous evening. Although he had just met them, James thought they were good blokes and he would miss this funny Australian company.

"Yep…our time's up," was the reply. Bandit never bothered to lift his head up to acknowledge James at all, his total concentration was on rolling a perfect cigarette, which left James wondering whether Bandit was tired of talking to him already. At that moment one of the younger stockmen called out to Bandit. "Boss, the swags are on the truck, we can't forget Tom, he's in the lock-up around the corner." Bandit looked at the stockman and said "Make sure there's no grog on board, you know the station's rules." That was it!

"Are you the boss, Sir?" James said approaching Bandit. "That's what they call me, young Jim," came Bandit's nonplussed reply. James wanted to work in the Outback and on a cattle station more than anything else and he worried that he may be pushing his luck here by asking Bandit for a job, but he had nothing to lose except a knock-back, and he was more than willing to learn all he could on a cattle station, no matter how hot or difficult it would be – he yearned to live the Outback way of life his Grandfather had frequently talked about.

"Would you have any work for me?" asked James hesitantly. "I'll have a go at anything, to the best of my ability, Sir." Bandit slowly looked up from under the brim of his hat as if giving James's question considerable thought then said, "Number one, don't call me Sir again, the name's Bandit, and number two, can you ride a horse, and not just a bloody rocking horse?"

"Yes, I can ride enough to get by," James answered, while wondering if his horse handling days on the family estate back home in England would put him in good stead for this position.

"Well, I'm a man short in the stock camp right now…arr McKenzie…

yeah…McKenzie broke his leg last week while mustering and won't be any good to me for a while, so I'll give you ago." Bandit stood up straight, grabbed his duffel bag and threw it clean through the open truck window where it landed safely on the front seat of the Bedford, then told James to be on the footpath out the front of the hotel where he would pick him up to leave for Campbell's Run cattle station in half an hour, or, "As soon as I can rescue our Tom from the police station lock-up."

When Bandit returned from the police station in the Bedford and parked at the front of the Victoria Hotel, James loaded his expensive suitcase and new swag, which had been hurriedly purchased from the haberdashery store across the street. James then climbed into the tray of the truck and as he did one fellow volunteered, "Get comfortable, it's a long way…Bandit will work you to death once we're at the station." James acknowledged this as he slipped down into a small open space between the crew from Campbell's Run, who were preparing to stretch out using their swags as back rests and pillows to get comfortable as they strived to find sleep lost from the wild evening before. James couldn't help but smile to himself while thinking how entertaining these Australian fellows were last evening, and he hoped they had another evening like it sometime. It wasn't long, and not a mile out of town, when most of the still well hungover stockmen were sleeping and snoring loudly, so loud the boss's blue heeler cattle dog constantly moved about the truck in search of a quiet place to lie. Which left young Tom from the lock-up, who was quite sober now and similar in age to James, as James's company on the long drive to Campbell's Run Station.

Eight long tiring hours after leaving Darwin, and after many pit stops for the recuperating stockmen to relieve themselves and to quench their thirst from the cool hessian water bag that hung from the bull bar of the Bedford truck, young Tom nudged James awake with "Twenty mile to go to camp, can't bloody wait." James woke and sat up immediately from his cramped position to find the boss's blue heeler dog seriously eyeballing him. They had been sleeping side by side, face to face, and James's first thought was he hoped he hadn't upset the dog with any loud snoring of his own as they needed to be friends if sharing the same camp on Campbell's Run.

James sat up resting his back against his new swag and looked around trying to take in as much of this new wild looking country as he could but couldn't believe his eyes – there was no sign of a road. Bandit was weaving the Bedford in and around gullies, through gaps in the ranges and crossing creeks and rivers without any trouble at all. Tom piped up to share his local knowledge with "It's a tributary of the Victoria River," followed quickly by "Grab Blue Dog, he gets excited when he spots a croc." Then Henry, probably the untidiest looking of the stockmen, rolled over from his cramped position and said to James, "You gotta watch the crocs here, they really like the Poms'… soft…sweet…meat," then laughed exposing his tobacco stained teeth.

"Lay off it, Henry," Tom volunteered. "Henry tries to put the wind up every new man who comes into our stock camp; no wonder they don't stick the mustering season out, or take a boggy (bath) in the river while they're with us. Well, yeah, when we're mustering along the river, it only takes a splash in the river water and the new chums see themselves as croc dinner, and they roll their swags and they're gone." Henry chuckled to himself, he'd had his fun and went to roll over to get comfortable in his swag again. "Yep…it's all because of you Henry," said Tom. With that suggestion untidy Henry, or Cranky Henry as he was more commonly known, came to life in one hell of a hurry by throwing a rolling punch towards Tom which never connected, although it started a full-on pantomime in the tray-back of the Bedford truck. Men flew out from their swags throwing random punches, others still half asleep had no idea of what bought on this circus. Blue Dog was in the middle of it, all bristled up and planting his two-bobs' worth where he thought it was most needed. Luckily, James was sitting up resting his back against the truck cabin directly behind the driver. Then all of a sudden while in the middle of a shallow creek crossing, Bandit, who had noticed punches were being thrown in the vehicle's dusty rear-vision mirror, suddenly planted his foot down hard on the brake pedal, throwing most of his fighting and unbalanced stockmen straight into the clear cold creek water.

With this James wanted to laugh out loud – his new Australian mates had got into it again. These skirmishes among the stockmen never bothered James, he felt no fear of mankind and found it all quite entertaining – apparently this was all part of a stockman's way of life, he thought. Plus James's physique was equal to the best of the blokes, being tall, fit and extremely broad shouldered from his days breaking and handling the family's well-bred horses that were favoured by the hunting and equestrian folk of England.

With the dishevelled and wet stockmen in the middle of the creek, Bandit kept up a steady pace in the Bedford until he pulled it to a halt on the opposite river bank. Bandit opened the truck door and began to seriously scratch around behind the driver's seat as if looking for something important that he'd lost. Watching Bandit, James wondered what could be so important that Bandit had to find it right now, and out here in the middle of nowhere it seemed. Then with an "Ah good, found yah," Bandit stood tall holding up two long bars of yellow Sunlight washing soap in his hands. "Catch this, and wash up," he barked as he fired one of the bars of soap to the saturated stockmen in the middle of the shallow creek. He then headed towards a nice clear spot of water further up the creek for himself with the other bar, but not before telling young Jim to make the most of the creek to wash as "We're short of water for bathing in the camp."

The last twenty miles to Campbell's Run passed in no time, and with the stockmen all washed and refreshed from their swim in 'Middle Creek', the mood on the back of the Bedford truck had improved considerably. By the time Bandit parked the truck up out front of the station's cookhouse everyone seemed genuinely glad to be back on the station. Bandit got out of the truck and walked into the cookhouse and out again in no time, then signalled to the boys to load the stock camp's cartons of tinned stores and tobacco rations onto the tray of the truck. "Make sure they're tied down," he said, adding "I won't be long and we'll get going."

"Not you Jim, come with me to the big house, where the Boss's wife, Shelia, will put you on the books for the stock camp." James followed Bandit towards the big house where they were met at the front door by the Boss's wife clad in neat fitting jeans and a white double-pocketed shirt, her brown and sun bleached hair pulled up high on her head in a loose ponytail giving her the appearance of fresh youthfulness.

"Hello Brock, and this is…?" asked Sheila while eyeing James up and down. "James Wentworth, madam," answered James in his refined accent as he extended his right hand to shake Sheila's. Bandit never missed much and thought Sheila held on to James's hand far longer than was absolutely necessary. "You have a fine cultured English accent, James, where does it come from?" she asked before noticing

Bandit's loathing look towards her, making her drop James's hand immediately. "Is something wrong Brock?" she blurted out. With a silly smirk on his face, Bandit answered: "We don't have time for a history lesson or even an English lesson Sheila." At that moment James realised the name Bandit was really Brock's Outback handle. But in the fleeting seconds of Bandit introducing James to the Boss's wife, Sheila, James couldn't help but sense that there was some connection between them. It's not my business, James reprimanded himself, but Bandit struck James as a person who wouldn't allow another to speak to him like that…no, not even a woman.

CHAPTER 11

Beginning of a Dream

Next morning James woke to the flurry of flapping wings and a wild mix of honking and chatter from thousands of brown swamp ducks at the Conga camp – a beautiful billabong overflowing with Australian native bird life, thought James as he sat quietly absorbing it all from the confinement of his swag. Suddenly, the peacefulness of the morning dawn was shattered by the harsh clang of the cook's huge camel bell, his cookhouse gong. Cookie rattled and shook the darn bell until it very nearly got on the boys' nerves, but it certainly got the stockmen up out of their swags and around the morning's campfire quick smart.

"Help yourself, with the porridge, the steak and kidney is in the frying pan, black tea over there," said Cookie as he pointed towards the drum of black tea with his long bladed boning knife that he used to pick his teeth with in-between cutting his breakfast steak.

James was as hungry as the rest of the stockmen and took an enamel plate and mug handed to him by Tom. In no time James had his plate loaded with steak and kidney and the tin mug full to the brim with well-brewed black tea. The men grouped close to the early morning fire, probably more for comfort than warmth. Some shared old tree stumps, others were lucky enough to nab an empty flour drum that could be used as a seat, while each man made sure his pannikin of tea was placed safely on the ground between his boots before getting stuck into breakfast. Earlier, Tom had whispered to James that the cook said he only boils the flour drum once for tea at meal times, so don't knock it over. James simply nodded his head in answer to Tom. "The camp cooks are often cranky old buggers, like to assert their authority around the campfire now and then...mostly good people but you can get the odd grouchy one though," Tom offered.

"Where is Bandit this morning?" James asked Tom. The evening before James had noticed that Bandit had carried his swag a good hundred yards away from the rest of the stockmen and the camp. "Bandit never camps near us men, always out on his own," Tom replied. "I suppose he's a bit of a loner in some ways...I think Blue Dog and Bandit like the quiet open space out there on that claypan flat." Just as Tom finished, Bandit and Cranky Henry rode up to the campfire on horseback, and while Bandit dismounted, picked up a twig and called for the stock boys' attention as he cleared a patch of red dirt with his well-worn riding boot, Cranky Henry remained sitting on his horse and watched and listened from above.

Bandit began to draw lines in the sand while dedicating points of the coming muster to certain more knowledgeable individuals as he began to give his men the day's orders. "James, you stick on the tail, until you get the hang of it; Henry will select a steady horse for you to ride today. I'm going out to scout ahead, north and east of the river. We'll put a mob together, bring 'em down the river to the wire yard by sundown." That was it, Bandit stood up, pulled the girth on his stockman's saddle to check it was tight, followed by a neat swing up into the saddle, and he was gone.

James looked towards Henry, who said, "The yarramin (horse) is in the stockyard waiting for you to ride him." Then with a wicked laugh that exposed his tobacco stained teeth, Henry tipped his hat to the young stockman, slipped his shiny new spur into the lower rib of his fine looking black colt which galloped and pig-rooted its way back in the direction of the old wooden cattle yards.

"Yes Sir," was James's prompt reply, and he immediately jumped up to wash his breakfast plate in the flour drum of warm water the cook had ready and standing in the cooling coals of the campfire for that very purpose. But there was something Bandit had said that still bothered James – he was to stick on the tail. Well whose tail was he to hang onto for goodness sake? James wanted to get it right because he was grateful to Bandit for giving him a chance to experience the Outback, even giving him the opportunity of working in his stock camp on Campbell's Run Station. Before James left for the cattle yard where he was to collect his horse, he went to Tom and asked, "Whose tail is Bandit talking about, I don't understand Tom?" With that Tom gave a good belly laugh. "My mother has said that we have a language all our own in the bush, so I understand what you're asking me. Bandit telling you to remain on the tail today until you get the hang of the way he musters simply means the tail is the south end of a beast, or where the calves, old, crook or lazy cattle hang. Usually on a long day's muster they're on the tail of the mob, the stragglers. Bandit wants you to keep them up, you know, push them steadily along with the rest of the cattle, you savvy, do you understand James?" Young gun Tom felt quite important helping cultured James with the Outback lingo so he told James that, "Someone has to do it, and you're the new chum in the stock camp James, and it's always the new chum's job."

"I'm not complaining Tom, thank you, I'm more the wiser now." James chuckled to himself thinking you fellows sure do have a language of your own out here. With that sorted, James made his way to the cattle yards to pick up the horse that Henry had selected for him to ride in the muster today.

At the cattle yards James walked towards Henry without speaking. Henry in turn pointed towards a rough-coated bay gelding that was constantly pacing around the perimeter of the old wooden yards. The animal looked rough. James stopped and stood still for a moment as if sizing the situation up before asking Henry if he was to use the nearby saddle and bridle on the bay. "Yep, that's it, he's all yours," volunteered Henry, without even bothering to lift his head from cleaning out the hooves of his own black beauty. Then with the bridle in hand James walked slowly towards his new steed but stopped for a moment to let the bay horse pick up his scent, the smell of another stranger. As James moved steadily forward he rubbed his free hand roughly under his armpit before offering the same palm to the stockhorse. By doing this, James hoped the horse would realise he wasn't Cranky Henry, the horse breaker. But while performing this old ritual James ran his eyes over the animal and noticed shockingly raw and scabby cuts under the belly area, and terrible rope burns around the bay's neck region. As James went to take another step closer to the animal it immediately began to snort and quiver all over, before rearing up and galloping off around the stockyards. James stood still and watched the bay for a moment, it seemed uncomfortable around people. James wondered if this could be the result of breaking the animal's spirit as his older brother Morgan had suggested to him when breaking a horse in to halter and saddle at Rosengarten. James took a moment to size the situation up and stopped to study the animal. He could no longer hear Henry using a rasp to file his own horse's hooves down, and from the corner of his eye he caught Cranky Henry leaning against a wooden post of the cattle yard puffing on a tailor-made cigarette and blowing circles of smoke high into the air. But Henry was watching James too. James thought that for some reason Henry seemed to have taken an instant dislike to him and wondered why. Was it because he was English and from the old country? Was it because he was a Pom? If this was the case things could possibly get a lot worse with Henry.

"Is it gonna take you all day to get on that bloody horse?" asked Henry in his slow Outback drawl. "You told the boss you could ride a bit, well, how about it." James turned and asked Henry, "Has the bay been freshly broken?" "About a week, or could be three days," came the casual reply. Henry was beginning to feel rather pleased with himself thinking he'd set this uppity Pommy fella up for the ride of his life by selecting the worst horse in the stock camp for him to ride on his first day of the muster.

Then out of the blue, Tom arrived at the stockyards on his own piebald mare. "What's the hold-up James? Bandit sent me back looking for you, he wants you working the tail, come on pronto, hurry up." James held the bridle up to Tom, to show he was on the job and said, "The bay's freshly broken and still extremely frightened of man and saddle. If I can ride him, I sincerely hope he doesn't make a mess of the muster for you all."

With that young Tom turned on Henry. "What do you think you can prove with James riding that bay, Henry?"

"Yeah, well why not, if the Pom can ride, he'll get the ride of his life," uttered Henry as he climbed to the top rail of the wooden yard to give himself a bird's-eye view of what he thought was to come.

"Well bugger you Henry, you know we haven't got all day," shouted a flustered Tom. "Come on James, I'll ride my horse into the yards to give the bay a bit of company." With that Tom walked his quiet pie-bald slowly through the yard gates and towards the frightened bay gelding which stood wide-eyed with ears pricked.

At that moment Bandit arrived at the stockyards looking like a massive thunder cloud ready to release a bolt of lightning at any moment. "Geez, James," said Tom, "we're sure gonna cop a good sized blast now from Bandit, I just know it, he needs both of us on the job." But while Tom was worrying himself about the 'telling off' they were about to get, James had caught his bay gelding and had the bridle securely on and tightened. He then led both horses towards the wooden yard rails where the saddle blanket and old worn saddle were both hanging. Bandit hadn't started on the two young fellows yet, but seemed to have a bit to say to Henry as he clambered down off the top rail to meet Bandit.

James wasn't too pleased putting a saddle onto a sore horse, but it seemed he had no choice. James had made sure that each of his movements were steady and positive as he placed the saddle on the bay gelding and girthed up the frightened horse. With the piebald companion horse still close by the bay horse's side, James took the opportunity to throw his leg across the well-worn saddle. But the very moment James's backside hit the saddle, the big boned bay gelding hit its straps too, pig- rooting, snorting and twisting, while spinning in the air, just like a fine 'saddle bronco' horse in full flight. Tom, who was in tune with the whole situation, promptly tapped his horse on the right flank, pulled down hard on his right rein and galloped towards the cattle yard's heavy metal gates. Flinging them both wide open, he hoped to give his friend the opportunity to hit the black soil flat beyond the wooden cattle yards where James and his big bay could sort out their differences in the wide open spaces, well away from the confines of the yard that seemed to hold immense fear for the newly broken gelding.

"Dig in deep with yah heels, sit straight," bellowed Bandit, who now realised that Cranky Henry had set the new man up for a fall.

"Hang on for yah dear life," yelled young Tom. Even Cranky Henry, who probably got the biggest surprise of all after selecting the worst horse in the entire stock camp for new chum James to ride, shouted, "Yahoo, you can ride 'em young fella."

As James held on tight to the bridle and a bunch of matted horse mane, his knees and thighs battled to hang a firm grip on the mad-dened bay as it tried every angle in the geometry book with its bucking, twisting and snorting, fighting with James to dislodge him from the saddle. James was not prepared to give in so easily to the bay – he had no fear of horses, and felt he could ride the bay gelding on the tail of the mob of cattle today, if only he could just give him a bit more time.

Now that the bay had begun to accept that James wasn't out to abuse him in any way, the animal's terrifying twitches of fear began to fade. With horse, saddle and man drenched in perspiration from the stifling mid-morning's high humidity, the bay eased its frantic pace. James felt he had control of the animal through his hands and thighs as he steadily trotted it around the black soil flat once more. It was only now that James felt he could relax and feel at one with his horse, but he also felt confident and pleased that he hadn't looked a fool in front of the boss and his cranky horse-breaker Henry.

"Good on yah, that was a real neat ride James," Tom said while flashing a mile-wide smile at his new friend. James acknowledged Tom's excitement with a nod towards him, then James looked towards Henry as he rode the big bay gelding to a halt directly in front of him. Yes, here's the problem thought James to himself as his horse began to shiver and snort and paw at the ground near Henry. Henry offered far more acknowledgment than James had expected. "You rode him boy, you rode him well." There was even genuine warmth in his voice, and with that Henry mounted his black beauty and rode off at a steady trot in the direction of the stock camp. Then Bandit barked "We're behind time now, get a move on lads towards the river to find these cattle," as both James and Tom teamed up with the boss and turned their horses in the direction of the thick undergrowth of the river.

After a while James dropped his bay gelding from a fast trot that was occasionally peppered with a fancy buck or two, to a steady walk-ing pace, which put him behind Tom and Bandit with their trotting horses. James worried that the girth on his saddle would begin to aggravate the scabby pink wounds he had spotted earlier on the bay, and he worried that if they worsened he would probably be on foot out here, in the middle of nowhere and quite possibly lost.

James battled to keep the boss and Tom in sight in the thick green prickly scrub that grew wildly along the river's edge. He certainly didn't want to lose sight of the men, and with this thought he gently tapped his horse on the flank one more time while asking the bay to pick up its pace. This rough looking animal is doing extremely well considering what he must have gone through with Henry, thought James. "I'll call you Aussie," James said out loud. "Yes, it's Aussie from now on. You're my first Australian horse...I doubt I'll ever forget you."

James rode his horse along the steep banks of the river, keeping his eyes and ears alert for any wild cattle, when out of the blue, Aussie's ears twitched, his nostrils flared, and he let go with a high pitched whinny while tossing his head about the air. James had also thought he'd heard cattle calling and bellowing from the far side of the river. He immediately put more pressure on his horse by forcing him to step down over the crumbling black soil on the river bank and into the still water that was shrouded in darkness from the over-hanging paperbarks and huge wild fig trees that thrived along the river bank. James decided he would attempt to cross the river by following a sand bank while hoping he would eventually catch up with the stockmen from Campbell's Run, where at last James thought he'd be able to pull his weight and do the job that Bandit had employed him to do.

At this point, James was beginning to feel slightly overwhelmed by the Australian Outback, with no roads, no signs and the vast distances between people and civilisation, and he was sure he had become lost after losing sight of Tom and Bandit who had possibly caught up with the other stockmen and the mob of cattle somewhere further along the river.

However, the emptiness did give James time to ponder and think of his family back home in England. James knew his Grand-mama, Lady Elizabeth, was an extremely strong and very capable woman and that she had always run the family empire with an iron but fair rod. Although James had been reared on the breast of a wet nanny who had been breast-feeding a baby of her own at the same time, he did love his mother Gabrielle, and thought of her nearly every day. He still worried about the state of her health and the 'depression sickness' that seemed to have constantly plagued her all through his childhood memories. It was a terrible shame, thought James, that his father, the now Lord Alexander Wentworth III of Rosengarten Castle, at times expressed such incredulous ways and had a need to constantly pursue other women, in a seemingly wild and wanton way.

Sadly, older brother Morgan had been tarred with the same brush as his Grandfather and father before him. Oh well, thought James, that has been the way of our life in England for centuries, and as the youngest in line to the Wentworth family title – a title I really have no need for, or so Grandfather said – it's up to me to break the mould. James believed he would break that awful cycle, and that living in Australia would help him do just that. He wondered if there might be a telegram or letter from the family waiting for him at Campbell's Run homestead on his return from this muster.

As James gently guided Aussie across the river he pondered that a little news from home would be nice and he couldn't help but wonder what his lady friend Catherine was doing now. Catherine was certainly of marriageable age and seemed more attractive and spirited than ever on her last visit to see him in England. Yes, thought James as he helped manoeuvre Aussie from a deep patch of water in the river, I believed there was an opportunity for me to escort Lady Catherine.

James gently guided Aussie through the knee-deep ink-black water. He picked up on a terrible stench, a sickly rich fruity, but also musky smell that hung thickly in the humidity. Just as Aussie began to panic, the high-pitched screeching and flapping of webbed wings of thousands of squabbling and urinating flying foxes clouded the sky, dropping partially eaten fruit on them and extinguishing what little light there was in the river bed. "Steady...steady Aussie," James soothed as he gently tried to calm his new steed. But Aussie was frantic with fear as he fought James, tossing his head wildly about and whinnying loudly while attempting to dump his rider.

"Hold up boy, steady Aussie," James said as he straightened his own back and gave a little slack to Aussie's reins to let him buck and pig-root all he wanted in the soft sand and cool water until the horse realised no harm would come to him. James thought the ride was far more comfortable than the one Aussie had handed out to him back at the stockyards that morning, but for some reason his horse still seemed unsettled. Then both James and Aussie could hear the cattle calls again, and then a horse whinny and a cattle dog barking frantically. He tapped his mount on the flank so they could catch up with the cattle muster that was now close.

As James pushed Aussie up and over the crumbling river bank onto the opposite side of the river he heard, "Ayeee young fella, you make it," offered an older and smartly attired Aboriginal stockman who seemed genuinely pleased to have company working the tail of the mob of slow moving and freshly mustered cattle. "Yes, Mullicka, we made it," answered a relieved James. Tom had introduced James to Mullicka back at the station, and had told him that Mullicka was an elder in the area and a good stockman, highly respected by Derrick Dunn, the owner of Campbell's Run cattle station.

James was now feeling more settled and not so lost and disorientated as he was earlier, and was happy to feel so free in so many ways. James tapped Aussie gently on the flank and moved his horse slightly towards Mullicka. "Mullicka, Sir, what position do you wish me to ride in?" James asked. Mullicka, his grey hair and wild grey beard standing on end in the heat and dust, turned to James with a huge smile on his deeply lined face and said, "You know young fella, this is the first time anybody ever called me that...that Sir fella name," and he roared with laughter. James couldn't help but smile at Mullicka and thought how he liked this Indigenous man from the Australian bush, as the stockman let fly with a high-pitched 'yow yow' as he patiently pushed the loitering cattle along.

With this, Mullicka turned towards James and pointing with his arthritic index finger said, "Young fella, you ride 'em that side, and I ride 'em this side, you push 'em up." With that he turned from giving James his orders and swung his own horse around promptly to chase another wild beast that had the cunning to attempt a breakaway from the mob while the two men were deep in conversation.

James settled easily into the muster, and enjoyed the chase of every wild and stray beast that tried to make a break for freedom from the main herd of cattle that he and his new friend Mullicka had gently pushed along together on the tail. Certainly the cattle and muster on Campbell's Run Station was hugely different to those musters and rather woolly looking beasts his family grazed on their Rosengarten Castle Estate in England, thought James. Plus I don't remember having so much excitement in one day. I'll make the most of my time on this station...how right Grandfather was about the Australian Outback, there's just so much to learn here.

The mob of cattle swelled in size by week's end as the other stockmen led by Bandit travelled far and wide from the main mob to find and hunt out the stragglers that had dispersed to the far distant hills to find a safe place to hide their young. As Bandit readied the cattle for the return muster to the station yard, he sung out his orders to his nearest man: "Spread out, let the cattle water in the shallow part of the river." As Bandit passed this message to his stockman, he also held his arms high and spread wide above his head, signalling to the others as they emerged through the veil of fine river-bank dust to spread out and protect the cattle as they watered.

By now James was feeling confident and extremely pleased with his new steed's performance. He thought Aussie had done reasonably well working the long and sometimes tiring days in the mustering camp. And so James hoped that in the future he and Aussie would be able to attend many more musters on the cattle station together.

Just at that moment young Tom rode up on his sweat covered and slightly tired piebald mare. "James, turn your horse around, Bandit has told us to water our horses two at a time before we move on with the cattle." James acknowledged by nodding towards his friend and asked, "Good day Tom?" "You bet yah, I scored a couple of good size rogue bulls and pushed them into the mob by myself." James couldn't help but notice that mile-wide smile...Tom was over the moon and pleased as punch.

CHAPTER 12

Horse Killer

"Follow me, James," Tom sung out as he led the way around the mob of thirsty and now watering cattle. James noticed as the cattle had their fill of water they would move up and out of the river bed and onto the opposite side of the river's bank where green shoots had emerged from the once burnt tufts of black grass. There they were met by the more experienced stockmen who had mustered and rode on the wings of the mob all day long, ready to hold them together again.

"Come on James, hurry up, and watch for crocs, the river's known for them," said Tom as many of these prehistoric reptiles could be seen sunning themselves within the shallows and sandy sculptured bays of the river. James tipped his hat towards Tom before both men slid from their worn saddles and led their horses towards the dark cool water only to spook several young freshwater crocodiles lurking in the shadows. As the young crocs panicked and dived back into the river for protection and security, they created an instantaneous chain of white foam diving events throughout the remainder of the river. This caused James's still rather touchy horse Aussie to rear up abruptly above him in fright, time and time again. James tried desperately to hang on to Aussie's reins as his new steed fought desperately against him with all its strength and its will of steel. James felt he understood Aussie's fearful anxiety, and really didn't blame him for taking fright of the crocodiles as he did. James spoke softly to his steed as he tried in vain to bring him back to ground. "Calm Aussie…calm," James soothed, repeating it over and over again while keeping his strong voice steady but low and comforting. James made sure he never lost control of the horse's reins, fearful that out in the bush he may never be able to catch him again. What a waste, thought James, Aussie had come so far and done so well today. But as Aussie fought and dragged James towards the high bank of the river, he heard young Tom sing out, "Me and my horse will come up behind him, a bit of company might help." Of course James was unable to answer Tom. His total concentration was with his horse which was still showing extreme signs of anxiety and agitation as it fought desperately to yank its head free of the bridle and break James's hold on the reins. Then at that very moment, in among the flying dust and debris, James caught a glimpse of another horseman ride up behind Aussie. Unable to recognise the rider who spun his own big steed around and backed him up close behind Aussie, James was shocked to see his horse cop a powerful boot from the new-comer's hind quarters which nailed Aussie's rear end with both barrels.

In previous musters, Tom had witnessed Henry forcefully push his own steed into using this very same method of dominance over feral bulls and freshly mustered cattle that had continually broken out from the mob of cattle. Now he used it on Aussie to forcefully push him towards the river. Why in hell did Henry always have to resort to these cruel tactics, thought a now angry Tom.

"Back off Henry, back off, James has enough to handle without your two bobs worth," yelled young Tom, while showing immense courage as he rode in on Henry to get his message across. Tom had experienced this nasty side of Henry before when he was the new chum in the stock camp, and now he decided that Henry's bullying tactics had gone too far. With the confronting sight before him Tom slapped his own steed on the rump and rode in to try to intervene between Henry, Aussie and his friend James. However, by this stage Tom could see that Henry was in no state to be reasoned with. "You arrogant old bastard," Tom hollered, "leave them alone," which only seemed to aggravate what was becoming an extremely volatile situation. With this Henry became only more explosive and angrily swung his horse around and dug his spurs so deeply into his own horse's flesh that they instantly drew blood, causing his own steed to react alarmingly by pushing and shouldering into Aussie, who by now was equally worked up because of his fear of the unknown in the water. James, who had no idea of what Henry was trying to prove, eventually let go of his horse's reins to let him go free. But Aussie was consequently forced over the top of the crumbling river bank by Henry and his horse, and into a breakaway gully, and that was when James heard a distinct loud crack as Aussie fell towards him, striking James in the upper thigh.

"Now look what you've done," yelled Tom, as Henry swung his own steed around. Without even as much as a backward glance towards the destruction he had caused, Henry returned to the now watered and grazing cattle on the opposite side of the river bank.

"Heck James, are you alright?" asked Tom. "There's blood everywhere." Tom had slid from his saddle and raced towards James who was on the ground. "Is your leg broken James, I heard that crack?" But while aristocratic blue blood James bled profusely, he assured his young Australian friend that he had not broken his leg, but had received a laceration. He was an extremely tough and hardened man from his days of breaking and handling the family's Rosengarten horses, and now he was worried that his new steed was in agony while still caught up in the savage breakaway gully with a broken hind quarter of its own.

"You're right James, Aussie has broken a hind quarter. In fact it's so bad he's unable to even get up," said Tom feeling somewhat disillusioned. Tom glanced towards James and could see his English friend was bleeding heavily. As Tom had a closer look at the wound in James's right leg he let fly with, "Far out James, that's more than a cut in your thigh, you need bloody stitches or you could bleed to death." James realised his Australian friend was a self-prescribed doctor but was becoming panicky from the sight of so much blood spurting from his wound.

As Aussie whinnied with the most terrible cries of pain each time he tried to raise his broken body from the gully, James called softly to his steed, "Steady Aussie, steady boy, help is on its way." James felt awful, and hearing Aussie's painful cries only made him feel worse. Then Tom, who seemed to be working on an adrenalin rush, burst forth with "We bloody hope so, or we'll be up the creek, yeah, all three of us thanks to that bloody madman Henry."

By now young Tom had a grip on himself and had torn off the long sleeves from both his and James's work shirts to use as a tourniquet on his friend's thigh. He then searched his belt for his pouch and pocket knife, which had English James promptly lift his back from the ground while attempting to roll from Tom's reach. "Tom, please be careful with that knife!" James implored. "Aw, for God's sake, come on James. I need to cut your jeans with this pocket knife, how else can I attend to your wound?" Trying to lighten up the situation a little Tom added, "I suppose I could try and chew through your jeans with my teeth if you want."

At that moment the boss arrived on the scene leading a spare horse. Both Tom and James looked at Bandit but found his facial expression hard to read – he carried that steely dark look of a hard man. There wasn't a word exchanged between them, there wasn't time. As Bandit dismounted he held an old wartime .303 rifle, and within seconds of James turning his head away from the sight of his struggling horse he heard the most powerful explosion of all time. And then Aussie was dead.

"For the best boys, he was in shocking pain, nothing we could do out here, nothing at all that would have been kinder lads," Bandit offered. Bandit had a quick look at James's thigh and said, "Good job Tom. When you're done, help Jim onto this spare horse and head back to the big house at the station. Tell Sheila I sent you both," and away Bandit rode to catch up with his remaining stockmen and the mob of cattle.

"Is that it?" asked James turning to Tom. "Yep, that's it, you know it can get tough out here sometimes, but don't let it deter you from loving the Outback, 'cause we have some good times too."

Tom helped his friend up into the saddle of the spare stockhorse, and although James's thigh was beginning to hurt terribly he wasn't about to complain loudly to Tom. He thought of his stockhorse Aussie who had just began to trust him and who had worked extremely hard in the past week of the muster. Now he lay dead and would probably become some man-eating crocodile's next feast. James shuddered at the thought of Aussie's demise and promptly decided he would suffer his pain in silence as help would be available soon enough.

The two horsemen rode their horses at walking pace across the sun-harden black soil plains far out from the river, where only a rare tree broke the monotony of the vast open space. Tom pointed out to James the large circular area of dangerous cracks and breakaway gullies left behind from the burning sun as it sucked all moisture from the soil, leaving it as solid as a granite block. Tom and James had become good friends during the river muster, and even with James's thigh giving him grief, he couldn't help but smile at young Tom's amusing stories of the Outback as they rode their horses over the black soil plain and down through the station's horse paddock. Soon, Tom became conscious of a familiar sound, the throb of the Southern Cross engine, the station's generator. He turned towards James and said, "Can you hear that? It's the station's power plant, about another mile further and we'll be at the big house." James acknowledged what Tom had to say with a tilt of his now dusty Akubra hat – he wasn't feeling that well and his thigh had swollen considerably.

The young stockmen were greeted by a rowdy bunch of cattle dogs, blue heelers, red heelers and pure white bull terriers. The animals no sooner greeted Tom and James when they heard a high-pitched whistle, which came from the direction of the homestead. This high-pitch sound brought instant quiet to the pack of barking dogs and had them return promptly to shelter under the homestead verandah, which was supported by wooden posts four foot above the ground. Damn amazing and well trained, thought James as he grimaced in pain and looked towards the homestead. Then he noted in the shadows of the bull-nosed verandah was a much older and rather large man, who was leaning on his walking stick while watching them both intently as he expelled a strong stream of tobacco smoke from his pipe, which James's nostrils told him was possibly Jamaican, his own Grandfather's favourite pipe tobacco.

"Tom, who is that gentleman?" asked James. "That's Derrick Dunn, he's the owner of Campbell's Run," answered Tom in a somewhat solemn tone. Then as if he had an afterthought Tom added, "Remember Sheila, who signed you on to work here, well she's his wife." It took a moment for James to absorb this new piece of information. "Goodness he's an old man, surely old enough to be her father," said James to no one in particular. "You hit the nail square on the head there James," his friend replied. "It's an extremely sore point and unwritten rule in the camp not to discuss what some of us may think is a strange relationship between Derrick and Sheila."

As young Tom tied both stockhorses to the homestead hitching rail, he then helped James slowly dismount. James found the sudden movement brought only more pain and bleeding from the wound in his thigh, and with Tom's help, James slowly slipped towards the ground with his teeth clenched tightly together, hoping to muffle any sounds of pain that may try to escape him. James spent a moment resting against the hitching rail, he needed to as the perspiration began beading across his forehead and for the first time ever he felt nauseous and faint. "Jesus, hang on James, for God's sake mate, don't bloody pass out now, you're too flaming heavy for me to carry," muttered Tom. Then out of the blue James heard a woman's voice speak to Tom. "Tom, please give me a hand to get James into the wheelchair. Derrick has been kind enough to lend us his." James tried to convince the two of them he would be fine, trying to save himself the indignity of being pushed in the chair by his Boss's young wife. With James in the wheelchair, Tom took control of the chair and began to push it flat-out across the huge lawn towards the ramp at the front of the homestead, while Sheila, seemingly full of importance, told James she would have him well and truly back in the stock camp in no time. Sheila then left it to Tom to bring James up to the homestead, but not before assuring James that she would attend to his wounded thigh on the front verandah with plenty of warm water, and would get further instructions from the district's Royal Flying Doctor via the station's two-way radio and medical kit. "Yes, we're not quite as isolated as it may seem," added Tom as if to reassure James that all would be well. "The two-way radio helps to keep us in contact with the outside world."

Young Tom couldn't help himself and whispered to James, "What a way to meet the big chief for the first time, you're riding his horse." "What do you mean?" asked James in a much lower tone of voice. Tom felt quite knowledgeable and slightly superior to his friend James at times – he held a higher rank in the stock camp for one, had been on Campbell's Run much longer than most and he did have an ear for gossip, plus he did like his new Pommy friend James and felt if he did share some of his knowledge of the place and its people it may help keep James out of trouble one day. "Well, they say the chief came a buster off his powerful quarter horse in that black 'drummy' soil country about twenty years ago. The old Aboriginal people say there's a hollow sound that follows you in that 'drummy' country. Some horses become confused and spooked by it, they think they're being followed and take fright of their own shadows." Tom had a quiet laugh while thinking about it and then continued. "Apparently, that's what happened with the chief's flash quarter horse, it got spooked and sent him flying…the chief ended up in a heap on the ground. The only horse he rides now on and off is the one you're riding in, boring old thing, don't you think? Do you want to see if we can get a buck or two out of it James?" asked Tom rather cheekily as he attempted to swing the wheelchair to the left and right to get a bite out of James. "Definitely not, thank you Tom," was James's reply as he gritted his teeth tightly together, hoping to soften the fresh pang of pain.

On reaching the front verandah both men were greeted by Derrick Dunn. He held out a large pale hand but his grip was made of steel. "I'm Derrick Dunn. Welcome Tom, and I believe your wounded offsider here is our new hand, English James?" asked Derrick in his deep gruff voice that really did suit the sizeable man, thought James. "Yes Sir, I'm James, and I apologise for the state I am currently in," answered James ever so politely. "Well, you have youth on your side, you seem fit and healthy, won't be long and Sheila will have you back in the stock camp and on the job," offered Derrick. At that moment his much younger wife arrived with a huge enamel basin full of steaming hot water to bath James's thigh.

Young Tom stooped to give Sheila a helping hand with the basin, but was shocked to cop a nasty rap across the knuckles from Derrick Dunn's walking stick. Shocked, Tom immediately stood tall and faced up to Derrick Dunn. He wasn't about to be knocked around by anyone, not even by his moody old uncle Derrick, or Derrick's bent old walking stick for that matter. "Chief, what was that all about?" Tom shot back at Derrick as he tried to stand as tall as his mean old uncle. "Let Sheila do it Tom. Don't know why she wants to as she has all the help in the world around the house here. Then Derrick turned towards Sheila with "But you always insist, don't you my dear." His tone of voice with a hint of sarcasm was not the most endearing Tom had ever heard. James sat quietly and simply wanted his wound to be cleaned and treated so he could be out and away from the tension that was so visibly heavy in the late afternoon air. Tom also felt he'd rather be back in the stock camp, with the atmosphere so thick it could have been sliced with a blunt butcher's knife. "Well James, I'll leave you in the chief's and Sheila's hands. I must get back to the muster other-wise Bandit will have my arse," and with that Tom descended the back steps of the homestead two at a time, strode smartly back across the evergreen buffalo lawn and in no time was galloping his piebald horse across the station's horse paddock while leading the stock camp's spare horse close behind him.

As Tom hurriedly left the homestead for the camp, he never gave it a thought he may be leaving behind a totally confused James. As Sheila, under the watchful eye of her husband Derrick, gently bathed James's thigh in warm salty water before attempting to pull his wound together with many butterfly stitches found in the medical kit, James wondered to himself, where was he to go from here as he grasped the significance of his worthless situation.

"Sir," James directed to Derrick, "I realise I am not of much use to the stock camp at this time, would it be better if I resigned?" Derrick Dunn was immediately taken aback with James's upfront offer of resigning – good men were hard to come by in the Outback. There were always plenty of seasonal ringers and blow-ins, but there was something very different about this English lad. "Definitely not boy, there's nothing wrong with your hands. You can wax the station's sad-dles and bridles, which is something Bandit never seems to give any thought to these days."

With that the chief handed James a well-beaten and used pair of crutches while saying he wanted them returned to the homestead as soon as they were no longer needed. Derrick then pointed out the stockmen's quarters some one hundred and fifty yards away. "You can camp there until your leg is right...should be by the end of the week, and take your meals in the cookhouse with the windmill man and the station's cook." With that Derrick returned to the cool of the inside of his homestead while James hobbled slowly across the uneven flat towards the men's quarters on his borrowed crutches.

James found himself a comfortable bed, and then the much needed bathroom where he attempted to wash away the heavy dust that clung to his hair, clothes and body while keeping his injured leg out of the water. James had intended to wash after he had finished watering his horse back at the stock camp. "Now look at the mess you're in," James chided himself.

With his thigh still giving him grief, James wrapped a towel around his naked body and hobbled out the back of the men's quarters where he hung his wet clothes over the fence that circled the brown lawn. He was sure they would dry quickly in the mid-afternoon sunshine, and while waiting for his only jeans and shirt to dry, James took the opportunity to test his camp bed to rest his very swollen and aching leg.

James found it difficult to rest and get comfortable on the horse-hair mattress in the stockmen's quarters; the room felt like an oven as the intense heat and humidity sucked all moisture from his body. Eventually, James got up and hobbled about the unlined room on his crutches in search of a cool place to rest. Soon he discovered that every second sheet of corrugated iron could be pushed open with a wooden prop, creating a huge shutter window which let in the warm and extremely pleasing breeze. At long last, James was able to lie on his bed and rest his throbbing thigh, while his perspiration-drenched body was pleasantly cooled by the wafting gentle breeze that came through the window. As James drifted on and off, and eventually into a restful sleep, his mind began to play tricks on him as it flashed between England and Australia. One moment his restless mind would have it that all was not right at the family's English property Rosengarten, and the next it was having him lost in the sandy desert of the Australian Outback. As James dozed spasmodically, his body temperature had begun to rise. He heard a vehicle drive past the men's quarters slowly. He thought of Grand-mama Lady Elizabeth and his mother Gabrielle, there was even a thought for his rascal of a father, the current Lord Wentworth III of Rosengarten Castle, and his older brother Morgan. But his dreaming left his mind muddled and confused. Nothing made any sense. Then as the sun set over Campbell's Run to leave behind the timeless pastel hues, the bright evening star rose high into the night sky coinciding with James's fever which also rose to its own zenith. As the fever moved slowly throughout his once strong body, weakening it with a burning temperature, in his dreams it also heightened his sexual desire for the very attractive Lady Catherine, who James had walked away from and left behind in England. Eventually, after many hours of tossing and turning, James drifted into a deep and peaceful sleep only to be woken later by the sound of a door closing as it scraped across the cement floor somewhere in the darkened room. The sound was closely followed by a whiff of a musky oriental – or was it a sweet smelling – perfume, thought James. Muddled and disorientated, James's first thought was of Lady Catherine. He sat upright in bed confused, but while trying to clear his still bewildered and foggy mind James called out in panic to his friend, believing he was still in England. "Catherine? Lady Catherine is that you?" Then after a short silence Sheila answered, "No James, it's me Sheila. You have had a terrible fever and been delirious and raving loudly most of the night…you have been extremely unwell, would you please remain on the bed."

"Would you please forgive me, I hope I haven't said anything inappropriate that may have offended you," offered James now feeling somewhat embarrassed about his whole situation, and especially his respectability in the presence of Sheila – the chief's attractive young wife who was closer to James's own age than her husband's – as he battled to hide his near-naked manhood with a tiny bath towel. The sight of James's tanned and hardened physique would have been enough for any woman to immediately go into overdrive, and Sheila was no different. In the limited light put out by the kerosene lamp on the kitchen table James could make out a steaming bowl in Sheila's hands. "It's for you, the cook told me you never made it to the cook's dining room for dinner tonight. He kept you this bowl of beef broth," Sheila offered kindly. James glanced down at his naked suntanned body feeling terrible to be caught out in such a situation, and wishing he had his clean clothes that were still hanging over the fence behind the men's quarters. Now James wondered how he would get to them and restore his respectability. "I apologise for not presenting myself dressed in respectable attire. My clothes are washed and hanging out to dry on the fence at the back of the quarters," offered James feeling genuinely embarrassed. "Not to worry James, no one will pinch them, they'll still be there in the morning, plus I like what I can see," cooed Sheila with a mischievous twinkle in her green eyes. It had been some time since Sheila had seen, and been so close to such a fine looking male specimen – well, not since the last time she had been with Bandit – and now she felt a little guilty for openly speaking her thoughts out loud. By way of compensating her guilt, Sheila quickly handed James some tablets the Flying Doctor had earlier prescribed for him via the station's two-way radio.

Sheila sat down on the foot of James's bed, handed him the bowl of beef broth and a spoon. Then as James began to hungrily devour the warm soup, Sheila got up and tidied James's sick bed, and while doing so her firm breasts brushed gently against his shoulder. She hovered about the bed head putting more effort than was necessary into plumping James's pillows, before finally saying goodnight and that she would call in and check on him again in the morning. James was grateful for the medical attention given to him by Sheila, but he did feel so much easier once she had vacated the men's quarters and he was alone again. And now that James's mind was clearer, he knew that he wanted no part of whatever friction there was between the chief and his young wife.

James's thigh still throbbed, but his fever had subsided. He was sure the soup had played a part in this, and he chided himself that tomorrow he must remember to thank Sheila for her medical attention and kindness for bringing him a bowl of soup during the night, which compensated for the evening meal he had been too ill to partake of with the cook and windmill man.

Now for the first time since his friend Tom had helped him back to the stock camp, James wondered how the muster was going, knowing that Bandit had planned on having the newly mustered cattle back at the station yard by the following evening. James gave a thought to the death of his steed Aussie, but also realised that the bullet from Bandit's rifle was the only humane way to go for his horse in the end, particularly way out in this land of the 'never-never'. His mind also touched on the brutal way that Henry, the station's horse breaker, used his own steed to lash out at Aussie with its hind quarters, something James thought was unnecessary and extremely cruel. James made a mental note that when the opportunity arose he would question Henry of his reasons for such cruelty, although he felt much more like squaring the score between the two of them. However, now was not the time as his thigh was still in pain, and James thought this would only give Henry an added advantage over him as Henry struck James as not only a cruel person but possibly a dirty fighter too. Well, one day the timing would be right, thought James.

The following day James spent shirtless in the sweltering iron-clad saddle room. The corrugated iron constantly crackled and popped from the overbearing heat as he vigorously rubbed beeswax into the station's saddles and bridles for Derrick Dunn. Sheila arrived, dressed in a crisp white and blue polka dot sundress carrying a white envelope with his family's coat of arms stamped heavily into the wax seal on the back of it. Just this one time James wished the family crest had not been used on his mail.

"This is for you, James," said Sheila, as she passed the official looking envelope towards James. But instead of letting the envelope go into James's hand, Sheila hung onto it wanting to play games and tease James with his letter. As James was too much of a gentleman to play childish tug-a-war games with his chief's wife, he relented and let go of his mail which sent Sheila staggering back several feet from James. "That wasn't very nice of you, James, I could have fallen over," Sheila said with an odd twist to her smile. James apologised immediately. "I thought you were handing me the letter, not playing games with me Sheila." He then bent down and picked the envelope up off the wooden shed floorboards without another glance in Sheila's direction. James thanked Sheila and hoped she would disappear back to the homestead, but instead she hung around, hoping James would be tempted to open his mail from home, especially as it had his family coat of arms stamped heavily into the red wax seal on the back of the thick envelope. James folded the envelope and placed it securely into his jeans pocket and buttoned it up. He would read it later when he was alone. "Aren't you excited to hear of any news from your family in England, James?" asked Sheila. "I am but as you can see I am in the middle of greasing these saddles for your husband," answered James, not realising he had put extra emphasis on the noun 'husband', while keeping his head down and concentrating on the job at hand. The last thing James needed was for Derrick Dunn to walk into the saddle room and catch his young attractive wife hovering far too close to the newly hired hand. Sheila's closeness and womanly perfumed body was affecting his own emotions.

Back at the men's quarters, James anxiously opened his mail from home. It was written, as expected, by his dear Grand-mama Lady Elizabeth. He smiled to himself as he thought Grand-mama would always be the head of the household at Rosengarten Castle, well, until her dying day that is, and seeing that Lady Elizabeth had weathered several rough storms in her time, James felt it would be some time yet before Grand-mama would be leaving them for good. But James found her letter disturbing. It seemed Grand-mama was not entirely happy with father or his older brother Morgan, and Grand-mama believed their wanton ways were truly out of hand and damaging to the good name of the family. James found the news of his mother, Gabrielle, the most disturbing of all, as she had attempted suicide. The thought of his mother wanting to take her own life disturbed James greatly. But Grand-mama had not stopped there. 'Your older brother Morgan, as the common talk reports, has put Lady Catherine in child. My dear James, I had not wanted to be the one to break such terrible news to you. As you well know the family had hoped that one day you would return to your senses and your roots in England, after visiting Australia, and marry the girl. There is so much despair in the family, I cannot possibly burden your mama with any more of it as she finds most days impossible to handle and others she spends dancing through the meadows in near nakedness. Please, my dear Grandson James, could you find it deep in your heart to return to Rosengarten Castle at your earliest convenience to help sort this terrible mess. If not for a long period, then please come for a short time and I will try to understand, and then if you must you may return to Australia with all my blessings.' The letter was signed off, Your Grand-mama, Lady Elizabeth of Rosengarten Castle.

CHAPTER 13

Torn

Outside the men's quarters James sat on a bench clutching Grand-mama's letter in his hand. It was evident that her once elegant and fine handwriting was failing, and James wondered if it was the 'goings on' at Rosengarten that were affecting both his mother's and Grand-mama's wellbeing. Not even the shade from the towering box tree above could offer James relief from the searing heat as he reread the letter over and over again. To return to England was not something James had wanted to do. At this point he hadn't even left the Northern Territory. He had planned to visit Lonesome Downs in the Kimberley, and also Koorong in the hills outside of Adelaide where he hoped to meet up with Dr Nicholas's son David. Then there was Coolamun Downs on the Nullarbor Plain in South Australia where his nanny Gemma had grown up as a child. These were all places of interest to James, places he had always dreamed of visiting from the stories that Grandfather and Gemma had told him during his early childhood years. Right now, James felt his aristocratic family in England was about to cheat him out of his own life's adventures and future in Australia. If nothing else, this would cut his stay in the country well and truly short. And now, as he sat on the hard wooden bench and silently pondered his future, he realised that never before had he felt anger or even resentment towards his own family members or their Rosengarten Castle Estate in the past, and he hoped that he would not in the future. But at this very moment there was one thing that James understood, and that was he would not let the family or its estate of Rosengarten control him or be part of his future life. James knew these were rash thoughts of the moment, but he was extremely annoyed.

James had always been close to his Grand-mama Lady Elizabeth, and because she had written this letter to him begging his return to the family estate, he decided after another day of serious thought that he would return, as duty called, for his dear Grand-mama and mother Gabrielle, but only this once and for a short time.

"Hey, where are you at?" asked Tom as he rode up to the men's quarters on his tired looking piebald mare. "I can tell it's not a love letter that you're holding in your hand, or is it? You seem to be miles away, James." "I'm fine, thank you Tom. Has the muster been completed?" asked James, while wishing he was still part of the team. He did enjoy old Mullicka's company on the tail of the mob, and especially the adrenalin rush that one got when the opportunity arose to help push along the rogue bulls and wild cattle that were brought in to join the quieter mob of already mustered cattle. James folded the letter from home and placed it securely into his top pocket. He would wait a day or two then re-read the letter from Grand-mama before speaking to Bandit about having to leave Campbell's Run Station for England.

Tom could sense that his English mate had some sort of problem that he wasn't prepared to share with him right now. Tom wondered whether Derrick's attitude towards James on the day of the accident had anything to do with it.

"James, are you sure everything is okay with you? I heard you were unwell but you certainly are many miles away?" Tom asked. This was the first time Tom had felt that his English friend had wanted to brush him aside, and he wondered why. Young Tom slid down from his piebald stockhorse, tied the reins to the outside hitching rail and sat on the bench besides James. "James, I probably should have told you that Derrick Dunn is my uncle, he's my mother's brother. Derrick was the eldest son in my mother's family, he inherited all of the family's property...my mother got nothing." James sat and listened to Tom and thought how both his and Tom's family life seemed to have run in parallel. Then Tom said, "I suppose I'm lucky he's even given me a job, because there's no love lost between either of them."

"Do you know Tom, that some of our families use a very similar system, it's sometimes used by the old aristocratic families in England. I suppose they all work the same way," offered James who wasn't really that interested in who really owned Campbell's Run. "Well, yeah, it's all bull dust if you ask me…I mean Derrick lived in the city, you know, all cars and smoke and big buildings, and he was a flaming accountant before he inherited this place, this Campbell's Run cattle station from his old man, my grandfather," said Tom, who was feeling a little angry because his mother, who had worked here until her parents died, had never even got a mention in her father's will where the family property was concerned. All she got was a five thousand pound cash payment. It didn't take much for James to feel his Australian friend was not entirely happy with the treatment his mother had received for all her hard work on the cattle station, and so James decided to try to change the subject. He had a problem of his own that needed to be discussed with Bandit in a day or two, and James thought that he too would be needing to vent his anger with someone, somewhere. So James asked Tom how Bandit was going, which turned out to be a mistake.

"You know, James, that's where the thorn in my side comes from," said Tom, still as agitated as all hell. "What do you mean by that, Tom?" his friend asked. "It was Bandit who brought Sheila to Campbell's Run in the first place. Sheila was Bandit's girlfriend to start with, and because she was Bandit's girlfriend, she got the job as the station cook at the homestead." Tom's mind drifted for a moment. "Umm, her cooking left a bit to be desired I might add. But, as soon as she found out that old Derrick owned the cattle station and that he never had a wife, it didn't take her long to dump Bandit, as he was only the overseer, for Derrick. I can tell you Sheila dumped Bandit like a bloody hot potato, and she immediately honed in on Derrick. They disappeared and got married within three months of first meeting each other. How about that for earning a quick quid in one hell of a hurry?" James really did feel for Tom, and he understood just where he was coming from as the situation was very similar in James's case in England. James could see the age-old ancestral line in this case – there were no children between Derrick and Sheila, so Sheila would take Campbell's Run Station away from its rightful owners at the end of the day.

"Ah, let's get off this bloody subject James. The rights and the wrongs of it, it just bugs me sometimes, probably because my mother was left out of the family property deal, meaning Campbell's Run. I suppose because she's a woman, her old man thought she wasn't capable of running a cattle station in her own right, but he had obviously forgotten just how hard she had worked for him on this station, handling the horses and mustering the cattle, and all for nothing. Because I think of you as a good fellow James, and I won't repeat this warning, be alert and careful where Sheila's concerned. I think Derrick's awake to her slipping across the boundary fence of marriage occasionally." Then Tom, out of the blue, let forth a burst of raucous laughter, surprising James. "Something funny Tom?" James ventured. "You were just in the middle of theorising your family's rather serious and I believe confidential information, and now you're in fits and tears of laughter. What's the matter, Tom?"

"Well, I was thinking, I'd hate to be the poor bloke that old Derrick eventually catches with Sheila, because he has one hell of a bad temper. Yep, old Derrick goes bright red. You can see his scalp glow when he's angry. I reckon he'd beat the shit out of him with that mean looking walking stick of his." Then Tom suddenly brightened up and said, "What are we sitting here talking about all this family stuff for anyway, James? Let's do some handstands and cheer ourselves up." James couldn't help but like this Australian stockman. They were the same in age, and English James felt that his red-haired friend could even get a good laugh out of the kookaburra if he had to. "Come on James, hobble across to the homestead yards with me and have a look at the good mob of cattle that we all mustered together the last week," said Tom, trying to look on the brighter side of life now. Then, with a cheeky twinkle in his eye, Tom added, "You were with us on this muster, weren't you James?"

Three days later and true to his plan, James asked Bandit if he could speak with him after breakfast. "You're not pulling the pin on the job already, are you young Jim?" was Bandit's candid reply. For some unknown reason Bandit had expected this English lad to have stuck it out in the stock camp a little longer than most blow-ins, but you can never tell, he thought.

CHAPTER 14

Trouble Brewing

James explained to his boss that he'd received a letter from home, stating there were problems and his mother was not well. There was no way James intended to explain anything any further only that it was imperative he return to England as soon as possible. James thanked Bandit for giving him the opportunity to have worked in his stock camp, something he had always wanted to do. James also apologised for any inconveniences he might cause due to leaving mid-muster. Bandit assured James that the mustering camp on Campbell's Run would operate with or without him. "You're a good horseman young Jim. If you ever think of returning to Australia, look us up, there could be a job for you, if you're lucky," Bandit said, as a mischievous smile crossed his face. Bandit went on and told James that he would have Sheila make his wages up and see if he could organise a ride back to Darwin for him. They shook hands on it, which left James wondering had the boss broken his fingers as he wriggled and stretched them back to life after Bandit's vice-like handshake.

James no longer needed the help of the chief's crutches, and his wound was healing nicely with the help of medication given to him each morning by Sheila under the Flying Doctor's instructions. James hoped that by the time Bandit had organised a ride to Darwin for him he would be fit and well again. In the meantime, James was kept on light duties around the homestead. In the evenings he aired his suit and laundered his stained work clothes ready for the journey home to England. James couldn't help but smile to himself as he rubbed his jeans hard against the washing board in the corrugated iron laundry. If the laundry maid at Rosengarten saw the state his clothes were in now, she would possibly think he had never washed or changed his clothes since leaving England.

Then late one evening in the men's quarters, while resting in a hessian covered deck chair trying to read an old newspaper by the dull light of a kerosene lamp, James had an unexpected visit from Tom.

"Jesus Christ James, I hear you're going back to England. Why would you want to go back there, mate?" asked Tom, seemingly both flustered and angry to be losing a friend of similar age to himself. "I was going to travel west and further south with you remember? We talked of working on other cattle stations together."

Of late, James's mind had been so involved with his family problems, and especially those mentioned in his Grand-mama's letter of his older brother Morgan and friend Lady Catherine's association, that he hadn't given much thought to anything else around him. James felt terrible for not informing Tom of his plans to leave Campbell's Run and his urgent need to return to England, but he felt it was only fitting his boss was the first to know. "I'm terribly sorry, Tom," offered James feeling a little guilty that Tom had heard the news the way he did, "but I did plan on telling you. I've just had several things on my mind of late." "Ah, don't worry about it James, it was that letter from home, wasn't it? I could tell, yah know, it was written all over yah bloody face," muttered young Tom, who didn't want his mate to return to his home country as he'd found him to be a good friend and good company in the stock camp. Then, at that very moment as the two men sat opposite each other in the dimly lit room, Tom swore he'd heard a gentle tap on the front door of the men's quarters. Raising an eyebrow, he whispered to James, "Are you expecting a lady friend?" "Certainly not, Tom," answered a rather indignant James, who found it unbeliev-able that his friend would even consider him entertaining the chief's wife. "Sheila's a married woman, and I do have some morals, Tom," protested James, who immediately decided to drop the subject. "Sorry James old mate, a bit of a crude joke I suppose, but I'm real sure I heard a tap on your front door and what else was I to think?" Tom poked James in the arm and whispered, "I'm not bloody deaf, there is someone at the front door James." The next moment they both turned towards the sound of creaking floorboards to see Sheila dressed only in a flimsy night dress standing in the shadows of the room. "Can we help you?" piped up Tom, knowing that Sheila would be taken aback and surprised to see him there with James. Tom had walked across from the stock camp and there was no horse tethered to the hitching rail outside the men's quarters, which would have indicated James had a visitor. "No thank you Tom," answered Sheila rather abruptly, "I'm not here to visit you. I thought I would just pop over and ask James if he needed any pain medication for the evening?" Her visit surprised James, as did her offer of pain medication, as Sheila had not offered him any medication at all over the last three days. In fact his thigh was well and truly on the mend. "No thank you Sheila, shall I see you out?" asked James. "No, I will see myself out and thank you James."

When the front door of the men's quarters was heard to slam shut, Tom couldn't help but let out a chuckle. "She'll hate me even more for stuffing up her visit with you, James, but I did warn you. Watch her, she's had good men booted out of this cattle station through her lies when Derrick has caught her out."

"Anyway, where were we? Ah yes Tom, it was the letter. I plan to return to England for only a short period of time, plus Bandit has more or less offered me my job back on the station," said James, who felt so much happier now that his return to the old country was out in the open. Tom said he'd been thinking and reckoned he'd come up with a good idea. "Do you know what I've been thinking, James?" James sat and looked straight at Tom for a moment and really had no idea of what he would come up with next, but James was certainly prepared to listen to him. "I've decided to take a holiday…and I'm going to England with yah. How about that?" With this news James immediately straightened his back and sat upright. He could not believe his friend would want to leave the warmth of the Northern Territory for cold old England, not even for a short holiday. "Are you serious, Tom? Would you really like to travel to England? You can stay at my family home while there," offered a now somewhat excited James while beginning to think that his trip home may turn out to be rather a joyous one after all. James could be sure of one thing – his Australian friend would sure liven up old Rosengarten Castle and keep the family and staff members on their toes. "Well then, James, that's settled. I'll get a loan off old Uncle Derrick. I reckon the chief owes me and my mum that much," Tom said.

Bandit had arranged a lift for both James and Tom from a generous neighbouring cattle station owner who was on his way to the big smoke to pick up staff of his own from Darwin Airport. "Here we are, lads, don't forget to get all your gear from the boot of the car," the station owner said as Tom wrestled to pull his man-size swag from the station owner's car boot at the airport, while James's suitcase was only half the size of Tom's swag. Suddenly Tom realised James hadn't brought his swag with him. "Where's yah swag, mate?" James had no intention of taking his swag all the way to England with him. "I've left it in the men's quarters ready for my return to the station, Tom." "Well, James, we never travel without our swags mate. We can stop and make camp anywhere...hmmm," Tom thought for a moment. "I suppose I can split mine with you if need be, it's large enough, as long as you don't take up too much room that is."

James and Tom checked into the flight desk at the airport, and now Tom came in for his first real taste of officialdom when trying to convince the neatly attired airline attendants that he wanted his precious swag to travel with him, in the cabin of the aircraft. "All the way to bloody England mate, it's all I've got," and probably was, as he had rolled his clothing and personal belongings on the inside of his swag like all genuine stockmen do. So, after what seemed a long and heated discussion, the attendants eventually convinced Tom that his swag and personal belongings would be safe in the cargo hold with the other passengers' suitcases. Still, all was not well with Tom. James decided to take a seat close by while Tom sorted out what he classed as his travel problems. "There's just this one problem to sort out James, and I'll be with you, mate," Tom explained to James, before he leaned across the airline counter again beckoning with his index finger to catch the attention of the busy airline personnel. Then, in what Tom thought was a reasonably low tone of voice, he spoke to the gentleman. "Sir, where does that black box travel in our aircraft to England?" This question from young Tom to the attendant brought all reception staff and attendants in the area to a sudden stop; pens dropped to desks and the floor, some official looking staff stood rolling their eyes, while the weaker of the bunch seemingly slipped away from sight altogether. Tom couldn't believe that such a simple question would take these half a dozen attendants so damn long to give him the simple answer he wanted, so he explained some more. "You know, that black box they always hunt for when the bloody airplane goes down, you know, when it crashes," repeated Tom in what he thought was very plain English. Still not entirely satisfied that the airline personnel understood him, Tom proceeded to give them a verbal demonstration using his right hand as the flying aircraft that crashes dramatically into his open left palm. Crash...bang! Tom stood at the counter eyeballing them all, when eventually the most distinguished looking gentleman in the group stepped forward and asked Tom ever so politely, "Sir, would this be the first time you have ever flown in an aircraft?" Tom was quick to assure the gentleman that it was indeed his first flight ever and he hoped it wasn't to be his last. With that knowledge, the distinguished fellow promised an anxious Tom that he would have him seated right on top of that little black box for his entire trip to England. "Good man, good man," offered Tom, now feeling a hell of a lot more confident as he put forward his hand to shake on the deal, which left a look of slight amusement on the distinguished fellow's face. Tom couldn't help but feel massively relieved now, knowing that his precious swag was taken good care of, and that he had organised for himself to ride 'that little black box' all the way to England. With his travel problems sorted out at long last, Tom was content to take a seat in the airline lounge and wait for the boarding call to England.

After the many long days of plane travel, peppered with the customary stop in Asia where both lads found the heat and humidity even more trying than the Wet Season in the Top End, it was time to board their flight from Singapore via Europe to England. James was surprised to find that Tom had willingly left behind a smorgasbord of beauties he'd stumbled across the rowdy evening before. Tom was still by his side without even a mention of that black box that seemed to have worried him ever so much at the very beginning of their journey, and now he was a lot less nervous and much more content. A little socialising the evening before seemed to have done Tom the world of good, thought James.

Once James and his friend Tom had arrived in cloudy and cold England, James realised he would soon have to explain his family's situation to Tom. James expected that Tom, 'being Tom', would have many more questions that needed answering after his explanation of the family dynamics. Their time of arrival could not have been better, thought James. With the annual fox hunt season and its festivities in full swing, his friend would certainly not be short on entertainment for the duration of his holiday with the Wentworth family.

James hoped his sudden and unexpected arrival home with his Australian friend by his side would not create any shock waves throughout the Wentworth family household. There hadn't been enough time to write to his Grand-mama and acknowledge her letter to him. Tom had told James only weeks earlier that they were lucky at Campbell's Run to have the station's mail bag dropped off and collected once a fortnight. As it turned out James's plans to return to England had moved nearly as fast as the station's mail service.

CHAPTER 15

The Lions Entrance

The driver slowed the vehicle's speed as it entered the Rosengarten Estate via the grand entrance marked by two large granite lions. Tom immediately sat bolt upright from his lounging position in the motor vehicle, totally astounded. "James...are you sure we are travelling in the right direction mate?" Tom asked, while unable to take his eyes from the huge and rather impressive castle before him. James suddenly felt a twinge of guilt for not confessing his family's circumstances in England to his friend while in the Australian Outback. So he said to Tom, "Remember when you were divulging your family history to me on Campbell's Run? Well, it's a very similar situation here with my family in England." "What do you mean?" asked Tom quite bluntly, totally astounded at the magnificent sight of the stone castle before him which would have made the corrugated iron and timber homestead on Campbell's Run look considerably pale. With that, Tom decided to have a good look around by hanging out of the moving vehicle's window. This way, although possibly a tad bushy, Tom could pick up on a landmark or two, for he certainly did not wish to be lost in England.

"Well, James you're a sly old dog. Why did you stay so quiet about all this? I mean it looks so good, we should have come for a holiday even sooner," offered Tom, and then he spotted the stables. "Have you got a horse or two for me to ride while we're here in England?" James assured Tom there were horses for all courses in the stables, and he was sure he would find something suitable for Tom to ride in the fields. "It's the fox hunt season Tom…would you be interested in joining the hunt? I have checked the dates and there is a hunt with the hounds starting tomorrow?" "Sure would, James," was Tom's quick answer, and at that moment the driver brought the vehicle to a standstill out front of the servant's entrance where James was unexpectedly greeted by a much older and slightly emotional Muldoon.

"Master James, how unexpected this is, Lord Wentworth and your Grand-mama never mentioned a word of your homecoming. Welcome home Sir." James immediately introduced his friend Tom, who stuck out his rough and callous looking hand towards Muldoon's smooth one, but was greeted with a bow of the head instead. Strange mob thought Tom, but he knew he could handle it for his holidays here at James's family estate. Then Tom turned his head slightly away from Muldoon's and whispered to James, "Excuse me James, but who's this Lord Wentworth fellow, and what are we doing at his place anyway?" James couldn't help but smile to himself, but he really didn't feel the need to explain his whole family history to Tom yet. So James spoke just as softly back to Tom and whispered, "I will explain at the appropriate time. Please let's just be on our best behaviour and enjoy ourselves, remember it's only for a short time anyway." Young Tom gave James the thumbs up, and decided to go along with the charade. All of a sudden he felt he could handle whatever pomp the occasion called for, and with total aplomb. Tom immediately straightened his back and squared his shoulders, sucked in his six-pack of muscle, lifted his chin to equal Muldoon's stance and silently planned on being on his best behaviour for his entire holiday here with James and his family. Aussie Tom realised he was in another's territory, slightly out of my depth, he thought, but seeing James handled our Australian Outback with ease, I'm prepared to give the pompous side of the motherland my best shot too. Now with that all clear in Tom's mind, he turned to catch an inquisitive Muldoon eyeing off his swag.

"Mr Tom, I would like to place this luggage in the storage room out back, if you don't mind, Sir?" Tom was immediately taken aback. Fancy the old fellow wanting to plant my swag in a dingy dark room with the spiders, and somewhere out back in this huge castle – unbelievable, thought Tom. "Well not bloody likely," Tom muttered to himself. Instead he plucked up the courage to round his vowels off as well as he possibly could, and then proceeded to give his explanation of his swag and the directions as to where it was to go. "This here swag is my suitcase which is carrying my clothes and all my personal and precious belongings. It's my bed roll and my protection from the wild wind and rain, and I'm damn sure there will be a bloody lot of that here, plus it carries my rifle to shoot a killer (food) and my Green River boning knife to cut it up with. Where I go, it goes, and with that Tom immediately grabbed hold of his swag strap and said, "I can guarantee there's no bull dust attached to that Sir." Tom stood tall before Muldoon came up with another bright idea. Tom was getting the feeling that this Muldoon fellow was a boss cocky around here. Muldoon had arranged for a porter to transfer James's suitcase to his old bedroom, but not before he assured James he would take care of his Australian friend and have a junior footman see Tom to his room. "Mr James, I think it a good idea if you informed the Lord and Lady of Rosengarten that you are back in the establishment, and that you have a friend from the colonies with you." James then excused himself and told Tom he would meet up with him at dinner that evening.

"Sir…" muttered Tom, already getting a little tired of waiting around the servants' entrance, "please just point me in the general direction of a place that I may throw my swag down for the time I'm here with James. I won't bother you, I can find my way." Tom could always find his way around Campbell's Run Station which he figured was a hell of a lot larger than this estate that his friend James was attached to here in England. In fact, Tom thought Australia could swallow this island whole. With this said, Tom gathered himself, pulled his dusty Akubra hat down firmly on his head, lifted his precious swag and threw it over his right shoulder as he began to wander down a long corridor of extremely high ceilings in search of a place to camp. Gasps of 'unbelievable', and 'bloody hell' escaped Tom as he poked his head around door after door and saw elegant rooms filled with sparkling chandeliers and furnishings glistening with hints of gold, reds and emerald green like nothing he had ever seen before. Crickey, this must be a palace of some kind, thought Tom as he humped his swag further down the long wide corridors, investigating room after room. Tom hadn't spotted another living soul as he gazed in wonder at the furnishings, marble pillars, statues and glitter, and the hugeness of it all. Large portraits from an era long gone – all with deadpan faces with cold unseeing eyes surrounded by heavy gold frames – hung on the walls in every room at the same level. In fact they were beginning to give Tom the bloody creeps. Just for a moment, Tom stood still in the quiet surrounds absorbing the atmosphere of the large room. He felt somewhat overwhelmed by it all as he consciously studied the portraits one by one. There were men and woman with soulless eyes. Tom couldn't imagine any of these characters on the cold walls behind him being of any use on the cattle station back home. He again wondered how did his friend James fit in among all this luxury, when out of the blue Tom felt a tap on his left shoulder. Holy hell, thought Tom, what a bloody creepy house this is, and then Tom felt the tap again. Feeling spooked and alone in this cold mansion, Tom's instant reaction was to swing around to face his assailant. As he did so with his swag still on his shoulder it connected the young and unsuspecting footman about the head and shoulders, sending him flying to his knees on the floorboards behind Tom with an extremely loud thud. Frightened and in shock, the young footman immediately exposed his hands and palms out in front of himself to show he wasn't out to attack anyone as he tried in vain to blurt out that Muldoon had sent him to escort Tom to his room.

"Bloody hell, what in the heck do you think yah doing creeping up behind a man like that? Sing out next time mate…yell out yah coming mate," offered Tom, who was buggered if he could understand the silence of the castle. I mean so much room and so few people, and they're creeping around the bloody corridors like that. Tom promised himself that as soon as he found James again he had quite a few questions that needed answering. Then as if an afterthought, Tom offered his right hand and shook the young footman's hand while asking him his name. "Alastair Sir, and I'm sorry Sir." Tom shook the young fellow's hand, "Not your fault Alastair. I'll just learn to watch my back while I'm here." Alastair dusted himself down, straightened his horn-rimmed glasses and dusted off his footman's uniform before attempting to take hold and carry Tom's swag for him. "Nooo you don't," Tom said grabbing the swag as he eyeballed the footman. "Thanks mate, I'll carry it myself. Just show me the way to my room." The young doorman was slightly taken aback by Tom's serious attachment to his swag. The green canvas swag roll, dusty and stained in places, was tightly secured by two handmade leather bull straps from Campbell's Run Station, and hanging from a bull strap was the Australian airports tag with Tom's name on it. "See that name?" said Tom looking at Alastair to be certain he had his full attention. "Well, it marks my swag," Tom concluded with some seriousness and a sense of importance.

CHAPTER 16

Return to Rosengarten

James found his homecoming to the family estate of Rosengarten clouded with uncertainty and confused emotions. His Grandmama, mother Gabrielle and Muldoon were genuinely pleased to see him. But his father Alexander III and older brother Morgan, it seemed, were not – or was it the stumbling block of the male ego that they were unable to express their pleasure in having James home again, if only for a short time.

At breakfast the following morning, James introduced his Australian friend to all his family members, which included his older brother Morgan. Sadly, Morgan's surly early morning attitude towards others hadn't improved at all, thought James, as he watched his friend stand and extend his right hand in greeting towards Morgan, only to have Morgan rudely ignore Tom's offer of a handshake completely. Tom turned and winked at James, then whispered softly to him, "Don't let it bother you. I've sorted out bigger and better men than him back home."

Tom decided to leave the Wentworth family to breakfast together – he couldn't possibly enjoy his first cup of morning tea and breakfast at the same table as an ill-mannered blue blood. No way in hell, thought Tom, I'm outa here. Tom left the Wentworth family breakfast room and immediately located the servants' dining room where he was welcomed with open arms by the establishment's staff. As the young English kitchen maids huddled about this Australian bloke in the warm kitchen atmosphere, some giggling while others loudly introduced themselves and questioned him about his home in the Australian Outback, the older female cook happily served up a hearty breakfast for all. She's got a lot better attitude in the morning than our stock camp cook on Campbell's Run, thought Tom to himself. With breakfast finished and after a good yarn around the kitchen table about the Outback with his new-found friends, Tom took a stroll to the stables to select a suitable mount for the fox hunt which was to be held that day. Many friends and visitors of the Wentworth family were expected for the big event. Tom hoped they would have slightly better manners than what James's older brother Morgan had shown him earlier that morning.

James thought his mother Gabrielle looked well, with her mane of thick chestnut curls pulled high on top of her head, giving her a sleek and slender look while dressed in a beautiful sapphire blue gown for breakfast. James suspected she was still battling the terrible depression sickness, yet somehow a soft youthfulness seemed to shine through her. Maybe mother's happiness was attributed to her frequent holidays taken alone and to the south of France – they did her so well, thought James.

On the other hand, James's Grand-mama Lady Elizabeth had the look of a woman who was carrying the whole world upon her plumpish shoulders. She seemed extremely tired and a little grey in colour, certainly not her demanding self. Even her silk gown with its soft flecks of light, offset with its embroidered white collar and cuffs and her favourite large pearl necklace did nothing to help lift his Grandmama's appearance, thought James. Either Lady Elizabeth was not well or there are problems with the Rosengarten Estate that I must get to the bottom of while I am home, James promised himself. James felt responsible in some small way for his Grand-mama since his Grandfather, Lord Wentworth II, had passed away, and James realised that he probably understood his Grand-mama far better than he did his father or older brother Morgan. James felt he understood his own family well enough to realise there was a problem among the inhabitants of this huge household. Could it possibly be so bad that they did not wish to discuss it with the other family members, which would have been done at the breakfast table in the past when Grandfather was alive. Or is it so deep and dark and unspeakable that they wish for it to remain locked away in a cupboard and cloaked forever?

CHAPTER 17

Surprise Announcement

James had returned to England with his suntanned, muscular physique and his good looks reinforced by a greater sense of confidence. He had always had the mental alertness to perceive that there was a family problem, and now James had made up his mind that he would sound out both his father and older brother Morgan as soon as he possibly could. Whether either person was willing to cooperate was another matter. James looked past the well-polished silver candle sticks in the middle of the breakfast table only to catch Morgan with a smirk on his face. Morgan then leaned across the corner of the breakfast table and even closer to his father the Lord Wentworth who sat at the head of the table. Morgan then whispered to his father. It seemed sharp and rather abrupt. He then sat back in his chair and looked quite pleased with himself as he straightened his morning jacket as if in readiness for an important announcement.

A short time later, Lord Wentworth, still seemingly deep in thought, raised his lifeless eyes from studying the gold Wentworth family coat of arms on his table napkin, picked up his butter knife as if in a trance and tapped it heavily against his crystal water glass, asking for the full attention of the family. Then clearing his throat loudly Lord Wentworth began, "I have an important announcement to make this morning, for the immediate family first and for our guests at this evening's Hunt Ball." With the family's total attention directed towards Lord Wentworth he began: "Congratulations are in order for my eldest son Morgan, who will announce his betrothal to Lady Catherine this very evening." Gasps of astonishment escaped nearly all at the breakfast table, all but Lord Wentworth and Morgan. Gabrielle looked directly at Morgan. She had no idea her eldest son had been courting Lady Catherine and was shocked at the untimely announcement, especially now that younger son James was home. Lady Gabrielle had understood, as most other family members had, that her youngest son James would one day marry the attractive Lady Catherine. "Won't you extend your congratulations to your eldest son, Gabrielle?" asked Lord Wentworth, not at all pleased that his long-suffering wife Gabrielle needed a little time to absorb such good news. Then as if she had been hit with shocking news, Gabrielle was jolted back to reality and offered, "Congratulations Morgan, it's just that your betrothal to Lady Catherine was so unexpected dear," and as her voice trailed away, "I never realised…" In fact Gabrielle could not believe what she had just heard her husband announce, although others would probably put her slow response and acceptance down to her medication and the 'depression sickness'.

James looked towards his Grand-mama, Lady Elizabeth. She had been rummaging in her beaded handbag and then promptly pulled out her delicate tortoise-shell fan and began fanning herself furiously as if there was an immediate need to circulate the still air in the break-fast room. Obviously Grand-mama needed something to do with her hands, James thought, even though it was bitterly cold outside. Then as if Grand-mama had just remembered the important announcement at the breakfast table, she stopped madly fanning herself and leaned across the table, tapped Morgan's white knuckles with her fan and congratulated her eldest grandson on his betrothal to Lady Catherine, saying, "I do hope you love her very much, Morgan." And then with ever-so-slight sarcasm added, "I also hope for your sake that it is a love match made in heaven dear, for we do need some happiness at Rosengarten now." With that Lady Elizabeth stood up and went to leave the room but not before turning towards James and reminding him to meet her in her sitting room. "You must come and tell me all about your Australian experiences dear." Grand-mama's departure from the breakfast room was promptly followed by her daughter-in-law Gabrielle's, who also felt that Lord Wentworth's sudden announcement regarding Morgan's forthcoming marriage to Lady Catherine was extremely sudden if not a little bizarre.

James had churned over the news of Morgan and Lady Catherine's association even before he had left Australia for England, but this announcement was extremely sudden and he wondered if the rumours that Grand-mama had written in her letter to him while he was still in Australia carried any truth. James stood tall and moved towards Morgan to shake his brother's hand and to extend his own congratulations, but before he did so Morgan pushed back his chair, stood and said, "I want you to remember little brother, that Lady Catherine is now to become my wife in the not too distant future. I ask you to respect that, and to keep that in mind while you are visiting at Rosengarten Castle." With that Morgan ignored James's outstretched hand, and full of his own self-importance, he turned his back on his younger brother and his father Lord Wentworth and left the breakfast room immediately, leaving both James and his father in the room alone staring at each other.

For the first time since the two brothers had grown and become young men, blond and tanned James noticed that he now stood a good three to four inches taller than his dark-haired older brother Morgan. These few added inches gave James a feeling of exquisite empowerment, not that James thought he needed any power at all, but he couldn't help but remember the brothers' younger years as they were growing up together playing and riding their favourite horses around Rosengarten Estate, that Morgan had always been the heir to be.

How quickly the times have changed, thought James, as he let out a long barely audible sigh as he returned his chair to the correct position at the breakfast table, and how Lady Catherine and her ideals must have changed too. "Yes," murmured James to himself, "I'm excited to meet Lady Catherine again and hopefully it will be at tonight's Hunt Ball." Lady Catherine had obviously meant what she had said to James before he left for Australia, but why the hurry pondered James.

Shortly, James was to meet Lady Elizabeth in the privacy of her own sitting room where he hoped to gain some insight into what was behind his dear Grand-mama's fading appearance. Right now James couldn't help but wonder if his own father or even brother Morgan might have contributed to Grand-mama's ill health. The shock of Morgan's sudden impending marriage was really the last thing Grand-mama needed.

But first, with just the two of them in the breakfast room, James thought he would take this opportunity to approach his father. Could there be problems in the family, could it be that the rumours Grand-mama called 'common gossip' did hold some truth? Surely the problem could not be financial as the family had more than sufficient funds and farmland.

"Would you like more tea, father?" asked James, hoping his lordship would take more tea and that this would give him an opportunity to converse directly with his father without any interference from any other persons or family members. "No thank you James, I must leave for the stables immediately. I promised Patrick our head groomsman I would be there, and I am already late. I must leave now, right this moment." Blow, thought James. As he stood in front of his father and shook his hand, James looked deep into his lordship's eyes hoping to find some sign that something was wrong or bothering him. "Father," James started. "Not now James," replied his lordship, "some other time perhaps, but just not now," and his lordship turned, clipped his heels and left the breakfast room for the stables. James left the breakfast room for the privacy of Lady Elizabeth's green sitting room none the wiser. But there was one thing James was convinced of – the once laughing and mischievous brown eyes of Lord Wentworth III were no longer laughing, and were now replaced by dull lifeless dark souls. James couldn't help but wonder if the very secret his lordship was hiding from the family was as dark as the circles surrounding his lifeless eyes. Was it so bad that it couldn't be shared, a problem shared was a problem halved…wasn't it? Or was it so serious and unspeakable that it had to be cloaked and hidden in darkness forever?

James knocked on his Grand-mama's door. "Please do come in James." Lady Elizabeth had anticipated James's arrival to her sitting room. Her elderly companion stopped pouring fresh piping hot tea into fine china cups, and opened the door to let James enter. She then left the two alone in the privacy of her ladyship's green room. "Sit down dear, we must enjoy a cup of fine English tea together. I am so pleased to have you return to Rosengarten Castle dear, so soon after you must have received my desperate letter." James sat in an uncomfortable brocade-covered winged chair opposite Lady Elizabeth. He took a sugar cube and stirred it into his tea ever so slowly, wondering where they were to start or what news Grand-mama had to tell him now that they were alone. He hadn't used any sugar while in the Australian Outback because there wasn't any in the Campbell's Run stock camp, so this little cube of sugar was a luxury he thought. Then Grand-mama was again rummaging in her beaded handbag as the tears welled in her pale blue eyes. She pulled out a white linen handkerchief embroidered with sprigs of lavender to softly pat the tears around her eyes and cheeks away. "James, I am so sorry you had to arrive home to Rosengarten to be greeted by such an unexpected announcement at the breakfast table, and on your first morning dear." James couldn't help but feel for this once strong woman who had always been the backbone of the Wentworth family. Once Grand-mama had asserted her authority and laid any problems bare, the family together would then sort them out quickly. But of course she was unable to help with those problems where she had been kept entirely in the dark. James felt a sense of anger towards both his father and older brother as he believed either one or the other was to blame for the decline in Grand-mama's health. As James sipped his tea and devoured a rather large slice of home-baked fruit cake, something he missed in the Outback, he wondered again if the Wentworth family had a Pandora's box of unspeakable secrets hidden away somewhere in the attic. Could it be that Grand-mama has something to tell me, worried James, although deep down he believed not. After some considerable and careful thought, James believed that surely once Morgan had married Lady Catherine, all the tension within the immediate family would simply disappear. For now, James wondered how he could have ever got Lady Catherine's and his own feelings for each other so wrong. Of course James had no intention of remaining at Rosengarten Castle, now or in the future. His mind was made up to leave immediately once the important family announcement had been made. Surely this announcement would clearly solve the problems Grand-mama had written of.

But Lord Wentworth III, who had been prompted by Morgan at the breakfast table, had stirred the hornet's nest that morning by his abrupt, if not totally unexpected announcement of Morgan and Lady Catherine's upcoming nuptials. Grand-mama and Mother Gabrielle simply had no idea that Morgan and Catherine were so deeply in love, and felt the way the announcement had come about was in extremely poor taste. Neither Grand-mama nor Gabrielle had been given the opportunity to warmly and officially welcome Lady Catherine into the Wentworth family fold by entertaining her the way they should, with welcoming dinners and cocktail parties, as was the custom in their circle of society. Grand-mama believed that as soon as possible, if not this very day, she would speak with her daughter-in-law Gabrielle and have her immediately arrange, with the help of her lady's maid and excellent chef, a 'welcoming dinner' for Lady Catherine. This event would at least show that the family did still have some class among their friends.

James wanted to make it clear to his Grand-mama that there had not been an intimate relationship between himself and Catherine prior to his leaving for Australia, and that this morning's unexpected announcement of the intended betrothal between Morgan and Lady Catherine was something that James intended to handle with total diplomacy. He would certainly not say or do anything that would confuse his family in any way.

James did find Catherine extremely attractive and even more so in the weeks leading up to his departure for Australia, and he believed she had felt the same way. He had never seen her look so tantalisingly beautiful, and James found when Catherine was in close proximity to him, her beauty teased his emotions mercilessly. But James's upbringing and inner strength had forbidden him from bedding the playful and very attractive Lady Catherine when he was twenty-one years old, for he had believed she deserved far more from him than a casual romp in the straw. At that time he was not prepared to ask for her hand in marriage as he felt he needed more time to find himself as a man first. Now it seemed Lady Catherine had chosen to love and wed his worldlier and older brother Morgan.

That morning while having tea with Lady Elizabeth, James spoke of his work as a 'jackaroo', a trainee stockman, on Campbell's Run Station in the Northern Territory. He proudly told his Grand-mama how Cranky Henry, the station's horse breaker, had set him up for a fall from a badly broken steed, only to have failed as James described the rough ride from hell. James talked of the cattle station, the people he'd met and the Outback way of life, and that he planned to return to Australia as soon as possible. Lady Elizabeth's eyes opened wide in disbelief that anything so terrible could happen to her youngest grand-son, although she was extremely proud of James, and thought the time had come for her to grant and fulfil her late husband Lord Alexander Wentworth II's last wish, as described in his will. This wish would be granted to James before he returned to Australia and his beloved Outback. But for now, Lady Elizabeth would stand and support young James as she believed Morgan's wedding was to be held sooner than anyone would have expected of this sudden nuptial announcement. "James," said Lady Elizabeth, as her mind returned to England from the Australian Outback, "I would like to talk with you again dear, before your return to the Outback. Good luck with the hunt today James, and be prepared...and save some strength for the Hunt Ball this evening." James worried he hadn't relieved his Grand-mama's mind from thinking that he and Lady Catherine were an item before his departure to Australia, but he promised himself that when the appropriate moment came around he certainly would. With that thought James bade his Grand-mama a good morning, followed by a peck to her warm right cheek as he had always done as a child, and left for the stables where he hoped to find his friend Tom.

CHAPTER 18

A Highfalutin Fox Hunt

James found Tom down by the Rosengarten stables. "Tom, is this the horse you plan to ride for the hunt today?" No sooner had James spoken his friend's name than the flighty colt booted the crisp morning air with both barrels as it tried its best to dismantle the young Australian stockman from his shiny English saddle.

"Bloody hell James," Tom sung out between the bucking and pig-rooting. "This animal needs a bit of work. He's the last horse standing in these stables, so I guess I'll have to ride him for the hunt today."

James went to apologise to his friend for the roughly broken colt that had been left in the stables for Tom to ride, but before he could finish, Tom pulled him up with, "Let it go James, I think I'll rather enjoy trying to ride this untidy colt out among those polished gentlemen, all decked out in coat n' tails and mounted on their highfalutin horses. I can't believe it, I mean, are they really going to chase a bloody fox dressed in all that fancy red clobber mate?" Tom was starting to sound a little frustrated as he put a spanner in the colt's flight plan and brought the bucking horse around to stand by James. After a short silence James answered, "Tom, it's the sport of kings." James ran his hand through his wild sun-bleached blond hair wondering how to explain this situation to his rather bushy Australian friend. "Tom, look at it this way, in England we don't have the luxury of an adrenalin rush from chasing rogue bulls and feral cattle as you do on Campbell's Run Station. We chase foxes instead." James could see that Tom was giving this some serious thought before saying, "Well, I suppose it's a way of getting rid of the bloody vermin," and with a sudden burst of excitement Tom told James he was ready to join the others on the day's hunt. As the two mates rode towards the swelling group of respectably dressed and mounted horsemen who were surrounded by a bunch of madly barking and highly excited tail-wagging English hunting hounds, Tom wondered what the day would hold for him. He leaned towards James and said in a rather loud whisper, "James, these dogs look pretty worked up."

"Heaven forbid Tom, please don't refer to them as dogs in the presence of these gentlemen fox hunters, they call them hounds."

"I can handle that James, but, I was wondering, have you ever come across two foxes at once?"

"No, I don't think I have. Well, not on any fox hunt I attended," answered James with a slight smile, and couldn't help but wonder what was really on Tom's mind.

"I reckon it would throw some excitement into the show, James. I mean, could you imagine the bloody foxes, hounds and all these men on horses riding around in circles, and at one hell of a pace and in all flamin' directions." James looked towards his Australian mate. "It'll be a good day, Tom." With that assurance, Tom kicked his colt in the flank. It broke into a buck, and farted and pig-rooted its way in among the English horsemen, unnerving some while others immediately moved to distance themselves from the wild colonial boy as they spread out to get on with the hunt.

During the fox hunt Tom couldn't help but feel a little sorry for James. His father, the Lord Wentworth III, was in the group as was his older brother Morgan, but Tom noticed neither family member took the time to ride beside or have a jovial conversation with James, as most other horsemen on the hunt had done. I suppose our families are alike in some small way thought Tom. It would take some kind of explosion to get a long conversation out of old Derrick back home on Campbell's Run, and most times one wouldn't believe that we were even family. Yeah, mused young Tom, one thing's for sure, his Grandmama and his mother love James very much, and I'm his mate, but that's about as far as the similarities between our families go.

Then out of the blue Tom spotted a fox. "There goes the little brown bastard," he sung out extra loud, and immediately kicked his colt in the flank to get a bit more pace from his steed. But the colt took offence, bucked and planted both barrels into the horse closest to him. Unfortunately, it turned out to be Morgan's fine looking steed that copped it from Tom's flighty colt. Down it went on its left shoulder flinging Morgan into a thorny blackberry bush. Tom gave the colt its head, hoping the animal would let go of all its pent-up emotions naturally, then pulled gently on his horse's reins to steady it up. Tom got his wayward colt in hand and spun it around to give Morgan a hand, only to be faced with an extremely irritated and badly scratched Morgan. Couldn't have happened to a better bloke, thought Tom, who noted Morgan had been literally dumped in the middle of a huge prickly blackberry patch. Funny, mused Tom, Morgan seemed quite pale until his angry performance kicked in big time. Bloody hell, Tom chuckled to himself, looks like this spoilt kid has lost his dummy again. The angrier Morgan became, the brighter his complexion glowed, reminding Tom of his old Uncle Derrick's occasional war dance back home on Campbell's Run Station. Totally exasperated, Morgan clawed his way out from the thorny blackberry bushes, whilst tugging angrily at his tight white riding pants which the blackberry thorns had tried to strip from his body.

"So sorry Sir," Tom said with as much aplomb as he could possibly muster with his Australian accent while trying his best to hold back laughter. "Can I give you a bloody hand mate?" offered Tom pleasantly. "Definitely not," roared back Morgan. "I don't want your bloodied hand. You are getting my dander up considerably colonial boy," vented Morgan in an over-exaggerated regal tone. Instead of accepting Tom's offer of help, Morgan's bad temper had the better of him and he made the fatal mistake of flipping his whip towards Tom and his unpredictable colt, which took fright again, bucked and kicked out better than any rodeo buck-jumping mount Tom had ever ridden, causing Morgan to dash for cover and protection. Tom again got his steed under control, noted Morgan and his mount were unhurt, and decided to leave Morgan to his own devices while he set out to find the others and that little wayward fox again.

"Now, where has that little bugger gone?" Tom decided to follow the high-pitched barking of the over-excited hounds and wondered how anyone would ever get close enough to nail a fox with that wild racket going off, but it's the English way he told himself. James rode out from the group of horsemen and their hounds to greet Tom and found a crumpled and blackberry-stained Morgan trotting up behind Tom. James's good manners would have him acknowledge his older brother on their crossing of paths on the hunt. But after the breakfast table warnings from Morgan that his younger brother James was to 'remember that Lady Catherine was now betrothed to himself,' James was no longer surprised to be rudely brushed aside by Morgan as he rode right past the two men without acknowledging either of them.

"Are you coping well Tom?" asked James. "As well as can be... where's that little brown bastard of a fox gone, James?" asked Tom. "Up that log over there. Some of the riders say they will light a fire and smoke it out. I'm leaving the hunt and returning to the stables," James said. "I still wish to speak with Grand-mama."

"I'll stick around to see what happens with this fox James...it's the first and probably the last of any fox hunts for me," Tom answered. James chuckled, he couldn't help but like this Australian fellow, and before he turned his horse around to leave for the stables James reminded Tom of the evening's Hunt Ball to be held in Rosengarten's ballroom that night. "The maid will lay out a set of my coat and tails for you to wear this evening Tom. We're the same size. See you there, don't be late."

"I'll be there mate, I'm not one to miss out on a party," Tom replied before musing, if it's as boring as some of these snobby fox hunters we'll sure liven it up. He saluted James goodbye, then made the mistake of kicking his unruly colt in the flank which set it off all over again.

As James was no longer a party to the highfalutin fox hunt, Tom decided to make the most of his flighty colt's agitation by milking its wayward performance for all it was worth. Tom tapped the colt in the flank again, setting it off into one hell of a bucking and pig-root-ing spin. "Buck boy buck," yelled Tom. "Get it all out of your system while you can." Tom sat back in his English-style saddle, distributed his body weight evenly, his right arm held high above his head while pumping the crisp morning air, which helped maintain his balance on the fired-up colt. Tom was an excellent horseman – he had to be to hold a position as stockman in the wilds of the Australian Outback. During the colt's wild performance it bucked, kicked and farted its way among the other horses and gentleman fox hunters who were waiting patiently for the little brown fox to vacate the smoldering log.

Poor little bastard, thought Tom, when his colt had steadied up and given away the idea of bucking any longer. Even I wouldn't be too keen to leave home with all these highly strung and madly hysterical hounds going off out here. At that moment the smouldering fox flew out of the burning log. Hounds and horsemen tumbled over each other as each party forcefully pushed their way through the over-excited bunch for the attack on the wayward fox. Tom had had enough. He spun his unhappy colt around, and as he did it crossed his mind that a bullet would have been more humane, and returned to the Rosengarten stables to unsaddle his colt and bed him down.

CHAPTER 19

A Fine looking Filly

Boy...what a fine looking filly we have here, thought Tom as he rode closer to the stables. There, out front of the stables stood one of the finest looking chestnut fillies Tom had ever laid eyes on. Leading the horse around was an even better looking filly dressed in a stylish riding outfit with a mass of wild strawberry blonde curls blowing in the gentle breeze. Boy oh boy! For a moment Tom thought his eyes were deceiving him. He rubbed his eyes and then again, believing that when he looked towards the girl she would have vanished into thin air. Tom's eyes were certainly not deceiving him, his vision of a beautiful slender woman was still out there. As he rode even closer to the stables, the woman, as nimble as could be, swung up into her well-polished riding saddle, straightened her back as she pulled a silver handled riding crop on her filly, and throwing caution to the wind, galloped wildly across the flourishing green paddocks, showing a fine display of 'horsemanship' as she jumped fence after fence and far beyond.

"Phew, what a nice surprise colty boy. Hope you took note of that neat looking filly as well," Tom said out loud to his colt as he rubbed his hand down his colt's neck in a show of appreciation for the horse keeping himself reasonably together on the day's fox hunt. As the young colt threw his head high in the air, accompanied by an excited high-pitched whinny, it seemed the young stallion was also interested in the good looking chestnut fillies.

As Tom unsaddled his colt, he wondered why James had never mentioned this person before. James had to be blind to miss this beauty, thought Tom. She looked too beautiful to be real, with her long hair a tangled mass of unruly strawberry blonde curls which blew wildly about her head in the wind as she galloped away. A free spirit, thought Tom. It would be nice to meet her, but unfortunately she would probably be way out of my league. Tom wondered if she was a family member…James had never mentioned he had a sister, or was it possible the lady was a family friend of the Wentworth family. He made a mental note to question James at this evening's Hunt Ball.

The younger of the Wentworth sons had returned from the fox hunt earlier that morning, hoping to have time and privacy to speak with Lady Elizabeth before this evening's ball. In the past James preferred to unsaddle his own steed down at the stables, but chose not to on this particular day. Instead James rode directly past the grand entrance to the Wentworth family mansion where he spotted a well-bred chestnut filly still lathered in sweat and tied down to the same horse rail he had planned to use for his own steed. James was hurriedly met by Patrick the head livery man who said, "I'll take care of your steed Sir. Lady Catherine has just arrived and she is in the formal lounge room wishing to speak with you in private." On hearing this news James felt his body tremble. He immediately wondered why Lady Catherine would want to meet me. She is betrothed to my older brother…father is making a formal announcement to all family and friends at this very evening's Hunt Ball. James had kept repeating this same mantra throughout the morning to himself, as his mind was finding it difficult to comprehend the situation between his brother and his lady friend. At this point James wasn't sure whether to hand over his horse's reins or not to the stable hand, but as he hesitated the reins were taken from his hand and passed to a much younger stable hand who promptly moved off with James's mount towards the stable, leaving him no other choice but to face his friend, the Lady Catherine.

James fidgeted with his riding jacket, put his riding crop under his left arm and proceeded to the archway where Muldoon promptly pulled open the heavy wooden door with much aplomb. "Lady

Catherine to see you Sir." It's been a long time thought James as he took a deep breath and raised his smouldering deep blue eyes to meet Catherine's dull lifeless ones, while the smile on her beautiful face was a poor attempt at happiness, thought James. There stood James all six foot three inches of him, tall, suntanned and extremely fit looking, and his wild sandy blond hair only added to his charisma. Suddenly, it was all too hard for Lady Catherine, and she could no longer stay away from James. One day James will be mine, thought Catherine, I will make him see me for who I really am, I will make James love me. James realised that now he needed to be the one in control of this emotional situation. His own body throbbed from the want to hold and caress this woman on sight, to run his hardened hands over her porcelain sun-kissed arms, to caress her beautiful pouting lips and her swan-like neck. His body ached to hold her, to make passionate tender love to her. James's want for Catherine was close to unbearable. If I could just hold her, but not now. James steeled himself. Catherine hadn't waited for him to visit Australia and find himself. Of course it didn't help that Lady Catherine's last words to James before he left England were, 'Don't expect me to wait for your return James,' as she bounced off towards her own steed, leaving James feeling uncomfortable at her sudden outburst in the round yard of Rosengarten stables. It's all too late now, thought James, his muddled brain unable to tell the difference between true love and wanton lust. He had to remember that Lady Catherine was now to marry his older brother Morgan and Lord Wentworth would make the announcement this very evening.

"James, please James," begged Lady Catherine as she moved closer to him with her arms out-stretched, "it's important I speak with you in private, please." As she whispered her voice seemed panicky and urgent and the tears began to well up in her beautiful eyes. "Please James, I really must speak with you," Lady Catherine begged one more time with her voice and lips both trembling. James looked down into Lady Catherine's eyes. He could see she was extremely serious and couldn't help but wonder what could be so terribly wrong in her beautiful upper class and protected life that the lady needed to discuss any matter with him, and urgently. Lady Catherine's closeness to James and her warm body emitting the delicate scent of her oriental perfume – the same perfume she had worn before he had left for Australia, James remembered – left his own body pulsating with want for this beautiful woman. His own emotions were close to breaking point as Catherine's tears tumbled from her eyes leaving a soft silvery film over her high cheek bones. James wanted to gently kiss those tears away as Catherine clung to James tightly and begged him again to please give her a little time. She needed to talk with him privately, it was of paramount importance. They stood facing each other, looking deeply into the other's eyes. James was holding Catherine's trembling cold hands tightly, hoping to transfer some of his own body warmth and strength across to Lady Catherine in the hope that it might help ease her frightful anxiety. "Please try to gather yourself together Catherine," begged an extremely concerned James, when suddenly a high-pitched angry male voice came from behind them both. "Excuse me, I believe I am interrupting something. Is it that important Lady Catherine that you cannot discuss it with me, your future husband to be, or have you forgotten?" demanded an annoyed Morgan who was still in a total state of dishevelment after the morning's fox hunt. His brown eyes turned a deep penetrating black as they flashed angrily from Catherine to James. James dropped Catherine's still cold hands and took a step back from her. As a young child Morgan found it difficult to control his temper, and at times James felt there was a devil in Morgan's veins – many of his younger days had been peppered with frequent outbursts of loud and demanding tantrums. James believed Morgan should have outgrown his childish demands but not so it seemed, as Morgan impatiently began to flick his ivory handled riding whip about the ornate lounge room chairs, upsetting Catherine even more, while he waited for some kind of explanation from the couple.

"Not at all," answered James bluntly in response to Morgan's question to Catherine. Squaring his shoulders as he turned to look directly into Morgan's menacing dark eyes, James couldn't help but notice his older brother's untidy state, his white jodhpurs torn and stained by wild blackberry juice. "Not a good day?" James asked of his older brother. While fumbling with the small talk, he certainly had no wish to create an embarrassing situation in the presence of Lady Catherine, and yet James was determined not to let his older sibling intimidate him in any way, not now or anytime in the future, like he had often done when they were young children. Not really expecting an answer, James couldn't help but notice that Morgan's once athletic physique had now slipped to give him a podgy middle section, while his penis hung like an old teapot in his tattered tight jodhpurs. James slowly turned towards Lady Catherine, bowed his blond head and bade her a good afternoon, with "You will probably need the time to dress for your big announcement this evening, my lady." James turned and without a backward glance towards Lady Catherine or Morgan, he left the room more puzzled than ever, thinking that this union never felt right, and certainly not like a love match made in heaven. James couldn't put his finger on the problem, but then it wasn't his problem anyway. As soon as he was able to have a long talk with Grand-mama James planned to return to the Australian Outback as soon as possible.

CHAPTER 20

The Ballroom

After James's unexpected meeting with Lady Catherine and older brother Morgan, he decided to put off his planned talk with Grandmama for the time being, thinking there would be other days he could talk with her before he and Tom returned to Australia and Campbell's Run Station. Instead James returned to the privacy of his rooms, where a junior valet had laid out his suit and tails for this evening's all important Hunt Ball. As James ran his eyes over his attire for the evening, he couldn't help but think of Lady Catherine's tearful eyes and beautiful face again. It bothered James to have walked out of the room on a distraught lady. He had never seen her in such an unhappy and emotional state as she begged for him to listen to her, which was what James had intended to do until Morgan burst into the room.

Suddenly, the atmosphere changed as his bedroom door slammed closed behind Morgan who stood with his back against the door, slapping his riding whip hard against the closed door, his breathing erratic. Still obviously agitated, he glared at his younger brother.

James turned around and looked towards an extremely angry Morgan. "I will say this once and only once James," said Morgan, whose eyes were black with anger, or was it his jealously of the younger and fitter looking James. "Stay away from Lady Catherine, not only is she betrothed to me, my brother, but she carries my child," and with that bold and rather brutal statement, Morgan turned on his heels and departed, leaving behind a devastated James. Morgan had now confirmed James's fears and the rumours relayed by Grand-mama. James lowered himself to the edge of his bed where he sat for some time with his head resting in the palms of his hands, then lay on his bed with both arms folded across his forehead as if blocking out all that Morgan had said. James found this information all rather hard to digest.

The evening came around quickly enough and by the time James had bathed and dressed in his suit and tails, it was time for him to collect Tom and introduce his Australian friend around at the family's annual Hunt Ball. Although James's mind was still busy churning over Morgan's blunt statement, he couldn't help but feel how unbelievable it all seemed. That a lady of Catherine's standing could be tainted by such gossip was unheard of – her family, our family, both tarnished for evermore, and this would surely be the end of Grand-mama. Morgan's words could not possibly be true thought James. But if there is the slightest chance that Lady Catherine is with child – just the thought made James tremble – then Morgan and Lady Catherine must marry immediately as the child cannot be born a bastard. James then vowed to himself he must never speak of this horrendous matter to anyone at all, not even Grand-mama or mother Gabrielle, although James couldn't help but think that his father should be able to help older brother Morgan through this unspeakable situation considering his own many infidelities over the years. James remembered the whispers he had overheard as a child through the lonely corridors of Rosengarten Castle. I'm sure father has had experience in these delicate matters, James thought. He decided to let this complicated matter rest and he would enjoy the Rosengarten Hunt Ball this evening as it could possibly be his last.

James, Morgan and Lady Catherine had grown up in the same circles of society. While both families had attended the season's hunt balls in the district, each had kept their individuality, and yet they were certainly no strangers to each other. James had seen more of Lady Catherine in the twelve months prior to his trip to Australia than he had in the ten years proceeding. As a young girl her love of fine horses drew Catherine to James, and yes, there had been the odd childish outburst of temper when the spoilt Lady Catherine found she was unable to bend James her way or against his will. James realised that ever since Lady Catherine's older brother Oliver was found dead at the bottom of a deep well on the family estate, the Hamilton family had closed ranks around their remaining child and protected and indulged her every whim.

The word was that Lady Catherine's family was extremely wealthy and owned even more farmland than Lord Wentworth III himself. This made Lady Catherine an outstanding catch as a bride and wife for any man. There had been many eligible and well-heeled suitors who had travelled from all over Europe and England to visit her family estate, hoping to catch a glimpse of the young beauty herself to temp her into their arms and away. It was widely known the beautiful Lady Catherine was expected to marry extremely well, and in the event of her making an unsuitable marriage, or to inadvertently bring shame on her father Lord Hamilton's family's heritage, Lady Catherine would lose all of her inheritance to her much older cad of a cousin Patterson – if he survived her. Lady Catherine was acutely aware of Patterson. At a hunt ball earlier in the season, Patterson, after indulging heavily on Black Hawk whiskey accompanied by huge rank smelling cigars, swaggered confidently up to his first cousin, the Lady Catherine, and whispered into her ear that "The gentleman she was conversing and playfully flirting with that evening would not be acceptable marriage material." It was Patterson's cold and calculating way of reminding his cousin that he too stood in line to inherit the Hamilton Castle Estate if Lady Catherine put a foot wrong, and how he hoped she would.

"James, there you are mate, where in the heck have you been?" came a rather loud voice with a slow Australian drawl from among the crowded ballroom. James looked through the well-dressed ladies and gentlemen in the room, then spotted Tom, dressed to the nines in his borrowed suit. "Well, well Tom, you suited up extremely well," offered James. "You're not too bad in yah glad rags yourself James," Tom fired back. At that moment a drinks waiter came by. Tom swung around and grabbed two fine crystal tumblers half full of the country's finest whiskey. "Here James, here's to us," offered Tom in fine spirit. The tall bronzed young mates talked and laughed together as they reminisced over the day's events. James looked around the ornate room beautifully lit down the centre by five massive chandeliers. Yes, this already seemed like another life he thought. Then James spotted gentle men and women he knew, and made a mental note to renew his acquaintance with them before the evening ended – he might not see them again for some time once he returned to Australia. Then there was Grand-mama, who stopped and talked to the guests whilst gently fanning herself with her tortoise-shell fan as she slowly moved about the opulent ballroom. She looked refreshed and beautiful in her royal blue gown and trade-mark large pearl necklace and earrings, while the simple tiara adorned with tiny diamonds and pearls added a touch of elegance.

"A flash sort of lifestyle you lived over here James, real grand mate, why would you want to rough it and live back of beyond in our Australian Outback?" asked a curious Tom, who by now was knocking his drinks back one after the other. Tom had never had it so good. "Well Tom, this aristocratic lifestyle can sometimes knock one about...see how some of those young fox hunters are staggering about already?" "Yeah, they can't hold their drink," offered Tom in a softer tone of voice. James laughed while thinking of his introduc-tion to the Northern Territory and Campbell's Run Station's overseer Bandit. Bandit, who had been keeping a close eye on his stockmen, noticed immediately when they were truly intoxicated and in the mood to wreak havoc with the hotel pool table. Bandit had grabbed one stockman after the other by the seat of their pants and threw them out of the pub onto the footpath. "Anyhow, I love the freedom and no restrictions in the Outback, Tom." Hmm, Tom thought, he wasn't sure he would want to give up his bed in this flash castle to spend his nights sweltering in a dusty canvas swag among the prickly spinifex on Campbell's Run in a hurry, but then again, there were a hell of a lot of benefits to both lifestyles. "Well James, I think I'll see if I can fossick about and find someone to dance with, I'm in the mood for a bit of the jitterbug right now." Tom placed his empty glass on a nearby table, and gave it a flick with his finger which sent it scooting across the top of the table to stop in the very centre. Tom felt good and very confident. He turned around to face James and gave his friend a mischievous wink before disappearing among the froth of evening gowns and well-suited gentlemen, his stockman's swagger more prominent than ever. Tom couldn't help but notice the sideward glances as he tipped his hat and swaggered confidently past some of the toffee-nosed fox hunters he and James had associated with earlier that day. What's more, he told himself, I bet I'll have a better time than they do tonight. This thought immediately had Tom straightening his lean back and square his powerful shoulders even more, not realising the powerful effect it had on several of society's older ladies.

James glanced about the crowded room until he spotted Morgan and Lady Catherine, only to have his heart skip a beat at the sheer beauty before his eyes. Powder blue really suits Catherine, James thought, and the diamonds around her swan-like neck threw off a brilliant radiance, as did those woven through her now tamed straw-berry blonde locks. James again reminded himself that the lady was now out of bounds to himself, betrothed to his older brother Morgan. It was time for James to go in search of his mother Gabrielle and father Lord Alexander as the announcement of Morgan's and Lady Catherine's betrothal must be imminent. James would be expected to stand centre stage behind Lord and Lady Wentworth, and by the side of his Grand-mama, Lady Elizabeth. This was needed to show the Wentworth family's united support of Morgan's and Lady Catherine's official engagement this evening. James's thoughts were suddenly interrupted by a firm tap on his shoulder. "Come now James, we must unite with the family this evening to throw our solid support behind Morgan and Lady Catherine's engagement." Then as an afterthought Grand-mama whispered to James, for only James need hear this she thought, "James, I'm sorry that we must do this, but please pretend you're happy with the idea." Then after a short silence, "I do hope Morgan does right by Lady Catherine." So do I, thought James.

The next moment the music stopped playing, leaving just a gentle excited murmur floating about the room as James escorted his Grand-mama to the podium where the other family members had already graciously assembled. James stood tall and confident, and was extremely handsome in the eyes of all women young and old attending the Hunt Ball. And yet, he couldn't help feeling pain and terribly uncomfortable for the moment, and wished that Morgan and Catherine's engagement announcement had been made official while he had been away. If only it had been made official then, thought James, but he knew the aching pain he now felt so deeply in his heart would have still felt the same in an Australian Outback stock camp. James had believed Lady Catherine and he had so much in common before he had left for Australia. As James's mind drifted back over the past he thought of their united love of their horses, fresh air and outdoors, her free spirit, their laughter and happiness when attending horse riding events on the downs, and of the ache in his groin the last time she had visited him at the wooden round yard by the stables at Rosengarten Castle.

After a fleeting glance about the ballroom, James chose to focus his stare on the back of his father's head. The butler had rung the gong three times, and now Lord Alexander Wentworth III proceeded to make the betrothal official in the eyes of the several hundred guests. There were prominent judges and bank managers from London, and many of the country's top equine stud producers, all gathered together with close family and friends. Yet as the announcement was made, amid loud cheers and congratulatory messages, James couldn't help but feel the intense scrutiny from the eyes of his friends as they tried to bore deep into his soul looking for an answer to this sudden and unexpected announcement between his older brother Morgan and the Lady Catherine. Yes, people had expected the betrothal to be announced between Lady Catherine and James sometime in the future, for ever since they were children and rode their ponies together on the moors, it was expected that the Lady Catherine and James would one day unite in matrimony. No sooner had Lord Alexander completed the announcement of the engagement and the merging of two of England's wealthiest landholders, than his eldest son turned towards the beautiful Lady Catherine, who seemed remotely sad and very distant on realising her engagement to Morgan was indeed official. Morgan squared his shoulders, his dark eyes boring into Catherine's larger green eyes forcing her to slightly bow her head as her eyes began to well with tears. It was as if Morgan's piercing and demanding glare was reminding Lady Catherine of the reason behind their betrothal this very evening. Morgan's stare never left Catherine's as he placed an enormous dark green emerald surrounded by many diamonds on her ring finger. Then immediately, as if proud of his catch, he held her hand high to show all family and friends that Lady Catherine would soon become his wife. Morgan kept a firm hold on Lady Catherine's delicate hand as she attempted to pull her hand away from his. The reality of what she had just entered into began to sink in as her body trembled with terrifying raw emotion. Morgan's brown eyes seemed to turn a smouldering black, his jaw firmly set as he tightened his firm grip on her hand, twisting it, hurting her and making her hand look even paler than it actually was. He bowed his head over the beautiful heirloom emerald ring and kissed it ever so gently before taking an extra firm hold of Lady Catherine's hand to guide her through the mass of gathered well-wishers and onto the ballroom floor where they would lead their guests in a slow romantic waltz played superbly by Top Hats, a well-known London band. Morgan was pleased Lady Catherine had not made a fool of him this evening whilst they were surrounded by so many friends from their upper-crust circle of society, and although he had worried some may have seen her effort to pull her hand free of his, or her silent tears while they had both stood on the podium together, his cocky arrogance told him to believe they were tears of joy. Morgan decided he would speak with Lady Catherine of this matter as soon as possible. He believed he needed to remind her of the reason behind their sudden nuptials at a later date, but not this very night! Morgan did feel extremely proud to have landed Lady Catherine for a future wife, although better circumstances would have definitely been an advantage. She is both beautiful and wealthy and probably far too spirited for him, but yes thought Morgan, the gain will certainly be all mine in more ways than one in the very near future.

After the announcement of the engagement that would unite two of England's largest landholders, James had intended to follow the family to the ballroom floor where he planned to join family and friends help celebrate this joyous occasion between Morgan and Lady Catherine. No matter how difficult it would be, he would put on a happy and brave face and attempt to be joyful. But before James could bring himself to join in and party the evening away with the others, he needed some time to stand alone on the podium, to give his muddled mind a quiet moment of thought and let it try to absorb all that had just eventuated before his very eyes. He must now convince himself that this was her wish.

'I must not show or have any feelings for Catherine, I must remain staunch and strong,' James told himself severely. 'My wicked dreams of Lady Catherine and I must be gone forever,' but he was still unable to pull his hypnotic gaze from the form of the beautiful woman in the powder-blue gown. His desire was stronger than ever! The orchestra struck up *A Beautiful Woman*, as Lady Catherine, trying her hardest to conceal her tears and unexplained sadness, was led in dance about the highly polished ballroom floor by James's older and controlling brother.

Then the murmur of joyous voices, happiness and laughter that had filtered throughout the large ballroom all evening changed suddenly, jolting James back to the present. The rowdiness became louder and more intense until a scuffle seemed to be gathering momentum among a group of the gentlemen fox hunters in the far corner of the ballroom. James immediately left the podium with the intention of assisting the doorman and asking the slightly intoxicated bunch to move themselves to the grounds outside the confines of the ballroom to sort out any differences. Extremely bad manners, thought James. What would his Australian friend think of the lords' and ladies' unruly behaviour tonight? Then out of the blue a loud ear-piercing whistle echoed throughout the high ceilings of the ballroom, so high pitched and piercing it caused a delicate tinkle from the crystals of Grand-mama's chandeliers. It was the same loud whistle James had heard Tom use to call the working dogs to heel in the stock camp at Campbell's Run Station. Dear Lord, thought James, Tom may be caught up in the middle of this terrible rowdy bunch of gentlemen. I must find him immediately. The music stopped and all dancing came to an instant halt. The chandelier light globes began flickering on and off and a slight hush came over the ballroom allowing the sound of fists hitting flesh to be heard from the direction of the brawling fox hunters. Another piercing whistle followed by "Hey James, up here mate." James quickly glanced about the swirling mass of gowns and dinner jackets that seemed to be moving closer to the outer circle of the ballroom. Then a surprised cry of "Oh James," from Grand-mama pointing with her tortoise-shell fan towards the high ceiling. "Do look at your Australian friend dear, he's swinging like a monkey from the family's precious chandeliers. Please James, do something about it quickly dear. Really, what has come over him?" James looked up towards the ceiling and the beautiful chandeliers to catch a view of his friend Tom in full flight as he swung from one crystal chandelier to the next, right down the centre of the grand ballroom. Fucking hell, thought James. He knew this expression was appropriate as the stockmen had used it often, and this stressful situation really needed it he believed.

James turned towards Grand-mama and calmly reassured her to leave the ballroom for the safety of the high-tea room, and then he would attend to this terrible situation immediately. When James once again turned towards the high ceiling he found there was no need to help Tom down from the flickering chandeliers as he had fallen and landed on a toffee-nosed fox hunter with whom he had had a run-in earlier that day. Tom's inappropriate landing zone immediately got the dander up of the well-dressed English gentleman, starting off another bout of the soft-shoe shuffle between the two men. James felt Tom could handle himself with the best of mankind, and he couldn't help but smile to himself when remembering his first meeting with Tom in the back of Bandit's Bedford truck in Darwin. There were many other stockmen who were well and truly hungover from the booze, all jammed in together like sardines with their swags and the boss's unpredictable blue heeler cattle dog. Bandit was the overseer of Campbell's Run Station and had refused to leave Darwin for the next cattle muster without his full team of stockmen on board the Bedford truck. It was the way of the North and how most Outback cattle stations operated. That morning Bandit went around to the cop station and bailed Tom out of the lock-up after he had spent the night in a sultry cell to cool off for brawling in the local pub. It was from that moment on that Tom and James had become friends. Suddenly James remembered Tom's current situation. He turned around to check on Tom and his new-found aristocratic friend. They were still doing the soft-shoe shuffle about the ballroom floor with each man taking a turn at throwing a few punches for good measure it seemed. James decided to let them be. They could sort out their own differences while he went in search of his mother Lady Gabrielle to direct her to join his Grand-mama and the other ladies who had sheltered together in the high-tea room.

CHAPTER 21

Blood on whose Hands?

W omen cloaked in floating ball gowns and gentlemen in smart dinner jackets clutched onto each other as some laughed and others cried as they hurriedly gathered themselves away from the masses who indulged in the wild and unruly conduct of the evening. For a moment James slowed and hesitated in his rush to help and support the family friends and guests – he reckoned most people were accustomed to some form of excitement at Rosengarten Castle's end of season Hunt Ball. James realised Lady Catherine was nowhere to be seen, but then reprimanded himself – Lady Catherine was not his responsibility and surely Morgan would look after her now. Glancing about, James wondered what had become of Morgan too, for not only was this the annual Hunt Ball, it was also the public announcement of his impending marriage.

Then all of a sudden a massive explosion sounded, instantly followed by another of similar proportion that again, and with even more intensity, rattled the crystals on Grand-mama's precious chandeliers. The second blast was extremely loud and was immediately followed by a whiff of gun powder that drifted into the vicinity of the ballroom. The sound brought an instant hush over the entire gathering as the frightened guests looked around for the intruder. One could have heard a pin drop, but the explosion had left James's ears ringing. Suddenly, there were high pitched and terrifying screams from the many women in the high-tea room as they clung to each other as many cried hysterically that there had to be a madman in the vicinity of the castle.

James went immediately to the far end of the ballroom to investigate, but the problem wasn't there. He then followed the surging throng towards an unused guest bedroom further down the cold corridor. James could hear spine-chilling screams followed by loud sobbing as female guests, who had viewed the disaster before him, came running back down the corridor, past James, holding their ball gowns high off the floor with one hand while trying to muffle their screams with the other as they ran stumbling to escape the terrible sight in the bedroom. As James's hurried steps carried him closer to the scene in the bedroom, the crowd of onlookers moved back in silence to allow him to pass. Several childhood friends reached out to touch James gently on the arm and shoulder as he passed them, as if to offer him some form of comfort. This situation may be too close to home for comfort, James thought as he hurried even more through the throng of overwrought people to the bedroom doorway with no idea who it could possibly be, or even who was making use of the ivory and gold guest bedroom which Grand-mama kept especially neat for her European guests and friends.

"Dear God," whispered an extremely shocked James, as he tripped and stumbled over a guest's elegant slipper that had unceremoniously been abandoned in her rush from the shocking bedroom scene. With his heart pounding heavily, so heavily in fact James had found it difficult to even draw breath, he moved without hesitation towards Morgan's lifeless form. Morgan's body lay naked and sprawled out across the luxurious ivory and gold tasseled bed cover that looked to be saturated in a large amount of his own blood. Close by on the same enormous bed and covered in blood and body matter, the auburn hairs on her pussy exposed to the world, was an overly endowed naked woman, the nerves in her naked torso still spasmodically convulsing with what little life was left in it. The woman, one of London's most beautiful socialites, was well known among the high end of society for her friendships and closeness to several extremely well-to-do married gentlemen. Now her beauty was no longer, her facial features spattered against the elaborate padded silk bed head behind her and over Grand-mama's ivory bedroom walls. James stood in shocked silence as he looked over both persons on the bed and quickly realised that the life was gone for good from both his brother and his mistress. What a damn terrible way to go, James thought as he fought back tears for the pair as he tried to pull the bloodied bed sheets across the bed and over both the naked and blood-ied bodies to give them a little dignity. Victoria, who was known to be quite condescending at times, was the brunette mistress the Wentworth family had been led to believe Morgan had dispensed with long ago, but obviously he had not, thought James. On the floor close by and covered in bloodied hand prints was a twelve-gauge shotgun and two spent car-tridges. Unable to stand the sight of the weapon any longer, James gave it a generous kick with his highly polished boot sending it flying out of sight and under the bed. In shock, James turned towards the handful of guests still close by, and seeing only many blurred faces, asked no one in particular: "Does anyone know of Lady Catherine's whereabouts? Does Lady Catherine know of this?" James's panicked questions simply tum-bled out of his mouth. The gruesome scene before him had put James in a terrible state of shock – to have found his only brother in such an awful and terribly puzzling situation was almost more than James could cope with on this most extraordinary day.

As James stood in the ivory and gold bedroom in an extremely confused state of mind, he couldn't help but hear the questioning whispers exchanged between friends and some guests who stood close behind him in the room. "Do you think Victoria had any knowl-edge of Morgan's association with Lady Catherine?" whispered one. "Was she the jealous type?" asked another. "Is it possible Victoria would do anything as terrible as this?" Then a much older woman piped up with, "Shame on them both, shame on Victoria. When that woman was a teenager she was the mistress of that boy's very own Grandfather…yes shame on her and some of our society's married men. Even some of their wanton wives around London were involved too. She had it coming for some time I'd say." The older lady, with her head held high, as only an English aristocrat could do extremely well, turned away from the grizzly scene to rush from the bedroom with the sound of her overly starched petticoats trailing behind her. After a short silence when all in the room were probably thinking over her bold statement, James heard the question asked of his most terrible thought. "Is it possible that Morgan was murdered? Could they have both been murdered?" Who would want to murder Morgan, thought James, but then Morgan's assumed ex-mistress was also dead. Then there is Lady Catherine, thought James. No, not at all possible, she would not lower herself to anything as terrible as all this. Dear God, James wondered, whatever could have happened to Morgan's sound reasoning? James immediately chided himself for allowing such a stupid thought to cross his mind. The whole situation was not pleasant and he felt instantly nauseous.

The next instant Lady Catherine burst through the crowd of onlookers and into James's arms sobbing uncontrollably while repeating over and over that "Something really terrible had happened to Morgan." James looked down at Catherine and noticed that Lady Catherine's beautiful powder-blue engagement gown and matching evening slippers were both covered in a light spray of blood.

"Can we all please leave the room?" James asked firmly of his fellow guests while still holding Lady Catherine's waist firmly, hoping to keep the lady's dress and shoes facing himself so that no other person could see what he had on the lower part of Lady Catherine's gown and right evening slipper. James then turned his torso to face the family guests. "There is nothing we can do, my brother and the lady are both deceased." James added that he needed to speak with both his parents and Grand-mama Lady Elizabeth immediately, and "Of course I must contact Detective Jackson of the London Police Department as well. I regret that the evening must come to an abrupt end, please don't leave as the police may wish to interview some of you regarding the scene. There will be whiskey and strong coffee in the green and gold lounge room for those of you who need it, the smoking room is available to the gentlemen, please help yourselves to the service." With this said, those remaining few friends who had been standing quietly behind James offering him support, walked solemnly from the ivory and gold bedroom out into the now vacant corridor. As the last person filed from the bedroom James took the time to look down at Lady Catherine. Her state of despair seemed uncontrollable as she clung tightly to his own tensed body. "Please James, take me away from here, something awful is happening around here," she begged of him. James could not help but feel uneasy about the whole situation that lay before his eyes. On the elaborate bed lay two naked people who had obviously earlier been engaged in some form of sexual activity, two well-known people who certainly should not have been entertaining the other on this particular evening at Rosengarten Castle. James felt the whole situation to be unbelievable, and yet if he hadn't been standing right in the very room and by the two deceased persons he would not, could not, have believed it at all.

Lady Catherine's arms were still wrapped tightly around her now deceased finance's younger brother James. Just the two of them were left standing in the cold silent room. James suddenly felt tired and unsure now of any feelings he had thought he felt earlier in the evening for the beautiful Lady Catherine. Nothing made sense any more thought James as he placed his roughened hands over Lady Catherine's soft ones to gently release her grip from around his waist.

James couldn't help but feel Lady Catherine's sudden annoyance by his actions. Her body immediately became tense and rigid, she let go of her hold of James and stood back from him to straighten her ball gown that was in a slight state of dishevelment. She took a delicate white lace handkerchief from her evening clutch before moving across the room to where there was light above the ornate mirror and began to gently pat around her eyes and neck with her handkerchief, all the while watching James's reflection in the mirror. James believed his eyes were deceiving him again, for he was positive there were red stains on Lady Catherine's white lace handkerchief. Is it possible they were blood stains, he thought. Lady Catherine immediately returned her handkerchief to her evening bag and promptly snapped it shut. As the only surviving child of the district's most wealthy landholder, Lady Catherine was accustomed to having her own way, and at the present time she was still carrying what she believed was an earlier rebuff from James Wentworth, who she thought preferred the Australian Outback to spending time in England nearer herself. James was another provocation for Lady Catherine as she saw it. She was beginning to feel slightly agitated with James – surely he knew she wanted him, to love and be held by him, and surely he understood that it was expected of them both to unite in marriage. Morgan had been the means to an end, and James will be made to understand that one day, mused Lady Catherine to herself. The now confident Catherine looked at James and smiled sweetly before turning and glancing momentarily at the two deceased persons on the bed. Tears welled in her eyes and she shook her head in total disgust before walking out of the ivory and gold bedroom ahead of James, leaving the gruesome scene behind her.

CHAPTER 22

Detective Jackson

As both Lady Catherine and James walked together in silence down the long cold corridor of Rosengarten Castle they were met half-way by an extremely anxious and slightly intoxicated Lord Alexander Wentworth III, who rushed towards the two of them on his way to the ivory and gold guest bedroom.

"James, Lady Catherine, my dear. I have just received the most terrible, terrible news." Lord Alexander looked directly at James, "Please, I beg of you James, tell me it is not so."

On seeing Lord Alexander Lady Catherine flew from James's side into Lord Alexander's outstretched arms, using her fingers to brush away the unstoppable tears from her beautiful face. Lord Alexander looked at his youngest and asked, "James, is this bad news really true?" For a few fleeting seconds Lord Alexander stared deep into his younger son's sad blue eyes, hoping to gain from deep within them his much wanted answer. But he quickly realised from the pain in James's eyes that his heir and eldest son was truly deceased. Suddenly, his father bent over, holding both knees with unsteady hands, knuckles whitening, and let forth the most animal crazed and haunting cry, the cry of terrible loss and pain that only a parent could feel on the loss of a child. With this frightening display of loss, James rushed to comfort his parent. Eventually, Lord Alexander gathered himself and said in a much more determined tone, "I must get to Morgan now, immediately." As James took a step back from his father, Lady Catherine pulled herself together and stepped back to give James room to place both his hands on his father's shoulders. "Father, I wouldn't advise you to go to the scene, it's a truly horrendous sight." But Lord Alexander insisted. "I must go to Morgan, please take care of Lady Catherine. She will be suffering terribly." "Father, I must warn you again, they are both deceased persons. I must call the London Police Department immediately. There will be a lot of questions asked and they will also need answers," offered James, who simply wanted to contact the police as soon as possible and then check how his mother and Grandmama were handling the shocking news of both Morgan and his assumed ex-mistress Victoria's death. Lord Alexander again took Lady Catherine back into his arms and gave her an overly exaggerated and unnecessarily long hug of sympathy, thought James, who had never noticed his father ever being so attentive towards Lady Catherine before. Lord Alexander then turned towards James. "Hold the call to the London Police Department. I will not have those officers running around and getting under my feet for the moment. I will call them myself and immediately after I have had time with Morgan." This idea sounded reasonable to James as his father was indeed the head of the family home anyway. Suddenly, as if his own life depended on it, Lord Alexander took a huge draw on his rum cigar before continuing on his way down the empty corridor towards the ivory and gold guest bedroom. James continued to escort Lady Catherine towards his Grand-mama's private sitting room where he hoped to find his mother Gabrielle as well.

On entering Grand-mama's sitting room Lady Catherine immediately dissolved into tears again, which left her face and body all hot, flustered and terribly uncomfortable. After receiving many words of comfort and condolences from the immediate Wentworth family, it was arranged by Grand-mama's lady's maid that Lady Catherine should take the time to indulge in a long warm bath filled with aromatic oil and salts, followed by a rest, before the police from London arrived to investigate the deaths of Morgan and Victoria. "It will be such a tiring time, yes, such a terrible time for all," said a somewhat exasperated Grand-mama.

In the meantime and while awaiting the arrival of the police, the immediate Wentworth family, shocked and immensely distressed, had gathered in the privacy of Lord Alexander's ornate ground floor office. Still unable to make head or tail of their terrible misfortune, each person repeatedly tried to piece together the ghastly events of their own day. Lady Catherine, with the help of Grand-mama's lady's maid to assist, bathed in a warm tub before taking time out to rest in the quiet of her luxurious guest suite on the floor above them. It was in this quiet time that Lady Catherine felt for the first time in her life a deeply harboured resentment towards her father's expectations that she should marry a son from the Wentworth clan whom she did not truly love. This was expected to proceed before the death of her own father, Lord Hamilton, who had been in ailing health for some time.

James excused himself from his father's office to check on the extended family and friends and the many other guests who had kindly attended Morgan's and Lady Catherine's engagement party. He was surprised to find some people still indulging heavily in straight Black Hawk whiskey on ice, which they obviously believed would help block out the day's terrible tragedy.

Detective Jackson and his sidekick Constable Robinson announced their arrival with a spray of gravel unceremoniously thrown from their vehicle's tyres against the lions-head entrance to Rosengarten Castle. Not for a long time had the London Police Department had a double crime to investigate in an aristocrat's castle. This would make the full front page of the *London Bulletin*, mused the young copper to himself, and there could be some interesting times ahead too.

James greeted the gentlemen and directed them immediately to his father's office where the remaining family members waited in silence. James had met Detective Jackson himself, hoping to stifle any titbits of staff gossip before any house member had the slightest chance of churning out front page gossip of their own. At this sad time we must all unite, thought James – his mother and Grand-mama certainly didn't need to hear any gossip of this horror day via their own lady's maids.

Detective Jackson was dressed in his usual uniform of a checkered brown and cream tweed tattered suit coat, while on his head was a matching cap that had certainly seen better days. Under his cap was the craggy worn face of a good detective, his trademark smelly cigar glued to the corner of his mouth. Jackson's sidekick Robinson, twenty-five years younger than his boss, had worked with Detective Jackson on serious crime cases before. The men were well known around London as a good team who could work together and would persevere at a crime scene until they cracked the case.

"Father, Detective Jackson and Constable Robinson from the London Police," James said on opening Lord Alexander's office door. The trio were met with a haze of strong cigar smoke from his father's chain-smoking habit. Lord Alexander rose from his seat behind the curved office desk and shook hands with both gentlemen. "Thank you for coming out to Rosengarten Castle so promptly." Grand-mama and Gabrielle both instantly sprung to their feet to greet the detective and his sidekick, both believing that now the detective had arrived from London he would be able to unravel the mystery surrounding the shocking deaths.

"Please, Detective Jackson," began Grand-mama, "this was to have been a good day for all our family and friends, but something has gone terribly wrong. My grandson and a woman are both dead. God knows what had become of them. That woman, what has she done to our Morgan? Only hours earlier he had become engaged to the Lady Catherine of Hamilton Hill Estate?" Grand-mama had found the news of the day extremely tiring and returned to her uncomfortable straight-back chair and began to search deep in her beaded handbag for another clean hanky to pat away her tears. Gabrielle, who had lost her extremely spoilt and tantrum throwing eldest son, got up from her chair and walked across the room to where a wood fire was burning gently in the hearth. She stood solemn and alone. Feeling more alone now than ever before, she allowed her pale vulnerable soul to absorb all the warmth of the fire while dwelling on her own sad thoughts of her first-born child's happier childhood years. Gabrielle moved closer to the hearth wishing she was able to throw herself into the hot flames and allow it to devour her pale and delicate body, for this was her son Morgan's very last day on this earth. She stood motionless with both hands clasped tightly together, as if each hand needed the other for strength, until her frail body, wracked with despair and emotion over the day's events, collapsed to the floor in a flood of heart breaking tears.

"Please excuse Robinson and myself," Detective Jackson said, "but I must investigate the crime scene and interview all. We have immense work to do. We must all meet here in this office once again in the morning." The two gentlemen were now full of authority and assured Lord Alexander and his family that they would leave no stone unturned in their investigation of the crime. "This is a most serious case with two deceased persons. We must move quickly and onto the crime scene immediately," said Detective Jackson as he and his sidekick moved off down the corridor with a notable bounce in their steps. It was now time to get on with the job at hand. With this final statement for the day both Grand-mama and mother Gabrielle rose from their chairs and left Lord Alexander's office for the privacy and comfort of their own sitting rooms upstairs. Grand-mama felt immediate prejudice towards that wanton Victoria, while the titbits of gossip fed to her earlier by her personal lady's maid only helped to raise Grand-mama's blood pressure and fuel her anger towards the woman. Gabrielle, on the other hand, was totally exhausted from the day's events and felt she needed to rest in her own bed and be left alone for a week.

Lord Alexander and his youngest son James both returned to check on their guests in the green and gold lounge room. James was left standing in the arched doorway alone as his father promptly made his way towards the whiskey cabinet, possibly to wipe himself out for the remainder of the evening. The rich green and gold interior in the lounge room with its exquisite European chandeliers, gave a touch of class to that intoxicated, staggering bunch of wild fox-hunting gentlemen, thought James. As James looked on, the room before him was slowly filling with the pungent aroma of cigar and tobacco smoke. Amid the smoke were several elderly gentlemen who staggered about the lounge room dressed in expensive coat and tails while still capable of holding their crystal tumblers of whiskey in the appropriate manner, with that little finger cocked high and out on the correct angle. Their other hand was busier than a horny octopus's tentacle, reaching out to pat the firm buttocks of any close at hand or passing young woman. Nothing has really changed here with the family party scene…booze, drugs and wild women. I don't belong here among all this lousy entertainment anymore, thought James. I have always despised it. James had spent his childhood watching from behind the curtains on the sidelines as his father and Grandfather's many friends partied hard. Only now that James had returned from the Australian Outback, and had not attended the wild party scene at Rosengarten for the past six months, did he notice just how immature it was. James found it odd that some persons had to be completely off their rocker on a toxic combination of drugs and alcohol to believe they were actually having a good time.

"Come in old chap, you'll need a whiskey or two to help drown the day's terrible, terrible goings on," coached an older family friend from the middle of the lounge room. "Not right now Sir, I have just remembered that I have several things to attend to. I will join you a little later for a drink," answered James politely while suddenly remembering he hadn't spotted his friend Tom for some time. James did an immediate about face and walked off in the direction of Tom's bedroom, not that James expected Tom to be in bed at this time, but it was as good a place as any to start his search for his Australian friend. Then as James was about to give up on his search for Tom, he was approached by Muldoon the head butler.

"Sir, I'm so sorry to have heard the terrible news."

"Thank you Muldoon. The police are investigating the scene as we speak."

"Can I assist you Sir? You seem a little lost, have you lost something?"

"No Muldoon, not a thing, but I have just realised that I have not been a good friend to Tom. The last time I spotted him was earlier today, when he and one of Morgan's wayward fox hunters were using Grand-mama's lounge room as a boxing ring."

Muldoon shuffled his feet before speaking. "If I may say so Sir, your friend from the colonies could probably take care of himself. He strikes me as a true colonial larrikin, a bit on the wild side I'd say."

James answered with a tired, "Thank you Muldoon." He didn't need to hear any more on Tom, he'd already copped a burst from Grand-mama earlier in the evening when Tom, who was reasonably full on OP rum, was caught by Grand-mama swinging from one of her precious chandeliers to another, right down the middle of the green and gold ballroom. Even James found Tom's form of entertainment hard to believe.

"I'll just take a quick look around the outside before returning for a nightcap and then bed," said James while hoping that Tom was not in any kind of trouble or up to any further mischief.

James, deep in his own thoughts, decided to make the most of his time alone as he walked slowly about the outside of the castle in his search for Tom, occasionally bumping into couples intimately entwined, some whispering quietly, others giggling and happy.

"James, is that you old chap?" James recognised the voice of a childhood friend, George. "Are you all right?"

"Yes thank you George. I'm looking for Tom, have you seen him about this evening? I haven't been the best of hosts." Before James could finish explaining himself to his friend, George pointed in the general direction of the stable complex. "I wouldn't worry too much Sir, I believe he may be looked after very well this evening." James thanked George and turned towards the distant stable complex where he suddenly noticed a tiny flicker of lamp light. As James approached the complex he planned on calling out loudly to Tom, but he needn't have bothered as James's favourite chestnut filly whinnied out a loud greeting to him instead.

"Hello there!" Tom called at the top of his voice. "Who do I have the pleasure of a visit from this fine English evening?" "It's James, Tom." "Come on in James, I believe you know Mandy. Mandy works as a kitchen maid in your family establishment," said Tom. James entered the stables, nodded his head in acknowledgement towards both Tom and Mandy before making himself comfortable on a conveniently placed straw bale, giving both Mandy and Tom time to fumble about tidying up their ruffled state. Poor Mandy was flushed and feeling somewhat embarrassed to be caught in an inappropriate situation by the boss's son and wanted to leave for her quarters immediately. James raised his hand beckoning Mandy to stay. "Please don't leave on my behalf, I've simply dropped by to see if Tom was in need of anything this evening," said James rather wearily. "I'll have a nightcap and head off to bed." Glancing about the stables, James wondered when Tom had moved his swag down to the stable complex from his guest bedroom in the house.

"Tom, are you really that uncomfortable in the house? Your swag, err your bedding, is here?" James asked pointing towards the rough looking swag laid out on the stable's clean straw.

Tom answered sheepishly in his slow Outback twang, "James, you know me mate." There was some silence before Tom asked, "James, ah, damn it mate, I overheard a guest mention to another that Morgan and a woman are both deceased. Was this a drunken rumour, or is it for real mate?" James stopped pushing the straw around on the stable floor with his boot. He looked and felt extremely tired, and it took all his willpower to stand up from his squatting position on the floor and face his Australian friend. The day's long and dramatic events were eventually taking their toll on him. Tom's friend, Mandy, let out a stifled scream when she too realised the rumour was indeed true. Not taking the time to say a proper goodbye to Tom or James, Mandy gathered up her possessions before making a hasty exit. She was sure her assistance would be needed in the kitchen at this sad time. Without another word, Mandy left the two gentlemen behind in the flickering light of the stables as she hurriedly ran across the dewy horse paddock to the castle's kitchen.

James looked so sad and forlorn standing there that Tom too understood without being told by James that the earlier gossip he had overheard was indeed true. Tom immediately wrapped both his burly arms around his friend, pumping James on his back. "Holy shit mate," he mumbled in his Aussie drawl, "why the hell didn't you say something earlier? I'm so sorry James, I really am. Family is family mate no matter what the circumstances. For God's sake James, do yah know what really happened? I mean, I heard it was a bloody mess, I mean this is England." It suddenly dawned on Tom that he was 'carrying on like a bloody pork chop,' and that he had better gather himself as his friend had truly lost his brother.

James fought hard to hold himself together in the presence of his friend before saying, "Tom, I know you're happier down here at the stables, there are a lot of tears and busy detectives nosing about the corridors. If you want to camp here, do so with my blessings, come to the house when you're ready. I must return now to the house to check on mother and Grand-mama. My absence will be notably missed."

Before James left the stable complex he walked slowly towards the horse yard with shoulders hunched and head bowed. A worried Tom kept an eye on his mate from the shadows of the stables; he couldn't help but feel a deep sadness for his aristocratic friend. Tom remembered his own mother once telling him after he had complained loudly about her miniscule share in the split of Campbell's Run Station that, 'Money isn't everything, it won't buy all life has to offer, young Tom'. Well, thought Tom, money didn't prevent Morgan from being murdered either.

Tom could see James's extraordinary wealth – the many large elaborate buildings filled with extremely expensive and extraordinary things, to say nothing of the many hundreds of wealthy friends – it was out there in the open for all to see. Yet Tom could feel in his gut that something was missing from his mate's life. If only James would confide in me, thought Tom, and if I knew, I could possibly help him.

James stopped walking and stood in silence, letting go of the present and returning to the past. He recalled the many long hours and days in previous years handling the estate's young horses, breaking and handling them to bridle and saddle for the family's once a year and hugely prestigious horse sale. Even Lady Catherine had spent some time leaning against a yard post studying both James and his beast at work until something more interesting took her fancy and she moved on.

The evening had become quite cool, and yet James felt a warm sense of calm come over him as he rested his tired body against the roughly sawn wooden panels of the round yard. James stared blankly towards the largest star just visible in the ink-black sky above. His mind drifted back over the many quality horses that had passed through his young hands at this very horse yard, telling himself that the days of the big thoroughbred horse sales will come again for Rosengarten Castle and the Wentworth family. It will happen, only it will happen sometime in the distant future, he promised himself. The heat and flies of the Australian Outback, combined with the will to still experience even more of the Outback way of life, as his Grandfather had done before him, was still very high on James's wish list. Yes, James promised himself, just as soon as this terrible tragedy had sorted itself out, Tom and I will return to the Northern Territory. There are many things I wish to do and experience there. While James's mind was spinning and processing his thoughts, he suddenly shivered on feeling the evening's cold moist air crossing the surrounding paddocks and beyond. He buttoned up his evening jacket and rearranged his collar high up around his neck for warmth before walking slowly back across the lush damp horse paddocks for home.

Tom had returned to his swag, set his back against a bale of straw and let his busy mind run back over the evening events at the ball. Tom remembered that he himself had had a lively time of it, and he even had the bruises to prove it. Now that Tom had sobered up he even had the decency to feel a little embarrassed for his shenanigans in the Wentworth family ballroom that evening. But Tom's sharpshooter eye had picked up on Lady Catherine's attempt to pull her left hand from

Morgan's while they were standing together on the podium. Tom was unable to remember if Lady Catherine had already accepted Morgan's large emerald engagement ring at that point or not. It will probably all come out in the wash Tom told himself, but something hadn't been quite right between that arrogant Morgan and his beautiful lady.

Rosengarten Castle had become a shell of itself the night Morgan and his lady friend died. The final hunt ball of the season, usually the most grand and lively of all in the vicinity, came to an abrupt end. Guests left in dribs and drabs, some in their elegant horse-drawn buggies used for special occasions – or to add that touch of glamour to an occasion – while others preferred to be driven to their homes in their chauffeur driven Bentleys. Those left behind supported each other by indulging heavily in whiskey and expensive champagne. Some very nearly choked and suffocated on their own cigar smoke that quickly filled the smoking room with a heavy dark cloud that hung from the high ceiling, while others mumbled in their stupor that the extra liquor was needed to wipe out the day's calamitous event.

CHAPTER 23

No Stone Unturned

The following morning came around all too quickly for James. Rising to sit on his bedside, his heavy head held in the palms of his hands, James still found yesterday's death of Morgan and his lady friend Victoria unbelievable. What had started out as a glorious occasion for two of England's wealthiest farming families – when Lord Alexander Wentworth III announced the betrothal of Morgan and Lady Catherine – had turned into a nightmare just hours later. Only this very morning the terrible incident had James feeling as if the family estate had already fallen on top on him, he could already feel the pressure. He appreciated that with Morgan's sudden death he would now be expected to fill Morgan's shoes as the next Lord Wentworth when the time came, and he secretly hoped it wasn't about to happen in the near future.

As James dressed himself in his best day suit, he remembered the meeting scheduled by Detective Jackson of the London Police Department was to be held in his father's downstairs office. It was time for James to scoot along to collect his mother Gabrielle and Grand-mama Lady Elizabeth. He would need to escort both ladies downstairs to his father's office. James knew that the detective and his sidekick were the very best of their kind in and around London. Both were known for solving some of the worst crimes in England,

and were extremely capable of tracking down culprits quickly. James hoped the detective had worked all night long on the crime scene in Grand-mama's ivory and gold bedroom, and that this very morning he may have some worthy news for the family.

James would make it his business to also check on Lady Catherine. He wasn't sure whether the lady was still a guest in residence at Rosengarten Castle this morning, or had she been driven back to Hamilton Hill where she would inform her father of the terrible catastrophe, and then take the time to gather herself and mourn Morgan's death in the warmth and privacy of her own home. James decided he would question Grand-mama first thing. James wanted to forget the sight of a light smattering of blood on Lady Catherine's pale blue evening gown and right toe of her elegant matching slippers. He really wanted to forget the whole terrible tragedy had ever really happened, but that wasn't at all possible.

Grand-mama and Gabrielle were ready and waiting on the balcony to meet Detective Jackson in James's father's office. Both were elegantly dressed in black French-lace mourning outfits most suitable for the occasion, and there was no doubt in James's mind that both ladies were hoping the detective had come up with some solid answers during his night's investigation, possibly something that would help solve the terrible catastrophe of yesterday.

"Grand-mama...mother," James said, greeting the most loved women in his young life with a light peck to their warmed cheeks. James noted how puffy and swollen the skin around his mother's face was, while her sad and bloodshot eyes spoke volumes to him. James believed his mother was still taking her sleeping medication for her depression sickness, as it had a similar effect on her face, but this morning his mother's appearance was worse than ever and it worried James. "Mother," James whispered, "are you well? Are you really up to the meeting with Detective Jackson this morning?" In a gentle voice as if speaking to a precious child, James tried to persuade his mother to remain in her sitting room and take more rest. "I will relay to you every ounce of news Detective Jackson has scrounged from the walls of Rosengarten, mother." Gabrielle lifted her sad brown eyes to meet her youngest son's, her voice barely audible. "I must be there James. I never realised that Morgan was so in love with the Lady Catherine. I had no idea at all, and this...this Victoria...I don't understand," her voice trailed away as she battled to sort it all out in her muddled mind. "And you Grand-mama, how well did you sleep?" asked James trying to make small talk with his Grand-mama. "Not as well as I could have my dear. In all my ninety years I have never been in a home of such tragedy. I must say that I am terribly saddened by it all, but I am made of sterner material than your mother dear, and I'm sure the Wentworth family will weather this last storm at Rosengarten Castle together." Then, out of the blue, "Who is this woman, this Victoria I believe her name is?" James was quite taken aback with Grand-mama's direct line of questioning to him. But before he could answer Grand-mama again asked, "Did you know of this person, James?" Lady Elizabeth still had the sharp mind of a detective thought James. "No Grand-mama, but I believe she floated around London's society circles. It's only rumour and gossip and not worth repeating," answered James, his voice trailing off with his own worried thoughts on the matter.

James delivered the two ladies to Lord Alexander's ground floor office where they were met by a very official bow of the head from Detective Jackson and Constable Robinson. Lord Alexander was already there. All were present bar Lady Catherine. James stayed standing while the other family members were seated around the office table. "I shall return upstairs immediately to escort Lady Catherine down from the Peacock guest room and I shall send a lady's maid to her room," offered James hesitantly as he glanced towards the detective and constable. "I had purposely left lending her my arm until last, believing she may need more time, considering Morgan's death."

Lord Alexander stood up promptly and addressed Detective Jackson. "Now that everyone is present I shall tell you the latest. Lady Catherine's father became seriously ill during the night. I know this because Muldoon woke me in the early hours this morning with the sad news. I, in turn, had the lady's maid wake Lady Catherine, and she was chauffeured home to her family's Hamilton Hill Estate almost immediately." Total silence filled the room before Lord Wentworth said, to no one in particular as he took his seat at the head of the office table, "How much more tragic could it possibly get for Lady Catherine?" Detective Jackson cleared his croaky throat a little too loudly, even sounding somewhat annoyed by this unexpected news. "Detective, could you give the lady a day or two with her sick father?" Lord Alexander asked. "I do believe he is very unwell. Then interview her at their Hamilton Hill

Estate if the need be at all. May I ask you to please remember that Lady Catherine had just officially become the intended wife-to-be to my eldest son Morgan only hours before this terrible tragedy?"

"Yes...yes," mumbled the very officious detective, "I will certainly be doing that. All persons who had visited the crime scene must be interviewed...now please, I wish to get on with this meeting, if I may? I would like to make it clear, I mean very clear, that at this point of my investigation no one is without suspicion." A gasp of horror escaped Grand-mama. "My dear man, I do hope you are not insinuating that this bold statement of yours includes our immediate family." All the while Grand-mama was trying to untangle her lorgnettes from her handbag, for she now felt the urgent need to have a damn good look at this outspoken detective fellow.

"Madam, at this point I emphasise one more time, no one is without suspicion, and furthermore, no one is to leave the vicinity of the Rosengarten Castle without a legitimate reason." Grand-mama, who was not used to being put back in her box, had become unusually subdued.

Lord Alexander questioned the detective. Did he have a suspect or thought of a motive for the terrible deaths in mind?" At the present time, the crime scene has the appearance of a murder-suicide, but it is all far too early in the investigation to rule anything out. We have a very open mind," the detective answered. Then Constable Robinson, who had been silent up to this point, piped up with, "Incidentally, what was the connection between your son Morgan and the deceased female?" Both Grand-mama and Gabrielle's eyes opened wide, before each of them admitted to having no knowledge of Morgan and Victoria's association. James then leaned towards Constable Robinson and whispered in his ear that he wished to speak with him in private regarding this matter at the first opportunity. Detective Jackson asked if the ivory and gold guest bedroom had been visited since the crime. This question was answered promptly by James, who explained that many guests had indeed gone into the room on hearing the shotgun blasts, including himself, and were devastated by the sight of the injuries as it was evident both persons were deceased.

"I then ushered the spectators out of the room while discreetly kicking the shotgun under the bed." "Can you explain the reason for this, I mean, booting the shotgun under the bed?" interjected Detective Jackson. After some hesitation, James answered that, "The sight of the gun covered in my brother's blood was all too much for me to bear…a most terrible sight indeed, Sir."

Gabrielle began to weep quietly. James asked permission for both Grand-mama and his mother Gabrielle to leave the room. "Detective, constable, neither my mother nor Grand-mama have any knowledge of this unfortunate event. I can vouch that both persons were in the high-tea room at the time of this terrible tragedy." Both officers put their heads together, then agreed that the ladies' presence was no longer needed at the meeting. Lord Alexander was asked to compile a list of all the guests' names and addresses. All persons would be interviewed, Constable Robinson said.

James then addressed his father. "Father, now that Grand-mama and mother have left the room we should enlighten these two gentlemen of Morgan and Victoria's past connection." Lord Wentworth grimaced and then very nearly choked on the thought for he would have much preferred that Morgan and Victoria's past connection not be mention ever again, but it was not to be. James went on to explain that several years earlier the deceased female had been known to be Morgan's mistress. Morgan had never spoken of the deceased female as such. It was noted how extremely protective Morgan was of her when they attended society's social occasions. I believe Sir, it was unspoken knowledge. It was rumoured the deceased female was ten to fifteen years older than Morgan but it had been kept under wraps for obvious reasons. Mother and Grand-mama had no knowledge of this matter. James explained he had been away in Australia but believed Morgan no longer associated with the deceased female. James added that there was no more information regarding this person that he could offer to help the detective and his colleague. What James could not bring himself to admit to the officers was that the deceased woman who had shared the bed with Morgan this night was the very same auburn-haired beauty who years earlier had ridden his dear Grandfather, Lord Alexander Wentworth II, to his death!

Lord Alexander added that he was of the same belief as his son James regarding Morgan's mistress and their association. He also added, as an afterthought, that he would much prefer if the detective and constable kept this discussion of both Morgan and the deceased female's activities entirely to themselves for reasons he was sure they would both understand.

Detective Jackson began to show signs of impatience, constantly tapping and twirling his pen on the office desk. "Please stop tapping the pen Sir," Lord Alexander asked the detective. Not only did Lord Alexander have a headache from the previous evening's entertainment, but it was damn irritating, he said. Detective Jackson stopped tapping and twirling his pen on the elaborate desk, stood up and began to gather his already dog-eared and slightly tatty notepapers, and as he did so, he said to no one in particular, "One would have thought the deceased persons would have picked a better time and place to rendezvous." Detective Jackson, who was known to be a rather cool, calm sort, had become slightly agitated with the morning's meeting with the Wentworth family.

He looked at Lord Alexander and said, "I must inform you that during our evening investigations of the deceased we found positive evidence of cocaine use by both parties."

Lord Alexander slammed both his fists down hard on the office table, and immediately bounced to his feet while sending his chair flying backwards. His red glare signalled that his blood pressure was at an all-time high as he demanded angrily from Detective Jackson what evidence the detective had to prove his eldest son had been dabbling in the drug on the very evening of his betrothal to the Lady Catherine. Lord Alexander Wentworth's instant display of anger and forceful show of protection for the family name came too late for him to try to fool this well-seasoned London detective, for the Wentworth males had built a reputation of their very own in the party scene.

"Wentworth, you know yourself that lately when boredom has hit our society's party scene, that those few with spare cash often liven themselves up with a little help from narcotics." The old detective reminded Lord Alexander that "The find was indeed fact, but the drugs had not killed either person. The cocaine may have contributed towards this terrible event of last evening." After a slight pause while he too lit up another foul smelling cigar, the detective continued with, "It was the two ounces of finely polished lead that did the damage Sir. And in answer to your earlier question Wentworth, the cocaine was on the bedside table, and also the coffee table by the far window." Then after a slight pause added, "I must leave now for my office in London. We have a load of work to follow up. By the way, both of the deceased persons were transported to the London morgue in the early hours of this morning. I will be in touch, goodbye."

CHAPTER 24

Under the Oak Tree

It was an extremely busy week following Morgan's unexpected death. The family home became a hive of activity with constant daily visits from other family members and friends offering their condolences on the loss of the Wentworth's eldest son Morgan.

Detective Jackson returned from his London office accompanied by Constable Robinson to comb through the ivory and gold guest bedroom one more time before they began to question every single staff member on the property. Detective Jackson's interest seemed focused on the shotgun. Did it belong to the Rosengarten Estate, and had it been kept in the gun and trophy room with all other hunting rifles? Was the room kept locked and where were the keys kept to the trophy room? The questions were endless. Lord Alexander informed the detective that the estate's trophy room was indeed where all the rifles were kept, and that the room was open to any guest who wished to participate in fox, pheasant or duck hunting on Rosengarten Estate. Therefore, there was no need to have the gun and trophy room locked at all on that particular day.

"I wish to inform you Lord Alexander, that Constable Robinson and I have interviewed the Lady Catherine of Hamilton Hill. During our conversation Lady Catherine had asked me to pass on her sincere condolences to yourself and the entire Wentworth family, and also to mention that her father's health is much improved. The lady will visit when she has had the time to mourn and gather herself in the privacy of her own home." Then in a slightly gentler tone the detective continued, "I believe Lady Catherine had left behind at Rosengarten Castle her evening gown and shoes that were worn on the night of her betrothal to your eldest son. May I see them, please?" This question brought a gasp of horror from James who was strung as tight as a violin. "Good God detective, why on earth would you want to see Lady Catherine's clothing? I mean, if they are here that is, they are the clothes of a fine lady." Lord Alexander jumped to his feet to defend his son's assumption on Lady Catherine's clothing and garments. He again slammed his office desk with both fists while glaring at the detective and telling him, "If the constable and yourself hadn't found enough evidence in the ivory and gold bedroom to come to a conclusion on the death of my son, I'm unable to accept that you will achieve anything further by looking at and touching a lady's fine evening gown. My good God Sir, this I will not hear of. It is outrageous!" Lord Alexander concluded as he calmed down and pulled his chair once again towards his office desk. "Simply all part of the investigation Wentworth," answered the detective in a tone that defiantly said, 'he was the one in charge here and you must not forget that', "but I will leave it be, for the time being that is." James breathed a deep sigh of utter relief – he was terrified the detective would have spotted the fine spray of blood on the lower part of Lady Catherine's pale blue evening gown and slippers. The sight of it would have been enough for the detective and his sidekick to conjure up all sorts of conclusions. The meeting between the four gentlemen had come to an end. Detective Jackson and Constable Robinson had not unearthed or disclosed any new information to the family regarding the tragic deaths. Their investigation had progressed no further than the belief the cocaine shared by both parties on that particular evening played a very minor part in the death of both persons. The deaths looked very much like a murder-suicide, and it looked suspiciously as if the female had shot the male in the back of the head first, which she followed by a fatal shot to herself via her right temple. The detective had stated that the case was certainly not solved or closed at this point. Lord Alexander was given permission to bury his son Morgan, and James had also been given permission to leave for

Australia on the condition that he return to England if the need for further police investigation arose.

As soon as the detective and constable had vacated Rosengarten Estate's premises, James made it his business to go immediately to the Peacock guest bedroom used by the Lady Catherine. He felt an urgent need to investigate if indeed she had left behind her pale blue evening gown and slippers at Rosengarten while in her haste to rush to the bedside of her seriously ill father, who sadly had shown signs of a temperature at the time and had remained at their Hamilton Hill Estate on the evening of her betrothal to Morgan.

James felt sick to the pit of his stomach on entering the Peacock guest bedroom used by the Lady Catherine. It was something a gentleman of James's class would never do. But James did indeed feel a real sense of urgency on entering the room. Why, he wasn't even sure himself, but the thought of the bloodstains on Catherine's beautiful gown wouldn't leave his mind. Deep down inside he believed Lady Catherine would never have become involved in any such murder. She was too much of a lady to have ever contemplated such an outlandish idea anyway. Why would it matter to her if Morgan had a mistress? James understood that theirs was certainly not what he thought was a love match made in heaven, but he was unable to work it out. Why and what was the connection between his older brother and the spirited Lady Catherine? James simply wished he had never spotted the red spray of blood on Lady Catherine's evening gown and slippers. And yet James still crept into the Peacock bedroom and began his quiet search through the huge wardrobes looking for Lady Catherine's pale blue evening gown. James was positive he would recognise it immediately as Catherine had looked so exquisite in it on the night of the ghastly tragedy. James had no wish to be caught in what was Lady Catherine's private room on the night following her engagement to Morgan. It was not only a bad look, but he wondered what excuse he would use if caught amongst the gowns in the bedroom closet. After what seemed an eternity of painstakingly checking every pale blue gown in the huge closet, James glowed bright red and began to stutter with embarrassment when caught red-handed in the act, with his wild sun-bleached head of hair caught in the beads and sequins of a pale blue tulle gown in the bedroom's closet.

"May I help you Sir?" came the soft English voice of a female servant. "You look to be in some kind of difficulties Sir. I mean, in among the ruffles and tulle that is." James had never been so embarrassed in his whole life, and to have been caught out by the new house maid at that. "I do apologise, I'm James. Are you new around here?" "Yes, I'm Annabelle Sir." The pretty, softly spoken girl also glowed with embarrassment as she tried to muffle a giggle. James went on to explain to Annabelle that Lady Catherine had used this particular room on the day of her betrothal to his now deceased brother, that she had been called away unexpectedly during the same evening and apparently in her haste to leave the premises, had left behind her pale blue engagement gown in the bedroom. "Have you seen it, Annabelle?" asked James, now feeling a lot more comfortable that it was all out in the open. "Oh yes Sir, it's certainly a beautiful gown," replied Annabelle, now feeling more confident around James. She promptly turned around and pointed to the pale blue evening gown that hung from a satin-covered coat hanger above the metal bath tub, and hooked on the lip of the tub were the matching high-heel evening slippers. "There you are Sir. I tidied the room the morning following Lady Catherine's departure. When I entered the room I found Lady Catherine's beautiful evening gown and slippers both floating in the bath tub." James moved slowly across the bedroom floor towards the bath tub while trying to get a better look at the gown and slippers. He spread the skirt wide as he studied the soft blue tulle intently, but there were no bloodstains. James then reached for the gown's matching slippers, and gently turned them around and around in his big hands. Again, there were no bloodstains. For a moment James felt confused, and he wondered had he imagined the bloodstains spattered across Lady Catherine's right blue slipper the previous evening? Or was he going mad with the worry of the horrifying tragedy of yesterday? A worried Annabelle piped up with, "I hope the gown or shoes aren't ruined Sir, I was extremely careful when I hung the gown up to dry. I did check for stains or marks of ruin. There are none, but I really did find them both floating in the tub full of lavender oil and bath salts on my morning shift Sir." "Annabelle…Annie, it's fine. Lady Catherine will be pleased you have rescued her gown from total ruin. Here, please do take this pound, and you must accept it as a thank you from Lady Catherine, for she will be so grateful that her gown and shoes are not ruined."

"Oh my goodness Sir, I cannot accept this! This is a small fortune," stammered Annabelle. "Please do," answered James as he went to move away. But before he left the bedroom, he advised Annabelle to parcel up the gown and slippers and have them delivered via courier to Lady Catherine of Hamilton Hill Estate. James then walked free of the room feeling as if a ton of lead had been lifted from his shoulders. Why had the bloodstains worried him so much? Was it really his problem if Lady Catherine went to jail? Did she really have anything to do with the murder, and where did the spray of blood come from then? James questioned himself over and over until he was nearly blue in the face. Could he ever forget that he saw the marks at all, James wondered, or had another soul spotted the bloodstains on Lady Catherine's gown and evening slippers? "Dear me old chap," James said out loud to himself, "you do really need a long walk in these beautiful manicured parklands to clear your clouded head before you become too mistrusting of all other persons." James began his walk remembering that shortly his older brother would be laid to rest on the distant hill.

Monday morning came around soon enough, and by ten o'clock a fine breakfast accompanied by the best champagne had been served to several hundred guests who had arrived early at Rosengarten. The occasion was to say their last goodbyes to Morgan Alexander Wentworth, the eldest son of Lord Alexander and Lady Gabrielle Wentworth of Rosengarten Castle. It didn't help that the rumour mill had run on overdrive since Morgan's and Victoria's deaths, while the gossip mongers also had a field day. James had been asked outright, "Why had Morgan wanted to marry the beautiful Lady Catherine when he obviously still had the hots for old Victoria?" Other persons presumed that the murderer had to be either female attached to Morgan. Was the murderer Lady Catherine or the late Madam Victoria? Then another arrogant young man dressed in full morning suit and top hat, and of notable heritage and full of anger because he had missed out on having had the opportunity to become personally acquainted with the Lady Catherine, outrageously suggested to James that Morgan had got his just deserts. Without thinking, James lashed out with a savage right hook to the young man's jaw, followed by a swift left to his upper jaw dropping his opponent to his knees. "Don't you ever suggest Morgan deserved this," James growled. "He wasn't always a man of

UNDER THE OAK TREE

good morals, but he never deserved what had happened to him. As for the Lady Catherine, I suggest you leave the lady out of this." James had had enough of the atrocious stories circulating about his brother and ex-mistress. It had been hard enough being home at Rosengarten under the circumstances as it was. But before James had the chance to offer his hand to the young loudmouth aristocrat still sprawled on the ground before him, his friend Tom arrived on the scene.

"Is this silvertail giving you a bit of trouble James?" Tom didn't wait for James to answer him, he simply grabbed the young fellow by the leg and dragged him bellowing across the lawn towards the currently empty grave site, muttering for the silvertail to shut his trap. "Good God Tom, what are you doing with the lad?" hollered James, who stood dumbfounded and shocked. Tom was a larrikin at the best of times, but he understood how James was feeling about the loss of his big brother, and if his mate James was in any kind of trouble, Tom made it his business to be right by his side to back him up.

"This grave is still empty James. Just thought I'd chuck this fella in the hole for a bit, might even shovel some dirt on top of this silvertail…might teach him to mind his manners at this serious time." "For heaven's sake Tom, please…please do let him go," begged James, now running up behind both Tom and the young man. The silvertail's expensive morning suit was covered in a mix of mud and horse dung. "Alright James, if you insist he can get up. I reckon he must have learned his lesson for the day." As soon as the cocky young aristocrat had both feet planted firmly on the ground again, Tom suggested it would be in his best interest to get his silvertail Pommy arse out of there quick smart. With this the toff disappeared to the servant quarters, where he understood his suit would be promptly cleaned and pressed to help save face and any further embarrassment on the day.

Tom paused for a moment before asking his mate, "How yah going James? It's a tough time mate I know, but don't let those cocky young guns get yah down." James stood flexing his fingers, he must have hit the young fellow harder than he thought. "Thank you Tom, you're a good friend to have around in these sad times." James glanced down at his wrist watch. "Tom, we'll have to move along, the funeral starts in an hour and a half. Wear my suit again, you looked extremely smart in it the other evening." Tom couldn't hide the lop-sided grin that crossed his dial, hoping he hadn't pulled too many threads in James's flash mocker (suit). Fuelled by a rather large amount of whiskey on the night of the Hunt Ball, he had accepted a dare from a toffee-nosed fox hunter to swing from the crystal chandeliers that hung down the centre of the Rosengarten ballroom.

"Tom, I'd like to leave England and return to the Australian Outback, say within the week following the funeral. Are you ready to return to your homeland too?" James asked. "Mate, I'm ready to leave whenever you are…as mates we must stick together, but I must confess that I'll miss a certain beautiful English maiden who works in your family establishment when I go bush again." James again glanced at his watch. "The time is getting on, let's discuss it later and make our final plans tomorrow." James and Tom shook hands on organising their travel plans the following day and went their separate ways.

James made a point of arriving early to the ballroom, dressed in his grey morning suit and top hat. He looked extremely handsome as he escorted his Grand-mama slowly down the grand stairway to the arched front entrance where Lord Alexander and his mother Gabrielle had already assembled to greet family and friends, some of whom had travelled great distances to offer their condolences and wish Morgan a last goodbye.

As James glanced about the family, he noted his father seemed to be holding up quite well, possibly with a little help from the whiskey bottle thought James. Grand-mama also looked to be in control, although her skin tone was greyish, which was unusual, and she did show signs of extreme tiredness. Yet Grand-mama stood tall and supportive, her two large strands of pearls obviously giving her strength at this sad time. As James's eyes lingered on his mother's frail but dark silhouette against the light backdrop, he couldn't help but feel a deep sadness for her. Morgan was her first child, and ever since his death she had cried continually. My mother is really battling the demons, thought James. Hopefully after today dear mother will find her strength again. Then an excited gasp was heard to escape the crowded ballroom. Lady Catherine had arrived looking more angelic and beautiful than any bride could possibly have wished to. Only she was dressed in an exquisite haute couture black French-lace morning gown, her head covered by a fine veil edged with the tiniest delicate pearls which allowed just enough light to expose her beautiful porcelain features to the mourners.

Lord Alexander rushed to take Lady Catherine's gloved hands in his own. "Do come and join the family my dear." Gabrielle began to pat around her eyes as her tears again flowed freely. Lady Catherine opened her black beaded clutch and produced a fine embroidered handkerchief to do the same. James's heart had begun to pound frantically. Lady Catherine's closeness to James in the family stand was having a devastating effect on him, yet throughout the service for Morgan, James stood tall and displayed the same strength his Grand-mama did.

Once the service was over in the grand ballroom of Rosengarten, a small group of family and close friends moved on to attend the final stages of the grave side burial for Morgan. James was anxious and simply wanted to have the burial over and done with now, and yet he had loved his older brother in his own special way. As the youngest of the siblings James had played second fiddle to older brother Morgan, who could be controlling and quite obnoxious at times. As a child Morgan had a favourite mantra which he recited continually while he and James played together on the farm's swing set. "I'm the lord of the castle and you're the dirty rascal," he repeated until one day it became too much for James to suffer any longer and he punched Morgan in the face giving him a black eye.

Morgan's coffin was ceremoniously delivered to the grave side by an ornate buggy pulled by his favourite horse. James had made sure of that. Morgan was buried in the Wentworth estate's private cemetery in the shade of the old oak tree beside his Grandfather, Lord Wentworth II, and other family members who had passed on before them.

With the service over, an elaborately cloaked Father O'Brian stepped back from the grave side to allow family access to the site. Lord Alexander Wentworth stood quietly gazing into the distance before offering a generous handful of fragrant rose petals to the open grave. James noted it was the first time he had seen tears in his father's eyes. Mother Gabrielle, who had not been in a good place emotionally of late, sat in her wicker chair at the grave side, quietly weeping as she rocked herself back and forth while attended to by her worried lady-in-waiting. Poor mother, she is not in a good place, thought James, before glancing towards his Grand-mama Lady Elizabeth, who was still standing tall and straight as a steel rod. It was at family funerals, James noticed even as a child, his Grand-mama's strength would shine through brighter than any other. "Would you like to take a seat,

Grand-mama?" James offered in a gentle voice. "No thank you my dear," answered Lady Elizabeth as she unconsciously placed her hand on the long strand of rather large pearls that hung around her neck. They were pearls that her husband had given her as a gift many years ago. "The past weeks have been extremely traumatic," Lady Elizabeth continued before asking James to get his father to arrange for the family doctor to visit his mother this very evening. "Gabrielle is not well at all. I intend to return to my rooms as soon as possible where I too can rest dear." For a moment Lady Elizabeth stood facing her youngest grandson before reaching out and taking hold of both his strong and well suntanned hands in her own. She then leaned towards James and spoke in a gentle voice. "Thank you James for enquiring. You do worry too much about your old Grand-mama dear, but thank you, and always remember that your family love you dearly." Grand-mama then lowered her voice considerably and whispered, "You are no longer the second fiddle dear."

James looked up from his conversation with Lady Elizabeth to be greeted by Lady Catherine's offer of a black gloved hand. Even if blindfolded James knew he would have sensed Lady Catherine's closeness. The scent of her exotic perfume not only had a tantalising effect on his heart, it also aroused his feelings for her.

"Under these terrible circumstance James, I believe you will now remain in England?" James felt the question was really a command or, was it more for Grand-mama's benefit? Whatever, it was news to James. Grand-mama butted in with, "This is something Catherine, that we must now discuss...I believe we will have a family meeting to decide your future James." As tired as she was, Grand-mama was unable to hide that mischievous twinkle in her eyes. Even with one of England's most beautiful woman standing by his side, James's strength also stood by him as he offered to both Lady Elizabeth and Lady Catherine, "Tomorrow I will talk about the future with father... today I will leave it be." James had already made up his own mind, and tomorrow's meeting with Lord Alexander wasn't about to change it.

CHAPTER 25

Return to the Outback

James woke to a beautiful morning following Morgan's funeral. In fact he felt so good he bounced from his bed to stand and gaze out across the estate's farming paddocks, noting that all the paddocks were enclosed by neat white picket fences. Standing at the window, James twisted and turned his slightly stiff upper body, before flexing his muscles, all the while observing Rosengarten's fine pastures. The cattle and horses grazed contentedly together, and yes he thought, how the Australian Outback really was another world compared to our English countryside. After spotting the farm's horse team, James had a light-bulb moment and remembered there were still two unbroken colts in the team. Now that Morgan was deceased there was no one to handle them. James decided he would approach Tom this very morning to assist him break and handle the colts to saddle. They could do this before they returned to the Outback and Campbell's Run Station, where James hoped they would resume where they had left off.

After speaking with Tom, James decided he would ride his favourite chestnut colt to the local post office to send a telegram to Bandit, Campbell's Run overseer. He wanted to inform Bandit of their impending return while requesting if their positions in the station's stock camp were still available on their return to Australia. Now, with the prospect of breaking the farm's two colts into halter and saddle, and making plans to return to the Outback, James was quite excited. Tom agreed it was time to return to Campbell's Run, but sadly he wasn't showing the same enthusiasm as James.

Shortly, the two men began to work on the unbroken colts. Both were extremely fit and in peak physical condition. In some ways they both seemed years younger than they actually were as each worked on their horse, exchanging some banter and much laughter as they went about their day's work.

That afternoon Lord Alexander III dropped by the farm's stables. He had heard a whisper that his son and Australian friend were both breaking the colts to saddle for the farm. This pleased him extremely. Lord Alexander told himself he always knew his younger son had never dodged hard work, in fact James had always seemed that one step ahead of the rest. He had also heard via kitchen gossip that James, who was now in line to inherit Rosengarten Castle and the title of Lord Wentworth IV, was also planning on returning to Australia in the not too distant future.

James looked up from cleaning his horse's hooves. "How are you, father?" asked James ever so politely. "Yes Sir, how the bloody hell are you?" echoed Tom before Lord Alexander could answer. Lord Alexander answered with, "I'm extremely well, and thank you both for asking. As you know it's been a trying time, but I feel your mother and Grand-mama are doing as well as can be expected." Lord Alexander choked and coughed and then corrected himself before butting out his foul smelling cigar against a yard post. "James, the reason I've dropped by the stables is to ask you to meet your immediate family in my office at 7pm this evening. Is that possible?" James stopped cleaning his horse's hooves and stood up before answering, "Yes father, I'll be there at precisely seven this evening." Looking most uncomfortable on his aged mare Dolly, Lord Alexander turned his steed towards the lions entrance, touched her right flank with the shining spurs attached to his highly polished boots and trotted toward home.

"Crickey James, that's an aged mare your old man's riding?" Tom commented. "She looked as old as those hills over yonder."

"That mare is Dolly, Tom, and you're right she is old, but my father loves her, and for both their sakes, I hope she has a few more years left in her yet."

"I know the feeling to lose a good horse, James, no different to losing a good friend...you know the feeling," offered Tom who had returned his full attention to the job at hand while thinking of Aussie, the gelding that James had painstakingly broken in on Campbell's Run only to have lost him weeks later to the stupidity of Cranky Henry, the station's irrational horse breaker.

James felt refreshed and ready to meet his family at precisely 7pm that evening. In fact he wasn't worried at all about the family meeting as he suspected it was an effort on his father's behalf to try to sway him to take the reins at Rosengarten now that older brother Morgan was deceased.

The remaining members of the Wentworth family again sat together in Lord Alexander's ornate office. Lord Wentworth III had already served himself a generous whiskey on ice. The butler served mother Gabrielle and Grand-mama both gin and tonics in their favourite Royal Doulton crystal glasses, followed by a small whiskey and water in a crystal tumbler for James. Lord Alexander waited patiently for all to have a tipple in hand before he began to speak.

"James, you understand that now that we have lost our dear Morgan you will become Lord Wentworth IV of Rosengarten Castle?" James answered with a direct, "Yes Sir, I do." Lord Alexander took his time to draw heavily on his huge cigar, again filling the office with a haze of smoke, all the while gazing steadily at James. Lord Alexander Wentworth continued. "I know that Morgan had been groomed from birth to take over Rosengarten and the entire estate, which has many acres of fertile farmland, and I suppose we hadn't given much thought to ever losing him, but due to these tragic circumstances the Wentworth lineage has prematurely landed at your feet." Lord Wentworth took a good swig of whiskey and ice from his crystal tumbler, and proceeded to unceremoniously crunch the ice loudly in his mouth before continuing. "James, how do you feel about remaining here at Rosengarten and on my death becoming the next Lord Wentworth?" James looked directly at his father, then his Grand-mama and finally his mother, Gabrielle, before answering his father's question. He hadn't forgotten how the butler had always shined Morgan's shoes better than his own, or how at one stage his Grand-mama had to speak sternly to his own mother because due to her ill health she had neglected to note that his shirts and trousers were crumpled and not pressed to the same standard as his older brother's. James wasn't about to remind his family of having to play second fiddle by most of the family members and staff throughout his early childhood years – he was prepared to let sleeping dogs lie. But James was unable to see the urgency of him remaining at Rosengarten Castle right now.

"Father, mother, Grand-mama, I would like to address this very important matter with you all. I understand that this will all become my heritage someday, that I will become responsible on your death father for Rosengarten Castle, the estate, the farmland and the title of Lord Wentworth IV. I am prepared to take on that responsibility when my time comes around, but…" James let his eyes drift across each member of his family, "but it is not the right time now, father." James sat with a straight back, squared his shoulders and directed his next thoughts out loud and directly towards Lord Alexander. "Father, you are not dead yet!" After a moment of silence James asked, "Father, do you understand what I am saying to you, do you hear me?"

Lord Alexander rose from his straight-back chair and poured himself another stiff whiskey while still chomping heavily on his cigar. Mother Gabrielle let out a gasp, her eyes welled with tears of disappointment. "Oh James, you must stay here now. We need you, I need you James." Grand-mama looked towards James questioning him with her eyes before saying to her own son Lord Alexander, "We could not control the sad circumstances that now cloud our family, as I could not predict the demise of your own father's death. It is unfortunate Alexander, but we will work this matter out between James and ourselves, just give James some time." James spoke quietly to his family. He reasoned with them that while Morgan was alive, hadn't farm manager Harrison managed the farms well and produced a profit? Therefore he must remain doing so. "Father," said James, "you're not dead yet remember, and I'll only be in Australia for a year or so. Then I will return to Rosengarten and do what I must do to work the family farms." Eventually the family agreed to James fulfilling his Australian dream. They toasted their decision with another drink before taking the evening meal together. Only Grand-mama requested another family meeting the evening before James was due to leave for Australia. She looked at the other family members and said that there was some well overdue business to be discussed and attended to with James.

It was several days before James and Tom were due to return to the

Australian Outback, and James could think of nothing else, although the Lady Catherine had frequently crossed his mind. He couldn't help but wonder what had brought two people so close to matrimony, for James felt deep within his own heart that it certainly wasn't love.

Tom was looking forward to seeing his own mother again and his station mates, but he felt he had fallen in love with Mandy the kitchen maid at Rosengarten. Tom was slightly confused. "James…mate, have you ever been in love?" he asked. "How do I know if it's real love I feel for Mandy?" James was somewhat taken aback. "Goodness me Tom, I think you're asking the wrong person. Why ask me?"

"I don't know, just thought you might know. You may have had more experience than me. It's just that I seem to have a constant gnawing in my gut, you know, a sick feeling in my stomach ever since you spoke of us returning to Australia. I'll miss her yah know." James couldn't help but feel a slight sadness for his Australian friend. Tom stopped working on his colt and stood staring blankly across the far distant hills as if searching for some of the answers to his own questions. "Well Tom, if you're coming with me we fly out Monday morning," James said. "The plane seats are booked and paid for. The decision is all yours, my friend."

Tom finished work at the stables early. "I want to shower and clean up James. I'm having dinner with Mandy in the kitchen tonight. "See yah at first light to ride the colts out again tomorrow." "Good idea cobber," James answered as the young bronzed horse-breakers looked at each other for a fleeting moment, a mischievous twinkle in their eyes. A cheeky smile crossed Tom's face before he let forth a loud "whoopee" as he punched the crisp afternoon air with his right fist, simultaneously clapping his heels together as he jumped high into the grassy fields in an extravagant display of excitement.

James stopped working, and with a huge smile on his face stood and watched his Australian mate bounce his way across the horse paddock towards Rosengarten's back entrance and Tom's home for three more days. That was presuming Tom was still returning to the Australian Outback with James come Monday.

Alone now, James had decided to saddle his own chestnut colt and take a leisurely ride towards the distant hills. This was something he did quite often before he had left for Australian shores. The 'Rise' was a special place on the farm for James. It was a reasonably short ride from home on his favourite horse. A tranquil place where James could sit quietly and think things through while gazing out over the family's farming estate and the many farming properties far beyond.

James picked his way steadily through Rosengarten's horse paddocks, pushing to step up his steed's pace once in the open space of the meadows. The harsh sunshine of earlier in the day had begun to fade rapidly. The meadows were thickly carpeted in sturdy blue cornflowers supported by their soft silvery-grey foliage, while the glorious spring weather gave off a feeling of total serenity in the soft late afternoon light.

James took the long way around to the 'Rise', not for any other reason than it was his favourite place and he wished to savour the beauty of the countryside. Morgan and Lady Catherine kept coming to mind, dashing any peace he may have hoped to find. On the spur of the moment, James decided to tap his colt on the shoulder and gallop these thoughts from his mind forever. The chestnut colt answered immediately to James's touch, and in no time the rhythm of man and beast became one as they moved to their own tune across the meadows and beyond to where a three-plank bridge crossed a fast flowing river.

James hit the top of the river bank then the three-plank oak bridge. The horse's hooves and the jingle of spurs and metal bits sent a terrifying echo up and down the river – just as Lady Catherine hit the entrance from the opposite side of the bridge. The thundering sound of horses' hooves on the dry timber caused both animals to rear up high and become unbalanced on the narrow timber bridge. There was not enough room on the bridge for either animal to pass the other by, let alone turn around. Frightened and fearful, both horses clashed on the bridge as each jostled furiously to prevail before unceremoniously ditching their riders. A tangled mass of panicked horses and riders rolled and fought to stop their own falls towards the boggy ground and the icy cold foaming river below. Loud whinnying came from the horses, while Lady Catherine's terrifying screams could have been heard for many miles. After landing in the mud below, James's chestnut colt sprang to its feet unharmed. Slightly battered and winded from his fall, James frantically tore at the straps and leathers of his saddle as he fought to disentangle himself to get to Lady Catherine who lay silent and still in the quagmire surrounded by reeds.

"My dear Lady Catherine," whispered James as he knelt down in the mud beside the lady to reach for her pulse. Dear Lord, she cannot be dead, it's all too terrible thought a fumbling and shaking James. "Please God no, please don't let it be," begged a frantic James who was now blaming himself for the cause of the shocking accident. How could I have been so stupid, thought a panicked James. Stupid to believe I was entirely alone out here, though in the past I had never come across another living soul on the bridge. James bent down over Lady Catherine as he frantically searched for the pulse in her neck, whispering and calling her name softly in the hope she would wake from this terrible nightmare. "Lady Catherine, my beautiful lady, please do wake up," whispered James. By now tears had begun to well in James's eyes as he begged her not to leave him, while rambling and explaining that he loved her. As James began to gather an unconscious Lady Catherine into his strong arms, lifting her from the boggy ground where she had landed, he heard her cough and groan softly. He lay her higher atop the river bank, then used his blue scarf to gently wipe and stem a large amount of blood oozing from a wound on her forehead. James then glanced towards Lady Catherine's highly strung filly which had broken a leg. There was no doubt the filly would have to be put down. What a terrible shame thought James. Lady Catherine again groaned and began to choke, and as she did so the second time, he placed both his strong arms around her upper body to help raise her from the ground. James held Lady Catherine close, resting her body gently against his own, hoping it would help her breathe more freely. Fearful for his lady friend's survival, James worried that Lady Catherine may have punctured a lung, and with hardly any knowledge of a woman's undergarments, James wondered if Catherine was wearing a tight-fitting corset under her riding outfit. Could it restrict her breathing? "Good God no," James said out loud to himself. James's arms began to ache as he held Lady Catherine's cold body firmly against his own, hoping his own body warmth would penetrate her smooth skin and keep her warm. All the while James prayed silently she would shortly wake fully, but for now James felt the heavens would come crashing down on him for his own careless stupidity.

James realised there was nothing he could do while Lady Catherine lay unconscious in his arms. There was no way he could leave this beautiful lady alone – to wake from this terrible knock to her forehead, or to wander dazed about the steep river banks that shouldered the swift, icy cold water below – while he rode to get the medical attention she so badly needed.

"Catherine, Lady Catherine, heaven forbid what have I done? I love you and I care for you deeply. Please do wake up," begged an emotional James. Only a week earlier his family had buried his older brother in the family cemetery under the aged oak tree on Rosengarten. Now this day has ended with the Lady Catherine, who had been betrothed to Morgan, laying semi-conscious in his arms. James gazed down at Catherine's serene face, even in her semi-conscious state and covered in blood and mud, James found her extremely beautiful.

"Lady Catherine, please do open your eyes," James repeated as he ran his hardened fingers back and forward across Catherine's forehead, hoping the stimulation of his touch against her delicate flawless skin would help bring her back to the present. Catherine's eyes began to flicker and James noticed her enlarged dark pupils in her green eyes before she closed them once more, only to open them again, and this time they stayed open. For a moment they gazed searchingly into each other's eyes before Lady Catherine whispered, "James… James, what happened? I'm sore all over?" Lady Catherine lifted her hand to her painful forehead. "Ouch…it hurts so much," murmured Catherine noticing her hand was now covered in blood. James took hold of Catherine's hand in his own, gently lifted it to his lips and kissed it ever so softly. Realising what he had done, James tried to brush off the incident with a panicked, "Thank goodness you have woken. I must get help for you immediately."

James went on to explain how they both entered the oak bridge at the same time. He said he blamed himself as he had entered the bridge at quite some pace. Lady Catherine seemed incredibly calm over the accident. James suspected she may have received a slight concussion and he wanted to get help for her from Rosengarten or Hamilton Hill Estate as soon as possible.

"Lady Catherine…" James started. "Please call me Catherine James…you always did when we were younger," she said, her voice soft as it trailed away. Lady Catherine looked sleepily into James's eyes. She was sore and bruised all over but felt extremely comfortable lying in James's strong warm arms. James wanted to make Catherine feel as comfortable as possible and stripped the saddle blanket from her own saddle to lay under her. The surrounding ground was wet and boggy and the cold would only encourage other illnesses, thought James.

After checking that Catherine had no broken bones throughout her body, and that the bleeding on her forehead had slowed, James said: "Catherine, I need to ride to get help for you. I will arrange for a doctor to be at the house on your arrival…" But before James could finish Catherine whispered, "James…I don't want to be left here alone. I want to go with you. I cannot stay here and watch my mare suffer with her own injuries…please James…please understand?" James tried to reason with Lady Catherine as she clung tightly to his arm – if he rode alone to seek help for her, he could ride at a faster pace, and it could be dangerous as he would have to take some risks in the dark that he could not with Lady Catherine by his side. James had planned to return to Lady Catherine with the farm manager's Land Rover. He could then ferry her safely to Rosengarten for the medical attention she needed.

Damn, thought James as he gazed down at Catherine's porcelain features that were just visible in the evening dusk. Her beautiful face now carried a deep gash to her forehead surrounded by her unruly strawberry blonde tresses that were partly matted with blood. They lay together on the ground, protected from its dampness by Catherine's red woollen saddle blanket. James, always the gentleman, held Catherine close in his arms to share his body's warmth with her. As Catherine dozed on and off she clung tightly to James. For a fleeting moment James wished he had never taken heed of Grand-mama's letter and returned to England and Rosengarten. Their closeness had his emotions at an all-time high, while the pounding in his heart was unbearable. I can't help myself, I must stop myself feeling for this beautiful woman, James scolded himself, and told his mind to stop right there. This was no time to think of Lady Catherine and Morgan or the reason behind their betrothal. As Catherine opened her eyes, James explained he would have to help lift her onto the back of his colt. This was not something he really wished to attempt alone for fear of doing more damage to the already hurting Lady Catherine. It would be an extremely long and slow walk back to Rosengarten Castle in the dark. James also realised that Catherine would probably suffer more pain as he lifted her into the saddle. But Catherine was adamant that she would not be left alone or left behind in the wild with the feral pigs, or to watch the foxes torment her seriously injured mare while James went for help. She wanted to be close to James. She felt safe with him, she said.

James accepted Catherine's determination, even with her body suffering pain she knew what she wanted, and again she had got her way. After much difficulty and excruciating pain on her part, James managed to secure Catherine to his colt, while he walked ahead leading them all slowly towards Rosengarten Castle.

That evening James was missed at the family dining table. Tom was called by Lord Alexander and asked to come to the family dining room as soon as possible. Tom was questioned about James's plans for the evening, but he couldn't offer any further information than that they had parted at the Rosengarten stables that same afternoon. The situation was fairly tense in the dining room with the family still in shock and deep mourning over the unexpected loss of their first-born son. Now, late in the evening, younger son James was uncounted for.

"Look," offered a stammering Tom. He had picked up on the worrying vibes of the family and now he too worried for James's safety. But there was one thing that Tom knew for sure, and that was that James was an excellent horseman, because if he wasn't, there was no way Bandit would have offered James his job back in the stock camp on Campbell's Run. Bandit never suffered fools! Sadly, thought Tom, accidents do happen, even to the best of horsemen.

"How about I go to the stables and take a look around for James? I'll check to see if his favourite chestnut colt is still stabled." Grandmama piped up first with, "That's an excellent idea Tom, please do that straight away." Lord Alexander said he would speak to the farm manager Harrison to question him before beginning a paddock search for James. At that moment Muldoon arrived with a note on a silver tray. "A note from Lord Hamilton Sir." Muldoon stood close by waiting for further instruction from Lord Alexander once he'd had time to study the note. "Muldoon, please make a phone call to Lord Hamilton. Inform him that we have not seen Lady Catherine today…and that James is missing also. Please make it clear to Lord Hamilton that we are about to commence a paddock search for both persons." Muldoon acknowledged Lord Alexander's request and promptly left the family's dining room for Rosengarten's phone room where he would immediately relay the message to Lord Hamilton, Lady Catherine's ailing father. In no time,

Muldoon arrived back in the dining room and offered to pour a stiff gin and tonic for Grand-mama and Gabrielle. It was times like these when both ladies really appreciated the offer of a second drink in the evening. Lord Alexander had his tumbler of aged whiskey on ice and offered a toast "To a safe return of both James and Lady Catherine." "Yes…a safe return," echoed both Grand-mama and Gabrielle. "And hopefully very soon," whispered Grand-mama to herself.

Tom hurried towards the stables and found them in total darkness. "James…James," Tom called loudly, so loud in fact it spooked some of the horses. Tom searched around the stables to where earlier in the day James had stabled his chestnut colt. It was gone. Tom then searched the tack room for James's saddle. It too was gone. Now Tom told himself 'you're no detective Tom, but wouldn't you say that James has gone for a ride somewhere and alone?' As Tom churned through these thoughts in his mind, he also did an animal count throughout the stables. There was only one horse missing, and that was James's chest-nut colt. Tom hurriedly saddled his horse and walked over to the gate that faced the meadows and the 'Rise', the far distant 'Rise' that James had been banging on about while they worked the horses that day. Tom remembered James saying it was his favourite place on the farm, and Tom was ready to bet his own pocket watch that that was where James had gone for a late afternoon ride. "Yes…that's it," said Tom out loud, "it would have been the only chance for James to visit the 'Rise' before we leave for Australia."

With barely a sliver of the evening's moon making light, Tom could just make out deep fresh horse imprints in the gateway. He returned to the stables, gathered a lantern and lit it up, carrying it on the off-side of his horse to protect it from the gusty cold breeze. Tom then returned to the gateway, climbed down from his saddle with the lan-tern in hand so he could study the fresh horse tracks in the pale lamp light. He needed to find out which way they would lead him.

Tom was no gun tracker, but he had been born and bred on Campbell's Run cattle station in the Outback of the Northern Territory. He grew up playing with Aboriginal children, and their favourite pastime was tracking goannas and snakes through the bush surrounding their camp site. So Tom felt that tracking James's colt would be a hell of a lot easier than tracking a bloody goanna's tracks, plus the colt's tracks were fresh, the ground was soft and damp, and the colt's imprints were also very deep. Tom plodded along the offside of what he believed were James's colt's tracks. In some places they stood out quite clearly in the lantern's light. Tom filled his lungs with the crisp night air. He couldn't help but feel pleased with himself for tracking the colt in what seemed to him to be in good time. Just as Tom reached the cornflower-covered meadow he stopped. Again he thought he heard a long drawn out horse whinny somewhere in the distant darkness.

"Hello James! Is that you James?" hollered Tom. "Hey James, where the bloody hell are you mate?" There was no response. Tom got down off his mount to again check the hoof prints that had sunk deep into the damp ground. The tracks were still clear in the lantern light and easy to follow. By now Tom had no doubt that these horse tracks belonged to his friend's chestnut colt.

For no real reason Tom suddenly felt a sense of urgency, it was the gnawing in his gut again. What if James's colt was spooked and it threw him, and what if he was lying somewhere in the dark and hurt? Tom decided he would push his own sturdy mount along a little faster as he had to find James and quickly. This time there was no mistaking another horse's call in the distance, it whinnied again and again, to be answered by the return call of Tom's gelding and the excited stamping of the gelding's front hooves. The animals were stable mates and would be together again tonight.

"James? James, is that you mate?" hollered Tom. Way in the distance the faint call of "Hello...hello there...over here...near the bridge," rang out in the dark of night. Tom was unable to see James's position in the dark. With no moon present it made riding directly towards James more difficult. Tom decided to give his gelding his head, and seeing the two horses were stable mates, he figured his horse would lead him directly towards James and his colt.

"Good God James, what the bloody hell happened?" "Are you alright mate?" asked an anxious Tom, wondering what the heck James was doing out the back of beyond. "I'm alright, thanks Tom, but Lady Catherine is in need of immediate medical attention," answered James. Tom was instantly taken aback, shocked and surprised to find his friend had never mentioned a word of his intended rendezvous with the beautiful Lady Catherine. Bloody hell, Tom thought, what a sly old bugger you are James, having it off with the lady behind my back. Tom quickly offered a genuine, "Pardon me ma'am," while still wondering how far he had gone with his coarse language in the presence of the lady.

At a much steadier pace Tom and James walked together with their horses towards Rosengarten, stopping every now and then to check on Lady Catherine who was sitting astride James's colt. Occasionally, gasps of pain could be heard from Lady Catherine. James would stop leading his colt immediately to help rearrange Lady Catherine's position on his horse, or to lift her gently down from his saddle to allow her to rest her painful body against his own as he cradled Catherine tenderly in his strong arms. James wished he could suffer Catherine's pain for her, he felt guilty and responsible for the accident, and for what would be the loss of her favourite mare. Both James and Lady Catherine loved their horses, and without speaking of it, both understood the inevitable. A bullet for the mare was the only humane way to go.

"Would you like me to ride ahead James, to alert your family that a doctor is needed?" stammered Tom, who was becoming quite worried on hearing Lady Catherine's frequent cries of pain. "No Tom, I'm sure they will pick up our lantern light and come to our rescue," answered James, thinking that it would be safer if they all stayed together on this moonless night. "Thank you Tom," whispered Lady Catherine, "I'm sure it cannot be much further."

Within half an hour Tom spotted the Land Rover's headlights manoeuvring slowly across the paddock. "James, if you stay put with Lady Catherine I'll ride out in the open with the lantern." "Good idea Tom", James replied understanding that the sooner Lady Catherine was attended to the better. Her cries of pain were now frequent, while the thought of her mare with a broken leg sent shivers down James's spine. James made a mental note to have Harrison, the farm manager, attend to the pressing need of Catherine's mare immediately. The animal would need to be put down.

CHAPTER 26

Safe and Sound

Lady Catherine sat propped against her satin pillows in the lilac room and looked more beautiful than ever. The large egg-like bump on her forehead had turned blue, and the doctor had said her stitched wound would heal nicely with little scarring. He believed Lady Catherine's aches and pains would fade and she would be able to return to her father Lord Hamilton and her own home to complete her recovery after resting in bed at Rosengarten Castle.

"Doctor, would you please arrange for James to visit me? I must thank him for rescuing me before he leaves for the colony again." The family doctor agreed to pass Lady Catherine's message on to James, and also agreed that she was extremely lucky to have been rescued. "It would have been an uncomfortable night out there by the river, and taken some real strength to survive the freezing cold. I will see James on my way out, please rest now my lady."

James went to knock on the bedroom door that was marked by a lilac flower painted on a white porcelain disc, but he hesitated. A housemaid went to pass him and he asked her to announce his arrival to Lady Catherine. James certainly did not want her or the establishment's staff to spread rumours connecting him and the Lady Catherine at this time. He certainly was not sneaking into Lady Catherine's bedroom – he simply came to wish her a speedy recovery and to say goodbye as he and Tom were leaving England for Australia at first light.

As James walked towards Lady Catherine's elaborately carved oak bed, he could feel the dampness developing in the palms of his hands. "James, how lovely to see you…please do take a seat," offered Lady Catherine, looking far better than she did the previous evening. Catherine extended her badly bruised hand towards James. James took hold of her hand and held it gently in his own, he studied the unsightly dark bruises around her wrist, knowing that they were the result of having had her wrist entangled in the bridle rein. James then raised his steely blue eyes to meet Lady Catherine's and said, "I am so sorry that this terrible accident happened. I blame myself for it. Please do accept my most sincere apology." "James…please, you must not blame yourself. I was as much to blame, really. Father says I had taken a selfish risk riding out alone, and so far from home. He was not pleased at all." Lady Catherine then offered, "I had to promise father I would never ride alone again. We worried our families terribly. How tragic their thoughts must have been James, especially after…after Morgan's terrible death." Lady Catherine began to cry softly and lowered her eyes to hide her tears. James went to let her hand go but she held on tightly. They sat deep in their own thoughts, holding hands, thinking. Then, "James, I need to speak with you before you return to Australia." "Catherine, we need for you to heal and get well first. Let's focus on your health for now. It really is the most important, and you really have been through enough of late. Please rest my lady." For fleeting moments James wondered whether Lady Catherine was still with child as Morgan had suggested on the eve of their betrothal. Surely the accident would not have done her body any good at all. Tears had begun to well up in Lady Catherine's eyes. James leaned closer to her bed, picked up her fine cotton handkerchief, turned her beautiful face towards his own and gently wiped away her tears. A weak smile escaped Catherine's delicate rose-petal lips. "Thank you my kind knight…thank you…you are a very caring and gentle soul James. May I write to you when you return to Australia James? The distraction will help me through all this." "You may. Grand-mama has my address. When you are well. You must learn to live and let happiness return to your life again Catherine," James said, now feeling much more confident. After a quiet moment or two, Catherine asked

James, "Please return to Rosengarten soon. I will need a riding companion James as father has threatened never to allow me to ride alone again." Lady Catherine again gave her hand to James. He lifted it to his lips, his smoldering blue eyes boring deep into Catherine's, then bent his head and gently kissed her hand. He felt Lady Catherine tremble, and he knew that feeling of anxious excitement was mutual.

CHAPTER 27

Tragedy on the Murrakai

As the aircraft wheels ground to a halt on the black top of Darwin Airport, James couldn't have been happier to be back on Australian soil. Tom, on the other hand, wasn't quite so sure. He had spent many hours of the flying time between England and Australia absorbed deeply in his own thoughts. James realised Tom was hurting and missing Mandy terribly. But one thing was for sure, Tom must have overcome his fear of flying as he never once mentioned the whereabouts of that 'little black box' on their long flight home to Australia.

The aircraft door opened to a blast of hot humid air. Huge dark thunderheads sat out on the distant horizon as many white cockatoos screeched their arrival only to be quickly moved on by two menacing kite hawks. James recognised a corrugated iron house roof in the distance, and then both lads received the true blue Territorial (Northern Territory) welcome of a swarm of big black sticky flies as they descended to the tarmac. "Welcome back to the Outback James," offered Tom with a silly smirk on his face. "It's the Wet Season mate, and it won't be long before the humidity will have you sweating like a pig again."

Within an hour of their arrival in the lounge of Darwin Airport they heard their names called over the airport intercom. 'Tom and James of

Campbell's Run Station, please report to the information desk.' Now that they were back in Tom's home country Tom took the lead again, just as James had done with his Australian friend while in England. Tom collected the note from reception and read it out loud to James.

'To Tom and James, stockmen of Campbell's Run Station. Please have bags and swags out front of airport by 2pm. Have arranged ride to station for you both via Dalgety's Station delivery truck. Be ready for paddock muster am tomorrow.' Signed Bandit. Campbell's Run overseer.

Tom said the telegram was sent via the Royal Flying Doctor radio that very morning. "Just enough time for us to have a drink and a feed before the long trip home, James." "I'll be in that Tom, I'm looking forward to seeing Campbell's Run again," answered James. The mates sat at the bar together where they could keep an eye on the coming and goings of the aircraft. "What do you think of flying now, Tom, would you do it again? Would you fly to England again?" asked James. "Yep, reckon I would mate," Tom said as he extended his hand to shake his friend's. "Thank you for allowing me to go and visit your place. It was more like a bloody castle though…and to camp there as well. Honest James, it's been one hell of an education mate, you know, to see how the other half live and that." James shook Tom's hand firmly. "Tom, it was a pleasure having you there." James laughed to himself when he remembered Tom swinging from his Grand-mama's crystal chandeliers. Then James apologised for the unforeseen circumstances that cropped up during their stay at Rosengarten. "Let's go James, Dalgety's store truck has just pulled up out front."

James found the trip back to Campbell's Run to be a long and tiring one on top of their three-day flight from England. The Dalgety's eight-tonner International truck had a simple bench seat in the cab that was shared by the driver and both stockmen. The driver was a big man who took more than his fair share of the front seat and was hell bent on making it to the next pub before closing time. The trip was one of constant pee stops – and refuelling the driver's pannikin with a little water and much rum throughout the day, which James believed contributed to the not-so-funny jokes told by their driver. A hessian water bag hung from the bull bar at the front of the truck, where the breeze kept the water cool for the rum.

A strange way of entertaining oneself, thought James. It's each man to his own entertainment out here. Eventually, the speeding and the slowing of the trip got too much for Tom and he purchased a bottle of rum for himself. "I like the aroma of good rum James. He's on the turps, and I haven't cut loose since the Hunt Ball at your place. Let's join the driver for a drink." Tom scratched around and found a couple of tin pannikins that had been rolling around under the front seat of the truck, he offered James a nip of rum in one saying, "This would kill a brown dog," but James wasn't up for it. Once they had left the hard 'black top' of the road and turned west onto the two-wheel rutted Murrakai track, James quickly realised the ride home to Campbell's Run was going to be a lot longer and rougher than he had anticipated. Not only was the big truck driver becoming quite pissed, but Tom wasn't that far behind him in the paralytic stakes. The many stops along the boggy Murrakai track to relieve their bladders and replenish their tin mugs with rum and cool water – which had begun to take the men longer and longer to do – had started to bother James, and he wondered if they were ever going to make it to Campbell's Run.

On each refuelling stop the trio were greeted by a distant call from the deep-throated bullfrog while simultaneously bombarded by thousands of huge blood sucking and whining mosquitoes. James could hear Tom cursing and slapping at the mosquitoes as they swarmed and attacked every part of his body that was left exposed.

It had been a long three days of travelling to Australia and now James was becoming extremely tired. All he wanted to do was take a little catnap, but he worried the burly truck driver and Tom had become totally inebriated. James wondered if it was such a good idea for him to fall asleep on the back of the Inter truck after all. It was a pitch-black night and they were out the 'back of beyond'. James realised that if he was spun around twice he would be totally lost out here, and there was nothing more he could do to help get the truck to Campbell's Run tonight.

Sometime later Tom offered quietly to James, "I think our driver could be slightly pissed. You take a camp mate. I'll help keep a lookout for straying cattle, sometimes there's the odd buffalo and wild pig as well to watch for." James thought there was a good possibility of the 'pot calling the kettle black' here. They were travelling through wild buffalo and feral cattle country and at night the animals would search out the high dry ground for its warmth. On their next pit stop to relieve their bladders and refuel their tin mugs with rum, James took the opportunity to roll Tom's swag out in the small gap left among the many cartons of station stores and drums of fuel on the back of the truck's wooden tray. James realised it was risky to leave the two intoxicated men in charge of the truck but in reality he had no control over either of them. As soon as the truck got going along the rough rutted dirt track James was quickly rocked to sleep. The vehicle's movement on the uneven road surfaces and the mundane drone of the truck engine had James sleeping like a baby in no time. The warm night breeze created by the moving vehicle gave some relief from the menacing and irritating mosquitoes.

Sometime later in the night, James woke to find the truck had stopped. Loud fiery slurred words were being exchanged between the truck driver and Tom. From James's previous experience in the Top End, and witnessing Bunderberg OP rum drinkers in the local pub in Darwin, James knew the potent brew in the brown ribbed bottle had a devastating effect on the average man's sanity, even turning some people into outright monsters. As the words between the truck driver and Tom became even more threatening towards each other, James hurriedly threw off his swag cover and clambered down over the side of the truck's tray to the damp ground below. As James groped his way around the truck towards the headlights at the front, he tried to convince himself that all the big brown snakes were bedded down for the night. Just as James made it to the front of the truck he overheard the truck driver yell to Tom from somewhere in the distant darkness.

"I'll get my own fucking water from the river." Tom answered the driver back with, "You stupid old bastard, you know it's probably got salt in it, and its big croc country." James piped up to no one in particular, "What is wrong…do we have a problem?" Tom answered, "We sure do have a problem. He's fucking drunk." James noticed Tom was having a conversation with the water bag that was hanging from the bull bar at the front of the truck. "That silly old bastard hasn't even enough brains to give himself a headache right now," muttered Tom. James couldn't help himself and burst out laughing for in some way it was hilarious – the truck driver and his spotter were both primed on OP rum, and now one was accusing the other of being drunk. This time the kettle was certainly calling the pot black. James worried that their truck driver could possibly wander off in the dark and become lost, and then they would really be in an awful pickle, he thought. "Do we have a torch Tom?" asked James, who was becoming extremely worried and frustrated with the whole situation now.

He began to pull swags and bags from the front of the truck, dropping each of them on the ground in his search for a torch or hurricane lamp. The truck lights were dull and lifeless and shone towards a large dark river. James wondered what life was left in the truck battery without the engine running. It gave James the creeps not being able to see where their truck driver had disappeared to in the pitch black of the night, and he knew it was also possible that he could run into a grumpy old buffalo bull. James tried his best to remain calm. He convinced himself their driver had done this station run many times before, and he was a well-seasoned Outback truck driver, which he had told the lads he was earlier in the evening. The night was steamy and humid, but James still shuddered as he listened to the overpowering mating call of one bullfrog to another. For some reason the night now felt eerily cold. James hesitated for a moment believing he should walk steadily towards the river bank and sing out as loud as he possibly could to try to persuade their truck driver to return to his truck. This wasn't something he really wanted to do, but seeing he was the only sober one among them, it was his responsibility, James believed. Then just as James had pulled the driver's seat forward to search for a torch, he heard the most horrifying scream, the scream of a man in serious trouble, followed by the sound of splashing and thrashing, followed again by terrifying cries.

"Jesus bloody Christ James! I bet a bloody croc got him," yelled Tom from the water bag at the front of the truck. Tom raced towards the driver's side door and frantically shoved James from the driver's seat. "Hop out of there James." In the dark truck cabin Tom frantically fumbled with the key in the ignition, and after several failed attempts of switching and flicking the ignition, he got the truck's engine running. Tom hollered for James to jump into the passenger side of the cabin, he wanted to drive the truck closer to the river's edge, ignoring his bush knowledge that they could become stuck in the boggy black soil and never get out again. But Tom was determined to locate their truck driver by shining the headlights of the truck toward the dark river water.

"Good heavens Tom, are you sure a saltwater crocodile would be this far inland?" questioned James, who was still shaken from the blood-curdling cry heard only minutes earlier. James didn't want to believe their driver had been attacked by a crocodile. He shuddered at the thought as he strained his tired eyes towards the river, while secretly praying their truck driver wasn't in there. "Yep, it's about where the fresh water and salt water meet, about here, the big fellas come up the river to shed their barnacles." James could swear Tom had sobered up in a hell of a hurry as he calmly manoeuvred the loaded Dalgety's truck towards the slippery river bank somewhere out there in the dark.

"Can't go any further with this truck, we'll end up in the bloody river ourselves. This black soil country is sticky, bloody slippery and boggy," offered Tom to no one in particular. James went to throw open the passenger side door, and as he did Tom spotted the biggest croc he'd ever seen slide quietly down over the river bank into the water. The huge croc sunk into the depths of the river's darkness leaving barely a ripple behind in the water. The muddy bank of the river had blended perfectly with the crocodile's skin colour, putting the wind up James. Tom screamed at James, "Bloody hell James, shut the fucking door mate! Did yah see that big bastard?" James immediately did as he was told. Shocked, he sat back in the truck mumbling, "Oh God no Tom, it can't possibly be true." As the most horrifyingly gruesome thoughts began to cloud James's mind, his own body began to react in fear. Even the biting mosquitoes weren't felt as James sat staring into the blackness, shivering and shaking and wondering had that croc really overpowered their truck driver. Both men began to feel terribly alone, although they had each other for company. Frustrated, Tom slammed the steering wheel hard with both fists. He and James agreed to take turns squatting on the truck bonnet with the mosquitoes while calling loudly for their truck driver to answer them back. As shaken as the lads were they sat out the long night, hoping against hope that their wildest thoughts weren't about to come true. During the night Tom flicked the truck lights on and off, and pointed out to James the ruby red eyes of stalking crocs in the black river before them. "See those James? That's a big bastard. You don't go near the water's edge in places like this, particularly at night."

James who was feeling totally useless, and not knowing what he could do to help, asked Tom, "Is there anything at all we can do? I feel absolutely at wits' end." Then the slow drawn out and mournful cry of a distant curlew didn't help the lads much. Tom sat quietly for a moment listening, churning through his own thoughts before answering James. "You know James, I've never been in a situation involving a croc attack before…that's if it was a croc attack."

The truck driver had told Tom earlier in the evening that the river crossing would possibly be too dangerous to attempt with the truck tonight. Tom decided to turn off the truck motor and the lights, and suggested they try to get some sleep, though he realised it would be highly improbable as they worried about their burly truck driver. The lurking crocs and the irritating bomber-size mosquitoes would make sure the only sleep they got was brief.

The lads really didn't want to leave the area without their truck driver. It seemed an inhumane thing to do. James never gave up hope they could find the big man and help him back to safety.

After a rotten night alternating between the bonnet and bench seat in the truck, the pair waited patiently for the first sign of daybreak. They talked softly of the horrendous catastrophe they had both witnessed the previous evening, wishing it was a terrible nightmare. They remained in their truck, willing the light of day to come quickly which would allow them to begin their search along the river bank for the truck driver.

Tom said he was sorry he and the driver had argued over the water bag the previous evening. He believed if they hadn't, the driver might have been with them now. Both lads were still in deep shock that morning, and found it hard to believe any person could possibly disappear as quickly as he had.

Both lads eagerly awaited the first glimmer of sunshine to rise up and over the nearby mountain range and disperse the morning fog which had hugged the river. But as the sun rose and the fog disappeared it left behind dark shadows among the mangrove trees on the island in the middle of the river. Tom and James hesitantly opened the truck doors to begin their search for their lost driver.

"Be alert James, there's a big bugger around here somewhere," offered Tom. He then noticed the driver's distinctive rippled boot tracks in the mud on the river bank. The tracks led Tom in a roundabout way through the grey mud to the river's edge. He saw where the driver stopped and had a pee by a cluster of mangroves. Both lads stood warily back from the water's edge, where signs of one hell of a struggle was evident. Even the crab holes were full of blood. Their worst suspicions were now confirmed on finding their driver's boot still containing part of his leg that had been ripped to shreds. Shocked and traumatised by their find, James suggested if ever they needed a stiff rum it was right at this very moment.

After a quiet discussion between themselves, they agreed to wrap the driver's leg in Tom's swag cover and secure it on the back of the truck. As Tom did so James urged Tom, "Let's please hurry Tom, I'm sure we're being watched by a large silent intruder out there." Tom stood up from fastening a rope around the swag and before long pointed out a huge stalking croc to his friend. "He's probably got the shits on, bet he reckons we're robbing him of something." James was amazed that this prehistoric predator could move towards them silently and without leaving as much as a ripple in its wake. "Don't you worry James, this has really got the wind up me too. Let's take what we have of our driver and get the hell out of here. I'm pretty sure that there is absolutely no hope in bloody hell of us finding our driver alive now." James felt terrible as Tom finished securing their driver's leg on the back of the truck.

After some hesitation the lads agreed to cross the Murrakai River at the low-level crossing and forge ahead to Campbell's Run Station with just the small portion of their driver strapped in the back. There was no Flying Doctor radio in the old red International, and their closest point of contact with the authorities would be the Flying Doctor radio at Campbell's Run homestead. They decided to share the remaining rum between themselves before dispatching the empty bottles out of the truck window. "That's it," said Tom. "We needed it," answered James. "I really appreciated that...thanks." Campbell's Run was an alcohol-free cattle station, and Derrick Dunn the owner tried to keep it that way.

The slow trip on the potholed rutted road had given the two men plenty of time to dwell on the previous evening's tragedy. Even the changing colour of the rugged Mitchell Ranges wasn't enough to cajole James into any form of conversation. In a trance-like state, Tom brought the Dalgety's old Inter truck to a stop out the front of Campbell's Run homestead. They were welcomed by Derrick Dunn's bunch of overly excited blue and red heeler cattle dogs, followed by Sheila, Derrick's young wife, who seemed extremely pleased to have two of Campbell's Run youngest and best-looking stockmen back on the property.

"Welcome back Tom, James," offered Sheila while extending her hand to one man after the other. "When did you take over driving Dalgety's store truck, Tom?" Sheila asked bluntly.

"It's a long story Sheila. We need to speak with Derrick and Bandit, and we need to hurry, it's an emergency." James turned to check that their driver's leg was still secured on the back of the truck, and that it was well and truly out of the cattle dogs' way. The men followed as Sheila hurried towards the homestead verandah to be greeted by Derrick Dunn and his station overseer Bandit. Bandit had arrived at the homestead only minutes earlier to discuss with Derrick the whereabouts of his two stockmen as they had been expected to arrive back in the stock camp the previous evening.

"What's the big hurry lads? Derrick asked. "Have you both seen a ghost or something? You're obviously happy to be back on the station." Derrick then asked his wife to organise some tea for the lads. Bandit picked up immediately that something terrible had happened. He noticed both Tom and James looked drawn and ghostly, and Bandit knew it would take one hell of a fright to have young Tom go white, and the Englishman James, well, Bandit thought he was tougher than he looked. It would take a hard knock or two to upset him as well.

Stammering, Tom blurted out, "A big croc got our driver." "A what...where did this happen?" asked Derrick Dunn in rapid succession as if finding it all totally disbelieving. "Yes Sir, we're sure it's a crocodile," offered James before Tom continued. "Part of the driver's leg, his foot and boot...there...there...wrapped in my swag cover... on the back of the store truck." Tom had barely blurted out the news before racing off to heave his guts out behind a bush in Derrick Dunn's manicured garden. Bandit immediately stood up tall, he was the station overseer and it was his job to get the ball rolling on this matter. "Where did this happen? Was it the Murrakai?" questioned Bandit before racing off towards the radio room in the homestead. That river has a dark past thought Bandit. He had been in this country for most of his life and understood the Outback. Bandit then returned to the verandah asking a series of rapid questions, before again returning to the radio room. On his return once more to the verandah, Bandit informed everyone that the police were flying out to Campbell's Run

Station immediately, that they had organised a charter flight and search party from Katherine, and they requested the use of a station four-wheel-drive on their arrival. The senior sergeant asked that both Tom and James travel back to the Murrakai River crossing with the police. Bandit looked towards his young stockmen, took his hat off and scratched his head long and hard before saying, "I'm sorry fellas...it must have been one hell of a night for you both, but the cops will need all the information they can get." Tom was back from behind the bushes and was no longer heaving his heart out. "Are you alright young fella?" Tom nodded his head towards Bandit. "James, how about you...you've just had one hell of an Outback experience?" James stood up and shook his overseer's hand and said, "I have, but I'll be alright mate." Bandit nodded his head in agreement with James. He knew both the lads would be alright, it was the initial shock that had got to them. The young stockmen downed their much appreciated mugs of tea and stood up to leave the homestead verandah. But before they did, James stuttered, "Um...umm...what should we do with the truck driver's leg Sir?" No one wanted to suggest to put the driver's leg in the cool room, as this was where the station's main beef supply was hung and shelved to age. Bandit said the cops were making tracks at this very moment. "How about we leave it where it is for the time being? It's up and safe isn't it?" he asked. Both Tom and James nodded – they understood what their boss meant by that comment – then left the homestead together for the men's quarters to shower and clean up before the authorities arrived at the station. Both lads were dreading having to relive the previous night's horrendous experience all over again.

The bush telegraph travels fast in the Outback, and the Royal Flying Doctor radio was always good for a 'galah' session among friends on neighbouring Outback properties. But most importantly it brought people together in times of need. So, it wasn't long before neighbouring cattle station managers were offering their much appreciated assistance in the search for Dalgety's lost truck driver as well. Campbell's Run Flying Doctor radio ran hot for the next hour with offers of support from far and wide in the Outback. Bandit was kept busy coordinating the arrival of those with small fixed-wing aircraft who had offered to fly the long winding Murrakai River to help with the search. Others offered to meet at the Murrakai low-level crossing with a dinghy and outboard motor. Bandit believed there was a fair chance of finding Dalgety's driver in the next day or two thanks to all the help offered from the surrounding cattle stations, or he certainly hoped they would.

But the two men stepped up as would have been expected of them in the Outback. They helped the police and volunteers with the search, while every now and then Tom would excuse himself to heave his guts out. It was a terribly hot and muggy day, with the humidity level as high as only hell could possibly be, thought James. The suffocating heat didn't help at all, and it was understandable that many persons were tense and on edge as they pushed steadily along the muddy river bank, while others searched in vain among the tall itchy spear grass and thick prickly undergrowth close by. The mugginess only helped tempers flare at the slightest mishap. The little skipjacks, with their dark bulging eyes, seemed to be the only happy souls along the river bank that day. They skipped and slid about in the black slippery mud and shallow water without a care in the world.

As the day wore on people became jumpy and irritable as some realised that they had begun to crisscross each other's tracks in their search for the truck driver. It was that time of the year when, without much notice, a huge monsoonal build-up of clouds would burst and torrential rains would quickly flood the nearby plains and countryside. In no time at all the flooded rivers would become twice as dangerous, making any movement in the area near impossible. This meant all persons would have to push themselves even faster and harder if they were to find the missing truck driver's body at all.

The first day of the search ended without a body or any further evidence of the serious fight the driver would have attempted whilst battling for his life. Nets were dragged by several of the more experienced boat captains throughout the river and in the general area where the truck driver had disappeared. A ripple of excitement spread through the searchers when the second drag retrieved the driver's blue chipped pannikin from the bottom of the riverbed. This was followed by catfish and black brim caught in subsequent drags. Eventually, the day came to an end with the authorities arranging an early start for the following morning. The following day's plan was to search the island in the middle of the mighty Murrakai River.

Tom and James were told by the police to remain calm and keep the search up along the bank of the Murrakai. The coppers and several volunteers travelled in two separate dinghies powered by small outboards to the dark, muddy and mangrove-covered island in the middle of the murky river. Some hours later the powerful sound of two gun shots broke the eerie silence, startling thousands of sleeping flying foxes from their perches high in the mangrove trees. One powerful blast was followed immediately by another just as loud. And then there was a deep silence. After another hour of waiting in the searing heat and humidity James and Tom began to worry that the searchers on the island may have struck trouble themselves.

"Come on James, let's go back down the river...opposite the island," suggested Tom. But as the lads stood up from their seat on a log, the distant drone of an outboard motor could be heard. For some unknown reason James felt a sense of relief. Soon after the second dinghy came into view. "Look Tom, there's something white on the front of that dinghy," said James while wondering what it could be. Their curiosity was short-lived. As the boat came closer to the shore, both James and Tom could not mistake the shape of a large human torso in a white body bag.

"We've found what's left of him, and it's not a pretty sight," the local copper said to no one in particular as the dinghy beached itself on the river bank. "No, not a pretty sight at all," he repeated shaking his head from side to side. "It had to be a big bastard that got this poor fella. It planted him up in the mud amongst the mangroves for later." Tom immediately began to heave his guts out again. He took off towards a huge paperbark tree further along the river bank where he found some privacy to let go of everything. He was relieved that the coppers had found the truck driver, and Tom understood why that big bastard of a croc had planted his catch – to let the body deteriorate some before he got stuck into it. Then loudly and shamelessly he heaved his guts out one more time. James wished he could be of some use to his friend as he helplessly watched Tom race periodically behind the scrub. There was nothing anyone could do to help him at the present time. Tom and James would eventually realise that only time would help Tom stop blaming himself for the crocodile attack on their truck driver.

It took some months before a feeling of normality returned to everyday life for the two young stockmen on Campbell's Run Station. But the heat and hard work in the stock camp soon brought the lads back to some form of reality. It certainly helped Tom and James to pull their weight alongside their friends – the Aboriginal stockmen and Cranky Henry the horse breaker – during a large tuberculosis eradication program that had started on the station. The Agriculture Department made sure every property in the district fulfilled its obligation to the state. While some property managers and owners complained loudly against the TB eradication program, it was necessary for the country to be TB free, especially if the Top End, including both the west and east of Australia, wished to retain its overseas beef markets. This was extremely hard yakka (work) but it did bring the laughter and back-slapping mateship back to the station's young stockmen. It also brought with it a pile of mixed emotions and some surprises, the like of which had never been seen before on Cambell's Run.

CHAPTER 28

Moving Forward

One night before the lads had left cold old England, they sat huddled close to a blazing fire pit at the stables. Tom came up with an idea. "James, when we return to the Outback, how about we both give Bandit a full mustering season back on Campbell's Run Station first? Then I would have repaid my loan to the old fella, you know, Uncle Derrick. With no obligations to anyone, we can roll our swags and find work wherever we please, you know, just as we had planned on doing before this trip to England came up, footloose and fancy-free. How about it James?" James agreed. He too thought it would be a fair deal, plus James remembered that Bandit had been very gracious in offering him his stockman's job back on his return to the Outback.

"Tom," James pondered for a moment, while thinking over what his Grand-mama had recently told him before he left England, "do you remember that night my Grand-mama called me to her private sitting room?" "Well...yes I do remember," answered Tom, wondering what could possibly have come up now to put a spanner in their well-laid future plans. "It was not simply for her to say goodbye, it was much more important than that," James continued. "Grand-mama informed me that I had inherited Lonesome Downs Station in the West Kimberley. It had belonged to my Grandfather, Lord

Wentworth II, and has never been part of Rosengarten's estate as I had always believed it to be." "You bloody beauty!" Tom exclaimed. "James, you've got your own cattle station now. Wish my own grandfather had thought as much of me when he died."

"Just letting you know Tom, that when we are ready to move on we do have somewhere to go. I would like to be there in twelve months' time if at all possible. Grand-mama would like me to report back to her on the property." Excited, Tom jumped up from his hay bale seat and gave his mate a big hug. "Congratulations James, you're now a cattle station owner. You've jumped to the big time mate, and you can count on me to always give you a hand."

It was six months into the agreement on the lads' planned future move, when back at the men's quarters at the station on a break between musters, James received a telegram via the Flying Doctor radio. It was from Lady Catherine of Hamilton Hill Estate, England. It read:

Dear James, I have liaised with your management whilst you have been away tending muster. I had asked for their permission to visit you on the cattle station. The owner, Mr Derrick Dunn, and his gracious wife Sheila have invited me to stay with them at the homestead. I have accepted. On my arrival in Australia a charter flight has been arranged to take me from Darwin Airport to the homestead. Under the circumstances I'm sure you will agree this break is much needed from cold England. It will help lift my spirits. Looking forward to visiting you and the Dunn family on the 13th of June.
Yours sincerely,
Lady Catherine of Hamilton Hill Estate

Dear me, thought James, is it too late to contact Lady Catherine via return telegram and inform her of my next move to Lonesome Downs Station? Grandfather had spoken of the property being extremely isolated, a great distance from any form of civilisation, and not a place he could imagine Lady Catherine would ever consider visiting – far too isolated. James couldn't help but feel extremely uneasy about the contents of the telegram. 'I mean, why visit the Outback of Australia now,' James said to himself. He believed it was the last place in the world Lady Catherine should visit at this time. It was definitely the last place her extremely wealthy but ailing father, Lord Hamilton, would want his only child to search out a husband-to-be.

After Tom and James had left England for Australia, and Lady Catherine had fully regained her health after the terrible riding accident, her father, the bed-ridden and seriously failing Lord Hamilton, immediately summoned the estate's Queen's Counsel lawyers and his only child to his bedside for a meeting of the utmost importance. It was here by Lord Hamilton's bedside that Lady Catherine was scrutinised for her resolve to carry out her father's most important wishes before his own time on earth came to an end. The frail Lord Hamilton made it quite clear that his only surviving child must almost immediately find "A suitable husband of good conduct and heritage who I expect will cherish and love you, my spirited daughter. There must also be three heirs from this one union, one for the job and two spares. I also believe this person will be an excellent land and property manager, as upon my death I wish for the two of you to take over the management of Hamilton Hill Estate and its counties." Lord Hamilton also reminded Lady Catherine that if she failed in her endeavour to find a suitable husband soon, or brought terrible shame and scandal upon the family before his death, that her older cousin Patterson would inherit part of the estate to act as her farm manager on her father's death. When the meeting of lawyers, bankers, family doctor and Lord Hamilton's only surviving heir came to an end that day, Catherine left her ailing father's bedside feeling extremely deflated.

Gathering her taffeta petticoats, her head bowed slightly so as to not expose any emotion, Lady Catherine hurriedly rushed past the staff room on her way to her own suite of rooms in Hamilton Hill Castle. Once inside the warmth and security of her own space, Catherine allowed herself to collapse on the soft down of her large bed where she felt free to cry herself to sleep. That night turned out to be a terrible long night for Catherine, for the turmoil in her mind wouldn't allow her sleep. When the early morning light peeped through her bedroom curtains, how Lady Catherine wished she had been able to communicate better with her father. Since losing her older brother Oliver to a most terrible drowning accident on the estate, then to have this tragedy followed closely by the death of her beloved mother, was, at times, more than she could bear. There were times when Lady Catherine would allow her charade of powerful strength and bubbly happiness to slip. It was in these moments of deep thought that she would be left feeling lost and terribly alone in the world.

Her father, a powerful banker and the extremely wealthy Lord Hamilton of Hamilton Hill Castle, had groomed Lady Catherine extensively for the position that awaited her upon his own death. Lady Catherine understood the task ahead of her. She wondered if her own father, or dear friend James Wentworth, would ever have believed her betrothal to James's older brother Morgan was totally loveless from her side. It was to be an arranged marriage to satisfy the powers that be. 'How little my father understands me. I could never ever have loved Morgan, not in a hundred years!' she told herself miserably.

James scratched around in the cupboards and draws of the station's corrugated iron men's quarters until he found a blunt lead pencil and an old school book left behind from persons long gone. Settling himself into an old canvas deck chair on the side verandah, James agonised over the wording of a telegram to his friend Lady Catherine back home in England. James was more than convinced the Outback of Australia was not the right place for a lady of Catherine's upbringing to consider a leisurely holiday. He worried that the terrible heat, suffocating red dust storms and at times an abundance of irritating flies and mosquitoes, which were ready to annoy the hell out of you at the first opportunity, would eventually wear her down. Then James remembered the large venomous king brown snakes he'd occasionally come across while mustering cattle. Dear, dear me, pondered a worried James to himself while nervously scratching his head with the pencil. This could all end up a total disaster for Lady Catherine and everyone else. By now James had experienced most of these elements himself, and with this knowledge alone James was sure the Lady Catherine would not happily endure her holiday here on Campbell's Run Station for long.

"James mate, where the bloody hell are you?" Tom bellowed as he ran a piece of wood along the corrugated iron wall of the men's quarters, creating one hell of a racket – enough of a racket that it even stirred up the placid temperament of the boss's blue heeler cattle dog. "Hey James are you in?" called Tom even louder. News travels fast in the Outback – there's not much that can be kept totally private for long, and James wasn't to know that his mate Tom had already heard the gossip that Lady Catherine planned to visit James and grace Campbell's Run Station with her presence in the very near future.

"Well James, I've heard the latest, why didn't you say you were expecting a visit from the lady herself?" Tom asked his astonished friend. "I've only just received the telegram Tom, how do you have knowledge of this matter?" James shot back.

"As far as I know James, your telegram came in several days ago while we were still out in the stock camp. Of course it came via the Royal Flying Doctor radio…Sheila told Bandit, and Bandit told me. He figured I would have known or that you would have told me…he asked me had I met the blue blood, seeing as I visited your place in England."

"There're no secrets around here James, Sheila will make sure the whole damn Outback knows that she has a real lady from England staying with her and old Derrick on Campbell's Run, I'd even bet my hat on that." Tom pulled up another canvas deck chair beside James and made himself comfortable. James had gone quiet with his own thoughts.

"James, I haven't told anyone that you have inherited Lonesome Downs on the west coast, and I've just told them that everything was big and flash over in your family home in England, you know all those rooms. I nearly got bloody lost mate, and those chandeliers, I'd never seen anything quite like it, really James." Tom's mind drifted back to the mischief he'd caused that night, and he sat silently with a stupid look on his face.

"Don't worry Tom, I guess everything comes out sooner or later. There's nothing to hide, it's just that I was going to try to dissuade Lady Catherine from visiting me here. I felt under the circumstances it would all be too much for her to handle right at this time." James went silent again before adding, "I suppose if the word is out and about Tom, she may as well come on out to Australia. I just hope for the very best for her ladyship and that she survives her visit in the rough."

"One thing's for sure James, Sheila will be floating on cloud nine over this, but I tell you I wouldn't trust her with any news – even about my sick dog, that's if I had one," offered a now reflective Tom. While the pair sat and reminisced over the last cattle muster they had completed together along the claypan flats east of the Wombrella Creek, Tom threw another log on the wood stove and James half-filled the large black kettle. They'd have a pannikin of tea each for a nightcap before Tom retired to his own quarters for the night.

Just as the two lads began to relax in the canvas deck chairs, with their pannikins of black tea on the cement floor by their feet, Tom went quiet and put his index finger up to silence James. The boss's blue heeler barked angrily and Tom was sure there was a stranger nearby. It was the only time the boss's dog got truly worked-up and agitated, and if this was the case, the blue dog would break its chain and attack strangers or animals not known to it. Suddenly, Tom rose from his seat as a gentle tap came on the back door of the men's quarters. He glanced towards James and asked, "Should I see who it is?" "Please do," James replied immediately. Tom opened the door to expose an extremely attractive part-Aboriginal woman cradling a much fairer skinned baby in her arms.

"Can I come in please Tom?" asked the woman standing in the doorway. "I don't trust the boss's blue heeler dog," she said rather quietly. James, ever the gentleman, promptly rose to his feet in the dimly lit room to greet their new visitor and child. The girl, surprised to see another person there with Tom, quickly dropped her big doleful eyes towards the rough cement floor, hugged her tiny fair child even closer to her own body and stared blankly at the floor of the men's quarters. James glanced towards Tom waiting for an introduction to the woman and child, but instead was surprised to see his friend absolutely dumbstruck for the first time ever, and James couldn't help but notice Tom's colour drain as his dark suntanned skin turned a ghostly white.

The kerosene lamp flickered in the light breeze entering through the still partly opened door. What little lamp light there was attracted several large bush moths to its glass shield. One could have heard a pin drop on the cement floor, thought James, as he looked first at his friend again for an introduction, and then towards the attractive woman with the beautiful big dark-eyed baby held protectively in her arms. James felt he needed to give both persons some time alone as there seemed a terrible awkwardness about the pair. James turned towards the kitchen stove, thinking he'd take his time and put another log on the kitchen fire – he was sure they could all do with a cup of hot tea. Tom suddenly put a hand out to stop James. It seemed James's sudden movement had awoken Tom from his deep far and away thoughts.

Stuttering, Tom said to James, "I'm terribly sorry James…terribly sorry for being so rude…Penny, this is my friend from England,

James; James this is Penny. Penny and I…we did our correspondence schooling here together in the old school house on the station and mustered Campbell's Run together as kids and as teenagers, until old Derrick got a bee in his bonnet for some reason and sent her away to a religious boarding college in Darwin." Tom shrugged his shoulders, he seemed to be in deep thought. "Yep, that's what he did James. Then several years later when I went into the Rural Stock Agency in town to collect fencing gear for the station I ran into Penny. She worked in the accounts department of the agency. We met up again in Katherine before I met you in Darwin, James." Tom's anxious stutter soon began to fade as Penny moved her baby to the other arm and tightened a little cotton blanket about the child. Tom looked towards James. "You must excuse me James, Penny and I need to go outside and talk in private. It's…it's been not quite a year since we last saw each other."

James had showered and settled into his own camp stretcher for the night when the boss's blue heeler cattle dog started to stir again before falling silent. Someone was at the back door of the men's quarters for the second time tonight, thought James wearily, only this time the banging was much more forceful.

On opening the door, James was greeted by Tom and Penny. Tom's pale complexion was replaced by a much more vibrant glow as he pushed past James into the warmth of the room to a table placed conveniently by the stove in the kitchen. It was here Tom confidently unwrapped the fair-skinned child from its protective cotton blanket. Holding the child high for James to see, Tom gushed, "See…see this little fella James…he's mine, his name is Tommy." James had never seen his friend so excited and he was truly happy for both Penny and Tom. "Yep, this little fella is both Penny's and mine. We'll look after him together." Penny hurriedly bundled the little boy in his cotton wrap and walked towards the back door. Tom, still with his mile-wide smile, was right by Penny's side. James felt happy for Tom, and stood silently back and watched as the overjoyed couple walked out of the men's quarters to disappear into the moonlit night and beyond.

The following week Bandit organised his best stockmen, which included Tom, James, Mullicka and Cranky Henry plus several younger boys to help clean up the cattle from their recent muster along the Wombrella Creek Flats. Bandit, being Campbell's Run overseer handled the main draft himself, meaning he'd draft out the meat-workers (cattle to be sold), the breeding stock and good bulls, followed by the young mickys (young bulls) to be castrated and young good looking heifers for spares. Tom was in charge of the ear-marking pliers, while James handled the station's branding iron, performing his task with ease. Mullicka and Cranky Henry were in charge of keeping the long cattle races packed full with stock. Bandit's orders to his younger stockmen were to "Keep pushing the mob from the holding pens into the receiving pens, staying out of the bloody way of any agitated or hormonal cows and bad-tempered scrubber bulls."

It was the time of the year when the skies were a bright blue, the days sunny and hot, and the nights absolutely beautiful. It was the only time during the mustering season – after the 'biggest muster' had returned good weaner numbers – that the owner Derrick Dunn would shout his stockmen several cartons of beer and two bottles of OP rum to celebrate a good clean muster. With the alcohol came conditions, meaning the stockmen would have to take their swags and friends down to the banks of the Bellina River. Old Derrick wasn't one to tolerate loud-mouth drunks making fools of themselves in the early hours of the morning, especially around his homestead and on his cattle station. Young Tom and Cranky Henry had felt the wrath of Derrick's temper over this very matter once before, so all the stockmen were more than pleased to abide by the rules and regulations set out by Derrick.

After a tough week cleaning out the cattle yard the lads were ready to party on the banks of the Bellina River. With the yard work completed, Bandit sung out to the men to gather their swags and a kerosene lamp from the quarters, while he visited the cookhouse to collect a round of rump steak, and a dozen onions and bread rolls which he had organised earlier in the day from the station's cook. Bandit had also organised for the younger stockmen to go on ahead and collect a quantity of good firewood that would see the evening out. He reminded the lads that the fire would first be needed for light, then after a few cool beers and rums, the unavoidable hunger pains would set in. "Good coals help cook good steaks," he told them.

The stockmen settled in on the banks of the Bellina River, some used their swags as backrests, while others who were lucky enough to entertain female company for the evening dragged their swags furthest from the fire and into the night's shadows. Earlier in the evening old Derrick Dunn and his much younger wife Sheila graced the hired hands and the stockmen with a visit. One 'sundowner' with his over-seer, Bandit, and the lads, was the way to keep the stockmen on side, Derrick believed. But it wasn't long before Derrick's attractive young wife found a valid excuse to move away from her husband's side and closer to Englishman James. "Good evening James," she offered in a voice just loud enough for her much older husband to believe she was simply being polite enough to make general conversation with a sta-tion hand. After all Sheila was the owner's wife, and believed she held a position of importance over the hired hands, whilst conveniently forgetting she was once the cook's offsider on Campbell's Run.

"James, how do you feel about this forthcoming visit from your lady friend from England, are you excited?" asked Sheila in rapid suc-cession as she sat down by the campfire to share James's swag roll seat with him. Her oriental perfume was far too intoxicating, and you're too close for comfort, thought James. Sheila let her jeans covered knee fall to touch James, she turned her body towards him exposing her naked breasts pushed hard up against the delicate see-through cotton of her half unbuttoned shirt. With her back towards her hus-band, Sheila brazenly ran her index finger gently along James's strong suntanned wrist trying to get him to acknowledge her want for him. James's instant reaction was to move as far away as possible from this woman. She was the Boss's wife and as Tom had once warned James, 'Sheila was trouble...big trouble, and many a good man had got the boot from the station because of her flirtatious ways.' James stood up, leaving Sheila seated on his swag roll. He threw another log on the fire, thinking the men hadn't grilled their steaks yet, and he was getting hunger pains. With his back to the campfire, James gathered himself and turned to face the Boss's wife, who he now realised was far bolder than he ever wanted to believe. Previously, James had brushed off Sheila's odd touch as being accidental, her flirtatiousness as being young and friendly. He reminded himself to be careful.

"Lady Catherine is a family friend. I was a friend of her now deceased brother Oliver. We had all more or less grown up together in England," James offered. "Her wanting to visit the Australian Outback was as much of a surprise to me as it possibly is to both yourself and the Boss," James continued as he glanced towards Derrick hoping to include him in this conversation with Sheila. Sheila stood up from the seat which she had shared with James, dusted the rear of her jeans off, leaned closer to James and said in a voice loud enough for her husband to hear, "Don't get me wrong James, Derrick and I would love to have your Lady Catherine visit us. I hope the visit turns out to be a wonderful Outback experience for her."

Sheila's older husband naturally overheard her conversation with James. "Your Lady Catherine is a very welcome guest here on Campbell's Run James. Sheila and I will certainly do our very best to see her ladyship has an enjoyable time while with us." Derrick then turned to continue his own conversation with Bandit. As Sheila went to rejoin her husband she left James with a whispered parting shot: "I just hope she's not too toffee-nosed, James."

"James, over here mate," yelled Tom as he moved out from the shadows. Then in a whisper, "Penny's there with our boy. She wants to remain in the shadows, you know, in the background for now." Tom then offered James another beer, as he turned to pull the bucket from the river where the beer had been placed to keep it cool. Tom again offered James some advice. "James, I know I keep repeating myself but watch that woman mate. She's out on the prowl tonight." He then suggested they shift the coals around in the fireplace and begin to throw the rump steak and onions on the hot plate to get the evening's meal under way. "Chuck on a few extra steaks James. Penny has a couple of girlfriends down from Katherine to keep her company for the weekend." James added the steaks, thinking he hadn't even acknowledged Penny and baby Tommy this evening, and reminded himself he must remember later to salvage his own manners and meet Tom and Penny's other friends as well.

CHAPTER 29

The Arrival of
Lady Catherine

The thirteenth of June arrived on Campbell's Run Station bringing with it the 'dry season' and the Top End's most pleasant weather. Gone was the horrendously high humidity that drained everyone of all energy. James couldn't help but notice that the station was a hive of activity this morning. One of the younger jackaroos was flat-out pushing a lawn mower around the homestead lawns, while another was raking the fallen autumn leaves into huge piles and burning them. Even Sheila was going mad on this particular morning, splashing water against the homestead's glass windows and then chasing the boss's blue heeler cattle dog off the verandah with the hose. There seemed to be action in all directions thought James. Watching all this activity spurred James into giving the men's quarters where he camped a thorough clean and scrub. Tom dropped by to borrow James's broom. "What's this James, getting ready for the lady's arrival?"

"Well, not really Tom. Just thought I'd follow suit."

"Only joking James. Can I borrow your broom and cobweb contraption?" asked Tom, while helping himself to the broom cabinet anyway. "The spiders are running riot down in the stockmen's quarters." As Tom was leaving to continue his own big clean-up, he popped his head back in the doorway and said, "James, hadn't seen you since the BBQ down on the Bellina, did it turn out to be a good night mate?" James stopped, wiped the sweat from his brow and answered, "It was most enjoyable, and lovely to meet Penny's friends as well." Tom winked and left his English mate to get on with it.

Within the hour the sound of the chartered light aircraft from Darwin could be clearly heard overhead as it circled the homestead to attract management's attention so it could be met at the station's airstrip. This was common practice in the Outback, as some airstrips could be many miles from the homesteads, depending on the property's terrain. James immediately stopped his cleaning spree to check out the circling aircraft and noticed he wasn't the only person doing so. Sheila was walking towards the station's Land Rover, followed closely by her husband and station owner Derrick Dunn. With the help of his walking stick, Derrick hobbled across the neat homestead lawn. He looked up and spotted James standing outside the men's quarters. Surprisingly, Derrick beckoned for James to join him and Sheila in the vehicle.

As the aircraft's wheels touched down on the gravelly red earth of Campbell's Run Station, the sound of wheels churning on the gravel brought back vivid memories for James. For this sound reminded James Wentworth of the constant coming and going of guests in their horse-drawn buggies and Bentleys during the hunt season on his family's estate in England. James's subconscious mind wondered whether this would be the beginning of something new and interesting here as well.

James stood slightly to the side of Derrick and his wife, with his concentrated gaze on the opened door of the aircraft. Then, there standing in the opened doorway, her hand reaching out for the handrail of the aircraft steps, stood Catherine. Clad in khaki trousers and crisp white linen shirt tucked into her trousers, her wild and unruly strawberry blonde locks blowing about in the Territory's warm breeze, James thought she was one of the most beautiful sights he had seen for quite some time in the Outback. For a split second their eyes locked on each other and Lady Catherine called out to James, forgetting for a moment that her invitation to visit Campbell's Run had come from the owners, Mr and Mrs Derrick Dunn. "James," called a trembling Lady Catherine, "I never dreamed that Australia was so far away from England, but I'm here now, and so glad to be here as the guest of the kind and generous Mr and Mrs Dunn." Sheila and Derrick stepped forward to be introduced officially by James. "We do hope it won't be too hot for you," offered Sheila sounding most sincere.

"You look as if you can handle the Territory, Catherine...hope you don't mind if we simply call you Catherine while you stay with us?" Derrick asked. "We always drop any 'handle' a person might carry in the Outback...sorry, but they don't really mean very much to us... too much of a mouthful. Hope you understand." Lady Catherine let forth a burst of laughter and said, "I would much prefer you call me Catherine. I hope James will do the same while I'm here." James answered with a twinkle in his eye, "I will try to remember to do so Catherine, and thank you."

Back at the station homestead, Sheila fussed about settling Catherine into her room. Derrick had invited James to have afternoon tea on the back verandah with them all. It was not common practice to have the stockmen sitting around on the Boss's verandah, but this was a special occasion to welcome Lady Catherine to the Outback of the Northern Territory. Under Derrick's instruction, the house help had strategically placed comfortable deck chairs to allow each person to absorb the late afternoon beauty of the distant and extremely rugged Mitchell Ranges. "Good job...a good job," boomed Derrick to the house girls, "we must let Miss Catherine see just how beautiful our country really is." The house help got the giggles, they were shy Aboriginal girls and Derrick Dunn was sure the girls' sudden burst of laughter was as much for the good looking James as it was for his booming compliment to them. During the long drawn out afternoon tea, Sheila outlined some of the planned entertainment for the week of Lady Catherine's visit to their station.

Sheila herself had first arrived on Campbell's Run cattle station as Overseer Bandit's girlfriend. She soon became the cook's offsider in the cookhouse, a communal kitchen some thirty metres from the main homestead. Then Sheila realised rather quickly her prospects could be even brighter if she married the older and very much single cattle station owner Derrick Dunn. Within three months Sheila had ditched her partner of two years and married her Boss. This was seen as progress in Sheila's eyes, for now she felt equal to her visitor, the Lady Catherine of Hamilton Hill. Sheila, as the lady of Campbell's Run Station, had loads of entertainment lined up for Catherine's approval. Sheila had apparently forgotten that Catherine's trip was to spend quality time with her friend James.

There was a planned morning tea when all surrounding cattle station managers and their wives were expected to attend, a luncheon incorporating their very own roast beef and locally caught yabbies, plus a BBQ of grilled barramundi. The list went on, leaving James astounded as to how much effort Sheila had actually put into planning all this entertainment for Lady Catherine's visit. James had found the stockmen's meals extremely basic but good, and once Tom, always the larrikin, had even hinted that James was eating their neighbour's prized steer!

There was even a day planned to investigate the beautiful Mitchell Ranges and its deep and well-hidden gorges, where the crevasses overflowed with ferns and the water holes brimmed with crystal clear spring water. Lady Catherine sat refolding her table napkin while quietly taking this all in. She would make an attempt to be involved with the entertainment and not show any ungratefulness, though she had really intended to spend as much time as possible with her dear friend James Wentworth, and certainly would have much preferred to seek out her own entertainment if the need arose. In her soft English accent Catherine said, "Please, you must not put yourself out for me at all Sheila...Derrick, but it does sound exciting."

Lady Catherine decided she would enjoy her visit here on the Australian cattle station, and was determined to spend as much time as she possibly could with James, even if the terrible flies and humidity did get to her. Somehow she knew she would survive this visit, she would make sure she did. For it was extremely important to Catherine that James understood she was a genuine, caring and loving person, and she was not the flighty hot-headed party person she was sure James believed her to be. This was possibly even more so after Lady Catherine realised that James had heard the gossip of her intended marriage to his older brother Morgan – and a shock it would have been for James – without having heard her side of the story. Her feelings for James Wentworth ran deep, as they had done since the tender age of six when as children they both galloped their ponies about the moors together, always competing, laughing and having much fun. But Catherine realised something had changed once each had reached puberty. It was about that time that Catherine lost her dear older brother Oliver on the family farm, and this was closely followed by the sudden death of her mother.

Lady Catherine's father, Lord Hamilton, constantly reminded his remaining child of her heritage and the lifetime of responsibilities it carried with it. Staunch and elderly, her father was now Lady Catherine's sole mentor, and he often feverishly drilled into Lady Catherine that she was his only surviving heir. It was not possible that she could ever forget, nor did she want to, but the once happy and playful Lady Catherine was beginning to disappear for she was acutely aware that her ageing father's wish for her to marry well had become his obsession.

"You do realise my dear daughter that you are exquisitely beautiful, extremely well-to-do, and the most valuable asset any suitable gentleman could possibly wish for in a wife?" Lord Hamilton could be an extremely harsh and at times controlling parent as he tried to instil his likes and dislikes into his only surviving heir, whose spirited, vivacious and flirtatious nature was constantly being downtrodden by her overpowering parent. It made her young life quite unbearable and miserable at times. To top this off was the fact her older and rather irritating cousin, Patterson, was forever reminding her that he was waiting patiently in the wings for her to slip up and marry an unsuitable partner or bring shame on Lord Hamilton's name. For upon her father's death, if the Lady Catherine had failed her father's stringent wishes, Patterson was more than ready to resume the role previously held by Catherine's parent as one of England's wealthiest private landholders. These terrible thoughts were never far from Lady Catherine's mind. In some small way Lady Catherine's fiery spirit and inner strength were the equal of her own father's for she had stood firmly against his wishes when he had a brainstorm one day after her brother's death and casually suggested his daughter marry her first cousin Patterson. This, he said, "Would solve all his worries for the future of his precious Hamilton Hill Castle and Estate." Not something his beautiful daughter had the slightest intention of agreeing to.

Lady Catherine wasn't fooled by her own importance, and while she realised James wasn't at all interested in her heritage, she believed her flirtatious nature may have bothered him. For James could be distant at times and seemingly unattainable. As adults, James and Lady Catherine had drifted apart; Lady Catherine's name was often seen splashed prominently across London's local newspapers, for she was often touted as the socialite of the season. James, on the other hand, who hadn't become a hermit and did attend the odd seasonal party, was preoccupied with the property's thoroughbred horses. James remembered how his ageing Grandfather worried over what he had called 'the neglected state of the Rosengarten thoroughbreds,' and James was determined as he grew older and stronger to take charge of the thoroughbred mares and beautiful stallions and make his grandparent proud again.

Sheila's kitchen help arrived to clear away the crockery from the verandah table. Lady Catherine wished the afternoon tea hadn't been so drawn out for she had so badly wanted to talk privately with James. *There is so much explaining I must do. I need to tell him the truth, and only one week to do it in*, thought a now tiring Lady Catherine as the late afternoon heat was beginning to take its toll on her. Lady Catherine hoped it was her tiredness playing havoc with her emotions, for she wondered, was James still holding onto that distant gap between them? *He seems quiet…would he still be unattainable?*

It was time for James to return to the security of the men's quarters, where in his own good time he would try to unravel the mountain of questions that had created a huge knot in his stomach. The feeling had only come about since hearing of his friend's intended visit to the station, for Catherine's beauty and closeness had a powerful hold on him.

Late the following evening, after a full day fencing in the intense heat with Tom and Bandit, James returned to his own quarters, showered, wrapped a towel around himself and sat on the bench placed conveniently on the back verandah of the men's quarters. The bench was placed on the opposite verandah to the main homestead which gave both parties their own privacy.

With a pannikin of tea by his side, James stretched out on the bench, allowing his over-heated body to absorb the late evening's cooler breezes. James hadn't seen Lady Catherine for the past 24 hours, and he wondered had the luncheon held in the main homestead gone well for her. James knew that managers, owners and their wives from neighbouring cattle stations had travelled great distances to attend the luncheon held in honour of Lady Catherine's visit to the Outback. James, Overseer Bandit and Tom hadn't been invited, not that any of the men wanted an invitation to the luncheon, and it was possibly the last thing they needed to attend. *But surely good manners would have allowed us the option*, James mused to himself.

There must be some relief from this heat, thought James as he allowed himself to doze spasmodically as his body temperature cooled with the evening and the last of the day became night.

"James...James is that you, it's Catherine," a soft cultured English accent whispered, her voice music to his ears. A panicked James sat bolt upright while trying to tighten his bath towel firmly around his lower torso. He must certainly preserve all dignity around Lady Catherine. "Catherine," blurted out a shocked James. "Heaven forbid...what are you doing walking around in the evening, there are venomous snakes around here." That was it, Catherine panicked and immediately jumped into James's lap. His bath towel broke loose and now barely covered his manhood. James was all but naked. Catherine's arms were wrapped tightly around James's well-toned body, and she was shaken and genuinely frightened. James's left arm held her soft body firmly against his own and his immediate reaction was to protect her. His nakedness felt her breasts pushed hard up against his own chest as his right hand fished frantically for the fast disappearing bath towel.

"Please take me inside your house James...where there are no snakes...please...please," Catherine cried for she had no intention of loosening her grip on James until she was safe inside his house where she believed there were no venomous snakes. James was not in a position to argue – they certainly could not be caught out in the dark in this compromising position. James stood up from the bench, both arms wrapped about Catherine while allowing his bath towel to drop to the ground. He told himself he would have to man-up and not be so embarrassed of his accidental nakedness. James carried Catherine inside his quarters where he lay her on the grey blankets of his roughly made bed.

"Please excuse me...I must dress Catherine," uttered a terribly embarrassed James. But Catherine had a hold of James's left hand and pulled him to her side whispering, "I have always loved you James... since we were both six years old...please believe me." James gently tried to peel Catherine's fingers from his own, but she held tight to his sweaty hand. "I have travelled all the way from England to confess my love for you, James." James could not avert his gaze from Catherine's any longer, and saw the love and want for him in her eyes was as deep as his own for her. James pulled a bed sheet across his nakedness – it was obvious his feelings ran deep for Catherine too. In his heart James knew without any doubt at all that the spirited Lady Catherine would never have travelled across the world to confess her love for him – or any other – if she hadn't been sincere. It was simply not in her nature to do so. But James still needed many questions answered before he would ever allow himself to really love and consummate a relationship with the beautiful Lady Catherine of Hamilton Hill. But the unanswered questions could wait for now, for this was the first time James and Catherine had sat and enjoyed some time together. It all seemed so long ago now since he had made that first trip to the Australian Outback.

James needed to get respectable, and disappeared into the bathroom. He hurriedly threw on his torn jeans and faded shirt wondering what Lady Catherine would think of their tattered and torn state. He then joined Catherine in his small clean kitchen, where the table was placed conveniently close to the wood burning Metters stove. When James had the luxury of spending a rest day in the men's quarters, he would frequently have the oversized black kettle constantly on the boil, ready to make tea for himself or his friend Tom.

At the kitchen table, the childhood friends sat opposite each other on hard wooden bench seats. James poured two enamel mugs of tea from the black kettle handing Catherine the red one while he kept the chipped blue mug. James took his bench seat opposite Catherine, his steady gaze locked with her own, her smiling eyes filling him with pure tender happiness. James knew he was a lucky man to have Lady Catherine travel across the world to visit him in the Outback. For the first time in a long while they were happy and at-ease with each other, and Catherine was able to share her first pannikin of real bush tea with James in his men's quarters' shack without the worry of Morgan walking in on them. Within the warmth and comfort of this little isolated kitchen on Campbell's Run Station in the Australian Outback, an unspoken loving truce was felt by both. Although Catherine, being Catherine, was still unable to contain her mischievous spirit and girly amusement at the sight of James's now rough and work hardened hands – studying them, turning them over in her own – she couldn't help but wonder when the day of their love-making came about… would these rough hardened hands tear up her silken skin?

In the kitchen, James turned the wick down low on the kerosene lamp. He lifted his gaze towards Catherine's thinking how her beauty outshone the lamp light. James pointed out the influx of large bush moths banging against the shutters to Catherine. He sincerely hoped the low light would keep the large bush moths at bay, for if her screams were overheard by management he would certainly have some explaining to do, and that could make his and Catherine's remaining time here on Campbell's Run Station a little uncomfortable.

"James," whispered Catherine, "I must explain certain things regarding Morgan and myself." Tears immediately began to well up in Catherine's beautiful emerald eyes and started to cascade over her high cheek bones and drop silently onto the well-scrubbed table top. A worried James leaned across the kitchen table and carefully put his index finger gently against Catherine's trembling lips. "Not now Catherine… not right now my dear. We still have five days before your planned departure for England, please wait until you are a little stronger."

The very next moment James was sure he heard a light tap on the men's quarters' heavy back door. Catherine froze and looked at James with worried eyes. "I don't think it's a snake," murmured James with a mischievous twinkle in his eyes. Just as James finished his sentence the back door creaked open followed by the patter of soft feet on the rough cement floor and there in the entrance stood Sheila in a light cotton see-through nightie.

James immediately jumped to his feet. "Heaven forbid Sheila…is there something wrong at the homestead, I mean, is the Boss okay?" asked a worried James for he had gathered from Tom that his uncle Derrick had his own bundle of health issues that needed constant attention. It had been some weeks since the Boss's young wife had found a feeble excuse to wander down to the men's quarters from the homestead, and it always happened when her husband was away attending a meeting in Darwin, James thought.

Sheila, not about to offer James an answer immediately, stood with the porch lantern behind her which left nothing to the imagination as she struggled to keep her immense anger in check at finding the beautiful English lady and station stockman James together in the men's quarters tonight. Again James asked, "Pardon me Sheila, has something gone wrong at the homestead?" James took a step towards his Boss's wife when she said, "How charming," and then after letting James sweat a bit, "There is nothing wrong at the homestead. Derrick is away in Darwin attending a cattlemen's meeting, and considering I was alone, I went to offer Catherine a nightcap but she wasn't to be found. I panicked and thought we had already lost her to the Outback, so here I am." A now discomfited Lady Catherine got up from her bench seat at the kitchen table and offered Sheila a genuine apology. "I'm terribly sorry for causing you so much trouble. The next time I go for a walk I must tell you." Ever the gentleman, James politely offered Sheila an enamel mug of well brewed tea, which was declined. As Sheila went to leave the quarters, she turned back and said with some attitude, "Catherine, on Campbell's Run Station, the men's quarters are just that, really not a place for a lady!" and she abruptly stormed out and left James and Catherine to their tepid tea. Lady Catherine looked worriedly towards James. "Oh dear me, James, have I upset the apple cart by visiting you now?" James pondered before lifting his head to look at Catherine and answered, "Can I suggest that you not dwell on what has been said tonight as I have it from a very good source…um… that the Boss's wife has a few problems of her own." Catherine agreed with James and then after some quiet thought offered, "I must say, it was lovely of her to say how charming we both looked sitting here together, James." James laughed for he had quickly learnt while in the stock camp with Tom that the term 'charming' also meant 'disapproval or disgust' in Australian slang, depending on how it was used – not something Catherine needed to worry herself about tonight, thought James.

CHAPTER 30

A Close Shave at Mitchell Gorge

Come dawn the following morning, all on Campbell's Run Station had to have been woken by the boisterous squawking of the red-tailed black cockatoos. The huge mob continually circled the homestead, alerting all that another day had begun, whilst leaving no gum tree, now loaded with gum nuts, unattended in their rowdy wake.

Lady Catherine bounced from her bed towards the verandah in search of the early morning alarm, and found the culprits close by. Then Sheila's house help arrived. "Good morning to you Miss Catherine," Katie offered.

"And a good morning to you too Katie. I believe we are visiting the Mitchell Gorge today for a picnic and swim, are you coming too?" questioned Catherine, excited and thinking how lovely it would be to have Sheila's house help join them for a fun day at the gorge. Katie's eyes dulled, she dropped her head and said softly, "Miss Catherine…I don't think that Miss Sheila likes us coloured girls much." Katie lifted her head and concentrated her gaze upon Catherine. "You talk to us… not like that Boss Missus." Before the conversation between Catherine and Katie could go further Sheila arrived on the verandah yelling heatedly. "Katie, clean that kitchen for me. I need to use it now…and quickly." Without a backward glance Katie hurried off towards the homestead's kitchen, leaving a shocked Catherine standing alone with Sheila in dead silence on the back verandah.

A good night's sleep hadn't done the Boss's young wife an ounce of good, for she was now taking her frustration and jealously out on others. Sheila looked Lady Catherine up and down, raised her eyebrows and thought it better to keep her own sarcasm to herself. The last thing Sheila needed was for Derrick to hear of her rudeness to their guest. She also understood that if her husband Derrick got wind of her own visit to the men's quarters last evening that he would shoot her attempted explanation down in flames. Sheila had been warned before! Now it was better to offer a half-hearted apology to Catherine for her previous evening's intrusion on James and Catherine, for Sheila had to remind herself that the two had been friends long before now. Nevertheless, Sheila's pain had quickly developed into savage anger at seeing James and Catherine enjoying one another's company in the men's quarters last evening. That was enough to rekindle that green-eyed monster in Sheila – or was it a psychological disorder hidden beneath Sheila's attractive exterior?

Catherine accepted Sheila's apology, then asked if the kitchen help, Tom and James and the other stockmen would come along for the picnic as well – the more the merrier thought Catherine. Sheila's answer was blunt and to the point. "Definitely not. Some of us must work around here." Shelia's attitude of last evening and her repeated performance this morning was beginning to leave Lady Catherine feeling most uncomfortable.

With the sun high in the sky, and after what seemed a long drive down a rutted dirt track, including fording several small swift flowing creeks and diverting around one huge gully in the station's old Land Rover, Sheila eventually arrived at the most beautiful gorge Catherine had ever seen in her life. The gorge, with its swift flowing falls cascading into a bottomless pool of crystal clear water, was at the girls' mercy for the entire day. All this beauty protected by the magnificent ochre cliffs of Mother Nature, who had somehow filled the gaps with wild fern and livistona palms.

Lady Catherine climbed out from the battered old Land Rover to stand on the cliff top, surrounded by nature's magnificent beauty.

Catherine stood for a few seconds to allow her perspiring body to absorb the soft cool mist rising from the furious tumbling of the waterfalls far below. She stood with her thoughts on the Boss's wife, thinking surely there was no need for any further tension between herself and Sheila today, for Catherine would forgive and forget, and was more than happy to enjoy this beautiful spot with Shelia.

"Well, here we are Catherine. I'll begin my day all over again…let's both enjoy this beautiful place together," offered Sheila, more or less asking for Catherine's forgiveness once again. Lady Catherine stood quietly taking in the gorge's natural beauty then asked, "Sheila, what is that spiral of wood smoke across the way?" Sheila stopped gathering their two picnic baskets from the tray-back of the vehicle to look at the spiral of smoke rising from the opposite side of the gorge. "Don't worry yourself Catherine," she said, "it's called a smoke signal, one clan of people signalling to another…possibly notifying them of our arrival here." Lady Catherine was intrigued with Sheila's knowledge on the matter and wondered if it was true. "Plus, many of the indigenous families from Campbell's Run and the neighbouring station properties use the area as a holiday camp while others for Aboriginal law I believe. Derrick says they don't mind sharing this beautiful spot with us, as long as we don't try and interfere in any way."

Now fuelled with excitement and her deep love of nature, Lady Catherine was anxious to begin their trek down into this magnificent cavity before them. Sheila led the way down the rocky outcrop while Lady Catherine followed cautiously at a much slower pace. Catherine hadn't bargained on clambering down over the many huge rock ledges while trying to keep her nerve as she balanced along some extremely narrow paths subject to frequent small rock falls. Dear God, breathed Catherine as she neared the bottom of the gorge, as beautiful as this place is, I will never attempt this trip again. For as brave as Catherine was to gallop a spirited stallion across the moors of home, heights it seemed were certainly not her thing. Uptight and extremely nervous, the now pale and shaking Lady Catherine willed her own body to remain calm so she could reach the sandy beach and that magnificent glistening rock pool that seemed so far below them in the gorge. All the while she kept wishing her dear friend James Wentworth was there by her side.

In the back of Lady Catherine's mind was her father's dream for Hamilton Hill Castle – she fully understood that a terrible accident would shatter her father's lifetime dream, and therefore her family's direct line of heritage would be lost to Lady Catherine's older cousin Patterson.

It was not the first time Shelia had visited Mitchell Gorge, she had come many times before to swim naked in the heat of day and bask on the sand in the warm summer's heat to dry. Immediately the two woman had reached the bottom of the gorge, both quickly disrobed and plunged into the pristine clear water, laughing and frolicking together, and calling out simply to hear their voices echo throughout the tall rock cathedral surrounding them. A pair of magnificent wedge-tailed eagles glided gently in the warm thermals high above the rugged escarpment, while the cockatoos' piercing squawks were ever present.

Cold and hungry, both women threw on their jeans and shirts and sat together on a warm rock ledge where they watched little fish swim in the crystal clear water beside them. Here they shared Sheila's corned beef and pickle sandwiches accompanied by a thermos of black tea. Lady Catherine thanked Sheila for her day out at Mitchell Gorge, adding in her soft cultured accent, how amazed she was at this vast rugged beauty hidden among these majestic ranges. "I think it is all truly beautiful, but certainly, most definitely not the place or life for me." Sheila flinched, for she had taken Catherine's comment personally, and her jovial mood suddenly changed and she asked Lady Catherine, "What is it you want in life? Is it James?" Lady Catherine instantly felt the tension rise between them, wondering whether it was any of this already married woman's business what I want or do. She quickly realised it was better not to elaborate on her own life for she may ruffle this woman's feathers even more.

Lady Catherine had been raised by a nanny and schooled by a grouchy old governess, who had once told her it was 'Better to bite one's tongue than to lower oneself and become involved in an unnecessary argument.' So Catherine answered, "Probably the same as you do Sheila."

Their day came to abrupt end as Sheila threw the picnic gear into the basket, collected her towel and headed for the cliffs where she called for Catherine to hurry up. "There are certain things I must attend to at the station before the day has ended." Sheila suggested Lady Catherine climb this vast cliff face ahead of her. But Catherine argued that her fear of heights was again with her, plus she had no idea where the safest path was. Seeing Sheila had visited the gorge often, wouldn't it be wiser if she herself took the lead? The Boss's wife pushed Lady Catherine in the back, telling her if she didn't make a move soon, they would still be trying to climb up the cliff face in the dark.

With her towel draped around her neck, and believing Sheila was pushing her ahead for her own safety, Lady Catherine cautiously lifted one foot after the other, praying to God that with each step she found a secure foothold on the rocky ledge. After a terrifying half hour and still on the cliff face, Sheila's directions had become more personal and abusive towards Lady Catherine. How Catherine wished she was not alone with Sheila today, and couldn't help but think that she had made it extremely clear in her telegram to Mr and Mrs Derrick Dunn that the purpose of her trip to Australia was to spend time with her dear friend James Wentworth. This is not to say Lady Catherine wasn't grateful to the Dunns for their invite to stay in their homestead at Campbell's Run.

Back in England, Lady Catherine was looked upon as a strong individual who could ride and compete with the best of society's equestrian set, but here on Campbell's Run Station, Lady Catherine felt uneasy around the Boss's wife, to the point where she felt her own resentment and distrust of Sheila building at a rapid rate. Her thoughts drifted to James, again wishing he was by her side as the steep climb to the top of the escarpment was beginning to feel near impossible for her. With her extreme fear of heights, Catherine had no alternative but to look only several steps ahead of herself and towards a narrow fragile ledge that she was sure no one in their right mind would ever attempt to cross.

Lady Catherine stopped climbing, although she only climbed at a snail's pace, as her fear of heights became overwhelming and her legs felt as if they were ready to collapse under her. Everything was becoming too much. Catherine could not move another inch, she could not even let go of the weak grip she had on a protruding rock. All she could feel was the powerful choking fear of her own heart pounding heavily in her ears. Exhausted and fearful, she allowed her weakening body to rest against the uneven rock face to absorb what little heat of the day was left before the sun slipped below the surrounding mountain range. This was the only way she felt truly safe.

"Get it together Catherine, move along," bullied Sheila. Catherine could barely answer for her fear of heights had now paralysed her against the rugged cliff face. "If you won't move, then please, get out of my bloody way," yelled Sheila, who could see for herself that there was room for only one person on the ledge. Sheila was becoming quite frustrated as she had wanted to get home before her husband Derrick returned from his cattlemen's meeting in Darwin. Plus her husband had suggested she not take Lady Catherine alone to the gorge for the sheer climb was far too dangerous. In addition, he had reminded her that the stockmen were due for a day off, and they should all travel together, it would be safer, and therefore they could all enjoy themselves in the beautiful water hole at the bottom of the gorge. But the green-eyed monster in Sheila wasn't about to allow Lady Catherine and James Wentworth an afternoon of sheer bliss together, no…not at all.

Lady Catherine thought she could hear voices somewhere in the distance as fear left her unable to open her eyes. Sheila yelled again and again for Catherine to move on or allow her to pass. Suddenly, rocks began to fall all around them and Catherine copped a force-ful shove in the back from behind. Next minute her grip slipped and she lost her footing. Catherine's ear-piercing screams could be heard echoing throughout the narrow walls of the gorge as she fell heavily against rocky ledges and bounced off others. Her beautiful body lay battered and bruised, and she was bleeding profusely from deep lacer-ations that soaked the yellow sand at the bottom of the gorge where she had landed.

Sheila glanced briefly at the falling Catherine, raised her eyes, and then climbed on steadily towards the top of the escarpment without as much as a thought to helping Catherine.

At 2pm, Derrick Dunn had returned to the homestead after attend-ing the quarterly cattlemen's meeting in Darwin. Sheila arrived and parked the Land Rover by the shed. Derrick was feeling extremely displeased that his young wife had not invited the station's stockmen along with Catherine and herself to Mitchell Gorge for the day. They had certainly deserved a day of relaxation too he thought.

"Where is Catherine, Sheila?" asked a now irritated Derrick. "For heaven sake don't tell me you left her behind somewhere?" Derrick believed no one could possibly be so stupid as to leave another behind in the Outback, unless of course it was intended that way. Leaning heavily on his walking stick, Derrick hobbled across the back verandah, placed his stick against a chair and grabbed his young wife by both shoulders, his fingers digging into her flesh as he demanded answers. Sheila screamed at her husband, "I don't know, believe me Derrick." Tears began to run down Sheila's face, as she continued to defend herself to her husband. "Catherine went for a walk in the gorge by herself. Please believe me. I looked, but couldn't find her. I came home to get help," cried Shelia. Derrick let go of his wife's shoulders, leaving deep red indentations on her skin.

Katie, Shelia's Aboriginal house help who had befriended Lady Catherine at the homestead, overheard Sheila's story to her husband. She quietly left the homestead by the back door, and ran frantically towards her own camp of people, where she relayed this terrible news to Penny.

Derrick immediately called Bandit on the station's two-way radio. "Need to speak with you urgently. Bring Tom, James and six good stockmen." Shortly a flurry of red dust was sighted down at the stockmen's camp, and in no time a vehicle arrived at Derrick Dunn's homestead gate. All the men leapt from the vehicle and hurried towards the back verandah where previous meetings of importance were held with their Boss.

Bandit had an inkling that something serious had happened to Lady Catherine after spotting Sheila peeking through the homestead's kitchen curtains. Bandit walked briskly towards Derrick, his gut telling him this was an emergency and somehow the Boss's wife was connected to it. The heavy pounding of Bandit's riding boots and the rattle of his spurs on the dry wooden floorboards of the verandah were enough to gain the attention of all in the homestead. One thing was sure; Bandit understood the old owner of Campbell's Run Station better than any other, and well enough to immediately sense that he was truly rattled. But what had gone wrong?

Derrick Dunn called his wife out from the kitchen and asked her to repeat the story she had told him regarding Lady Catherine's disappearance at Mitchell Gorge that day. Sheila sat beside her husband, pale and in constant tears as she twisted a handkerchief around her fingers. Prompted by her husband, Sheila repeated her story on Lady Catherine's disappearance at the gorge. Bandit's dark penetrating eyes bored deeply into his ex-partner's – somehow her story didn't ring true to him. After all, she had shacked up with Bandit before marrying old

Derrick Dunn. Bandit felt he had some understanding of the woman.

James immediately jumped to his feet. "Heaven forbid...we must find Catherine now...please let us hurry to the gorge." James found it unbelievable his friend would have disappeared into thin air while exploring the cracks and crevasses of the gorge. He more than any other there understood his friend, and he found it hard to believe that Catherine would have wandered off by herself in a region totally unknown and alien to her.

Lady Catherine was a pampered English woman who had previously travelled with a lady's maid constantly by her side and many servants at her beck and call. James was certain that Catherine would never have gone off alone. He had never been so sure of anything in his life.

Bandit's plans were promptly executed. He had stockmen on horseback to search the surrounding areas, while he, Tom and English James would ride in the vehicle with the two-way radio. This way Bandit believed all bases were covered. Just as Bandit went to pull the vehicle out from the homestead, Penny, Tom's girl waved for them to stop as she ran barefoot from the Aboriginal camp. Tom met Penny halfway down the claypan flat. They had a quick conversation before Tom returned to the vehicle and offered, "Penny believes Sheila is not telling the truth." Bandit then drove off at speed to begin the search for their missing English visitor.

Tom had never seen their overseer drive the station's Land Rover quite so fast before – in fact Tom was amazed the old thing had it in it. They arrived at the top of the Mitchell Gorge escarpment, confident they had enough daylight left to organise an evacuation if needed. All three were silent with their own deep thoughts as each man grabbed the necessary items from the tray-back of the vehicle. The homestead medical kit, ropes, a small container of water and a portable stretcher were all laid out on the lip of the gorge and ready to go when Tom piped up, "Hey Bandit, James...look over here." Thick smoke was spiralling up from the bottom of the gorge. Then Bandit spotted many footprints tracking across the sand from the opposite side of the gorge towards the cliffs below. "All those tracks can't possible belong to Sheila and Lady Catherine, there are too many of them," offered Bandit. At that moment a thin, sparsely clad Aboriginal man, closely followed by several others, walked out into the open space below, looked up towards the three stockmen and began to 'sing out'. They waved their spears and beckoned for the white men to climb down the cliff face and follow them. Bandit and Tom begun the dangerous descent immediately, but not before Tom offered a word of advice to his friend. "James, take it steady mate, there's a lot of loose rock. We will find the lady, just go steady mate, we can't have two of you hurt and at the bottom of the gorge."

As the stockmen climbed steadily closer to the sandy bottom of the gorge, each man noticed a large patch of red sand. "Bloody hell," whispered Tom. "Jesus Christ, this is all we need," muttered Bandit. "Heaven forbid...no," cried James, who was close behind the other two and close to the bottom of the gorge by now. On the sandy bottom they were met with the strong smell of wood smoke and goanna grease, and many scantily clad black men with their chests covered in raised tribal markings. Wrought from worry, James raced towards the red patch of sand only to be stopped in his tracks by a black man with a spear. The man pushed James back towards Bandit and Tom who were now in deep conversation and arm waving with the tribesmen. "Please...let's do hurry," begged James. "I'm sure that's human blood over there...please...if that's Catherine's blood she must be in serious trouble." Tom stepped back, put his arm around James's shoulders to show he cared too. "Come on James...this mob has dragged Catherine into a cave under that rocky ledge...she needed shade mate," Tom explained. "They say she is alive, but 'no good', meaning as soon as I get a look at her I'll climb back up the cliff face where I can get reception to call in the Flying Doctor aircraft to the station's airstrip as soon as possible. I'll also call Derrick to arrange a helicopter to land on the sandy bottom here in the gorge. They'll lift the lady from here to the station, and before dark the aircraft with a doctor will move her from the station to the hospital in Darwin." James thanked his friend for showing strength and calmness at this terrible time. "Come on James, this group of people are protecting Lady Catherine with their life. I overheard them telling Bandit in pidgin that a white woman was yelling at her, and one man saw that white woman push this one in the back, meaning Catherine was shoved." "Tom, are you thinking what I am?" whispered James who was feeling terribly unsettled now. Trying to show some diplomacy Tom said, "I don't want to jump too far ahead James, but honestly, I'd believe these tribal elders before I'd ever believe Sheila's report on this accident." Tom had a light-bulb moment and thought to himself, no wonder Bandit never lost any sleep over loosing Sheila to old Uncle Derrick, it's all starting to make sense now.

Bandit was with Lady Catherine first. She was unconscious and had several deep cuts to her head. Tom and James raced in to the cave, and weaved their way through the tribesmen and women who had formed a protective human circle around Catherine. Several smoky campfires surrounded Lady Catherine as she lay covered in blood on the ground before them. James panicked and grabbed Tom's arm whispering, "Why the bloody fires...for heaven's sake Tom." Tom whispered back, "Keep it together James, they're spiritual people... this smoke is to protect the lady from any further harm."

James knelt down in the sand beside Catherine feeling totally useless, shaken and horrified to see her in such a bad way. Bandit suggested they not handle the lady any more than was necessary, for her breathing seemed shallow and there was a rattle in her chest. "I don't want to frighten you James, and I'm no doctor, but I believe there may be some internal damage." With tears blurring his vision, James took hold of Catherine's hand gently in his own. He checked her pulse, for he needed so badly to know that his childhood friend was still with him. James sat back on his haunches while still holding her delicate white hand, closed his eyes and looked towards the heavens and prayed for help for the woman he loved so much. When he opened his eyes it was into the many black faces with their huge frightening eyes peering down on him.

The inside of the cave was filled with a cloud of wood smoke. This smoke was fanned around by the older women who swayed trance-like as they waved bunches of young gum saplings to the rhythm of a tribal chant. James sensed the serenity surrounding them all and he knew these tribal people were good folk, for here they were out in the middle of nowhere giving their best to help save Lady Catherine. Carefully, James leaned across Lady Catherine and softly kissed her bloody and bruised forehead, touched her face gently, then placed his ear to her chest, for he had also detected that distinctive rattle.

CHAPTER 31

Suspicion and Innuendo

Life had changed for many people on Campbell's Run Station the day after Lady Catherine's terrifying accident. Catherine had been successfully airlifted to Darwin Hospital by the Royal Flying Doctor. Her diagnosis of a perforated lung, broken ribs and collarbone, and deep lacerations was good considering her terrible fall. James had informed Bandit that he planned to resign from Campbell's Run Station for he wished to be by Lady Catherine's side to offer comfort and support as soon as he possibly could. James wasn't one to forget his manners, and he certainly hadn't forgotten that Bandit had taken a gamble when he had hired him on the footpath out front of the Victoria Hotel in the main street of Darwin. Back then, James was just another fresh Pommy fellow from England, and fully understood that Bandit had taken a gamble on hiring him at the time. James hoped he had proven his worth to Bandit during his time working in the stock camp on Campbell's Run Station.

Since Lady Catherine's accident, not only had the unspoken accusation and innuendo run rife on the station, but even that protective feeling of a once close-knit station community had changed – that wonderful warm and secure feeling that every person on the station understood, from the management down to the stockmen, that another always had their back covered, no matter what. But what had come over the Boss's young wife that day?

At the men's quarters James had packed his duffel bag and began to roll his swag when a loud banging was heard out back. "James...hey James...open up mate," bellowed Tom. James hurriedly opened the back door to his friend before shoving another log into the firebox of the wood stove and moved the black kettle over the direct heat for a quick boil. Over time, James felt he had got to understand Tom rather well, but this morning his friend seemed unsettled for some reason. A mug of good black tea would be a start to helping them both feel better, thought James.

Both lads sat opposite each other on the wooden benches either side of the kitchen table. "What's wrong Tom...is something bothering you?" James started. "You're packing...you're out of here, right?" Tom replied bluntly.

"You're right Tom, but not before you and I had discussed the plans we had made. I'm pleased you're here now though." Tom nervously moved his mug around in circles on the kitchen table and then said, "I'm out of here too, and not alone...Penny and our son are coming with me. I handed in my notice to Bandit this morning. He said he doesn't blame you for leaving the station as well after what happened. But old Uncle Derrick is in for one hell of a bloody shock because he's about to lose Bandit, the best overseer he ever had." Both lads sat staring into nothingness, absorbing this latest news. Eventually, James asked quietly, "Does Derrick know all this...I mean...I feel terrible that we're all abandoning him and Campbell's Run Station. Tom, do you think he can still handle the station alone...I mean he is getting on and he's not a young agile man by any means, plus aren't there a few health problems as well?" Tom pondered for a moment before answering, "Well James...I'd say the old fella and his young bride have had it coming for some time. Uncle Derrick never believed me when I told him Sheila constantly harassed any new stockman that had the displeasure of having to camp in these quarters – they're conveniently close to the homestead. Word has it she would be down here in her itsy-bitsy nightie whenever old Derrick was away overnight...and the next thing you'd know the poor bloke would be sacked 'cause he didn't go along with her wants. James felt himself burning from embarrassment – he too could have been sacked if Sheila had so desired.

"James, do you remember me telling you that woman has had many a good bloke sacked from Campbell's Run? She's got to be unbalanced for bloody sure...in fact I'm bloody positive she is. Either that or she's permanently horny and the old fella's not servicing her needs... bloody hell James." James felt he understood where Tom was coming from, for his old Uncle Derrick was obviously blinded by the youth of a beautiful young woman some thirty years younger than himself – hopefully he would wake up before it was too late and not meet his maker the same way as James's dear Grandfather, the Lord Alexander Wentworth II, had done back home in England. James wondered how he could ever possibly forget that his Grandfather had died from a massive heart attack in the middle of an overzealous sex act with his very young mistress Victoria.

Another harsh bang against the men's quarters' back door brought in Bandit. "Come along lads, Tom, Jim, we need to visit old Derrick on the homestead's back verandah and make a few things clear to him before we all pull the pin and leave the property." Tom bounced up from his bench seat with a "righto", and James said he agreed with Bandit. Once again the sound of 'men on a mission', with three sets of well-worn riding boots accompanied by the jingle of Bandit's spurs on the old verandah floorboards, was enough to have Derrick Dunn greet them all in a hurry. Sheila poked her head out the kitchen doorway and asked bluntly, "Do you want something Bandit?" Bandit stepped aside from the lads, excused himself from his Boss, put his head close to Sheila's and said, "Sheila...I suggest you join us in this meeting with Derrick...we don't want to tell tales behind your back...do we?" If looks could have killed, Bandit was sure Sheila would have disposed of him there and then. Derrick suggested his young wife gather herself and attend the meeting.

Derrick sat down, puffed his chest out and asked, "Well Bandit... what has brought all three of my best stockmen to talk with me today?" Derrick Dunn hadn't a clue in the world what he was about to be hit with. Sheila again began to fidget – when she wasn't tidying her shirt she was twisting her handkerchief around and around her pointer finger. So, starting with the overseer, followed by Tom and James, the stockmen resigned from Campbell's Run Station. All three felt terrible as Derrick's strong appearance faded quickly and considerably. His shoulders hunched and he paled frightfully. Tom was going to inform his uncle that the whole Aboriginal stock camp was moving away as well, but with Derrick suddenly looking so poorly he thought better of it. But Bandit thought it was time old Derrick was made aware of some of Sheila's failings. How many times had she pulled a loaded gun on him and others and threatened to shoot them at point blank range? Or held a boning knife to his throat – and her partner before him – threatening to slice each of their throats wide open? And no wonder the station medical kit was never fully stocked when needed, for Sheila had a tendency to raid the medical kit's more potent drugs for herself. Her past partners were much bigger and stronger than Sheila, and each man could have taken her down easily. But they didn't because she was a woman and therefore she got away with it. These men weren't prepared to lower themselves to her level by inflicting violence on her or detailing her manipulative ways. But not this time. Bandit and Tom went on and calmly explained to Derrick what the tribesmen had repeated to them in pidgin and sign language. These tribesmen had heard all the yelling and abuse, and were sure that Sheila had pushed Lady Catherine from the cliff face at Mitchell Gorge that day.

Immediately overcome by anger, Sheila began screaming at them all as she forcibly shoved her chair backwards, changed her mind, picked it up and threw it directly at Bandit, all the while screaming, "Liar…liar…liar, those old tribesmen wouldn't have a clue what they're talking about…you know what they're like, you can't believe a word they say…you're all a bunch of bloody liars, the whole damn lot of you." Sheila's anger boiled over as she bounced about the verandah screaming and throwing anything and everything she could possibly lay her hands on. Even her husband's boots were sent flying through the kitchen's glass window, smashing it to smithereens and taking the fine bone china drying on the kitchen sink with it.

This outburst wasn't at all new to Bandit, for he had expected a theatrical performance from Sheila, he'd seen it many times before. "Bloody hell," whispered Tom watching the Boss's wife performance, he'd never seen anything quite like it before. James just sat shell-shocked, and found the outburst unbelievable. He wondered why a good man of old Derrick Dunn's standing, well-educated and once an accomplished accountant, would tolerate such behaviour at all.

Patting the seat beside him, Derrick persuaded his young wife to calm down, stop and gather herself. "We can talk my dear…we can talk this through…now come here and sit down beside me," he soothed. Sheila calmed down but wasn't prepared to sit anywhere near the stockmen, and looked at them as if they all had the plague! The time had come for the three stockmen to leave this performance and the unhealthy situation behind them. Bandit, Tom and James stood up, said their goodbyes and shook Derrick Dunn's large hand. James looked towards Sheila, hesitated for a fleeting second, and then acknowledged her with a slight bow of the head. It was only his good manners that made him do it, but he was appreciative of the medical treatment she had tendered to him after his horse accident. Derrick then mentioned to James that if Lady Catherine wished to press charges against Sheila, they knew where to find her. James sensed Derrick was sad to see his stockmen leave Campbell's Run, and he was sure there was a tear in the old man's eyes as the three of them went to walk away.

CHAPTER 32

Time to Move on

In the passenger seat of Bandit's ute was his best mate, his devoted blue heeler cattle dog, and between them, his dusty leather brief-case with his name 'Brock Anderson' in large worn gold lettering on the side. His dusty swag roll rode in the back tightly secured. Bandit left Campbell's Run Station in his busted-arse ute for a new manager's position in the tough Gulf country of northern Queensland. He was a drifter, and never saw the need to spend up big on a new vehicle. As long as his ute got him from A to B – that was all that really mattered to him – he presumed everything else would be just fine.

The mates, James and Tom, found a new lease of life and went back to their plan to take over James's inherited cattle station in the West Kimberley. Travelling happily with them in the faded grey Land Rover that was towing an even more dilapidated trailer, was Tom's partner Penny, and their baby son Tommy. Earlier, James had telegrammed his family in England notifying them of his change of address to Lonesome Downs. How pleased this would make his Grand-mama, Lady Elizabeth, knowing at long last that James was accepting his inheritance from his dear Grandfather, Lord Wentworth II.

Neither of the lads had been to the Kimberley before and they couldn't help but wonder what this Lonesome Downs cattle station held in store for them. James did not know at the time of his Grandfather's unexpected death that he was to inherit a million acre cattle property in one of the Outback's wildest, if not last, frontiers. Nor did he have any clue that most of this property was mainly uninhabited, and had no neighbours around for a hundred miles in any direction from the homestead. His Grandfather had been in partnership with his long-time friend, a heart surgeon from the Adelaide Hills, but unknown to James, Lord Alexander Wentworth had purchased his partner's share of Lonesome Downs on his last trip to Australia.

James planned on spending a week with Tom, for they would both need to get some idea of the lay-out of this huge property that formed the Lonesome Downs Station lease. He needed to do this before he left to visit his dear friend Lady Catherine in Royal Darwin Hospital.

At the hospital reception desk James was given directions to Lady Catherine's private room in ward three. He had brought with him a pretty bouquet of frangipani, the colour of brilliant sunshine. James believed Catherine really deserved better, but it was all that was available to him from the little corner store at the time. As James Wentworth stepped closer to Catherine's private ward, the more nervous he became. He worried she would be angry he had not visited her bedside much sooner. Her doctor had advised James via the two-way radio that his friend Catherine would survive her terrible ordeal at the gorge and that her wounds would heal well, although there was a chance the lady would carry scars for many years to come. For the time being rest would be the best medicine for her.

Dear God, how I have missed this lady's smiling face and mischievous ways, thought James. Since Lady Catherine's accident, all his quiet moments alone on the station had been spent reminiscing over the happy times they had spent together in their childhood – galloping their favourite horses among the blue cornflowers on Rosengarten or across the damp moors of Hamilton Hill. The quieter times were spent sitting together on a fallen log under the old oak tree shading the Wentworth family's many gravestones discussing their plans and futures. They were both young at heart back then, and neither could see or even talked of a future together, for they were best friends. But in the last couple of years James realised their feelings for each other had changed dramatically, and his alone were far deeper than ever before. Now he felt an urgent need to hold and caress Catherine.

James tapped gently on the white door of Lady Catherine's private room. Everything looked so white and sterile, a vast contrast to the men's quarters at Campbell's Run, thought James. He cheekily held the bouquet of frangipanis around the doorframe first, to check on his welcome. There was a soft laugh, followed by a warm cultured English accent. "Please do come in James, I have missed you terribly." James hesitantly entered Lady Catherine's hospital room, and couldn't help but feel an immediate sense of relief to find her sitting upright in a comfortable armchair by the large bay window. James was truly astounded to find that even that terrible accident on the station was unable to diminish Lady Catherine's beauty in any way. Now, rays of sunshine entering the room through the bay window brought an abundance of light to her wild and unruly blonde curls. And with a racing heart, but not really wanting to expose his emotions at this time, James found he was no longer able to contain them. When Lady Catherine stood up and took a step towards James while openly crying tears of joy, James accepted her love for him had to be real. Catherine clung to James while offering him her lips, as if her own life depended on holding him close to her forever. With Catherine in his arms James was unable to contain his feelings any longer, reciprocating her love for him, lovingly and tenderly. As James held Catherine he told himself, the past was history, although he found it hard to forgive his deceased brother Morgan for his distasteful innuendo only hours before his betrothal to the Lady Catherine. For an extremely angry Morgan had made it his business to enter James's bedroom and say, 'The lady carries my child...stay away from her.' James now realised those words had to be untrue and made a silent vow to himself to never mention it to Catherine. The past was just that, history.

James returned by himself to the Victoria Hotel in the main street of Darwin to secure accommodation for himself and Lady Catherine. He entered the front bar, which was directly inside the front door, to find the bar propped-up by half a dozen sun-bronzed blue singletted and rough looking characters. Dear me, thought James for a moment and then asked himself, how will Lady Catherine accept lodging here among these tough looking men of the Outback? James hadn't forgotten the stories he'd overheard around the campfire one night from the station's horse breaker, Cranky Henry. One story stuck in James mind, and had him believe that the North of Australia really was 'the last frontier'. Cranky Henry had said the Northern Territory was often used by outlaws. It was an isolated area of rugged mountain ranges and wild flood plains, fit for tough men and resilient woman folk – a convenient place for those one step ahead of the law. He said once these folk believed their misdemeanours were forgotten, they'd move on again. Dear me, thought James, I will have to rethink our accommodation plans if Catherine is unable to accept this hotel.

Then, "Do you want a beer or accommodation mate?" the sunburnt bartender asked James. "Accommodation please," answered James. At that moment James was relieved to spot Molly who he remembered from his previous stay there. She was the owner of the hotel who prided herself in managing the reception desk and keeping the riffraff at bay. James waited patiently as Molly worked her way down the long narrow bar towards him. "Follow me," she said, without as much as lifting her head.

James picked up his duffel bag and swag and followed Molly to the little reception room out the back. "Are you new here, have you stayed here before?" Taken aback, James felt he was on the stand in a court room, then answered, "I've worked as a stockman for the last two seasons on Campbell's Run ma'am." Molly lifted her reading glasses a little higher onto the rim of her nose and studied James intently. "Actually...it was you ma'am who put me onto Bandit our overseer out there." James felt relieved to see Molly had remembered their first meeting here in her Darwin hotel, and now that she had, James hoped Molly would find a slightly better room than his previous well-used one for his friend the Lady Catherine. "Yes, I do remember you... you're the English gentleman," offered Molly, while flicking through her dog-eared reception book looking for a vacant room for James.

"I'm James Wentworth ma'am. I'd like one room for myself and another for my English lady friend Catherine, who will be in tomorrow. Could I request the very best suite of rooms you have for Catherine please?" "Can you afford all this on a stockman's wage?" Molly asked abruptly. "I have the Wedding Suite vacant...she can have that." Taken aback, James answered he could afford to pay and offered to pay upfront for both rooms immediately. Molly handed James the room keys. One for Lady Catherine in the Wedding Suite on the top floor overlooking the sapphire blue bay, while James's room wasn't that far from his previous one on the ground floor. James bent down to pick up his gear when Molly said, "Don't suppose I have to warn you…cos it seems you have a lady friend, but I tell them all just the same…I don't tolerate unsavory types, or wild drunken parties that go on all night long until they wreck my rooms. I throw them out. No questions asked." James looked at Molly and was sure that craggy face of hers caved in to a faint smile.

The next morning James contacted Tom via the Flying Doctor radio to assure him he and Catherine hoped to be back on Lonesome Downs the following week, providing all went well for Catherine once she was discharged from Darwin Hospital. He had also advised Tom to send his store order via the two-way radio. James planned to arrange for the station stores, Lady Catherine and himself to arrive at Lonesome Downs homestead on the one charter flight. Life would change for James now he had his own cattle station to manage. With Tom's help and advice, James planned on turning this once Outback holiday property of his Grandfather's into a working cattle station. James dreamed that one day Lonesome Downs would be able to pay its own way. James had come to realise that he truly loved the isolation and rugged interior of the Australian Outback, and looked forward to all the challenges it would throw up. He now fully understood this country was as unforgiving as it was loving. James's need for a successful outcome with Lonesome Downs was to show his appreciation and gratitude to his Grand-mama Lady Elizabeth. His grandparents, Lady Elizabeth and the now deceased Lord Wentworth II, had always been there for James throughout his mother Gabrielle's constant sufferings of the depression sickness and his father's unfathomable need to constantly associate with other women outside the boundaries of his marriage.

CHAPTER 33

Lonesome Downs

On the day of Lady Catherine's discharge from Darwin Hospital James was a bundle of anticipated excitement. Not only had he accepted they were both free to allow their feelings to develop in the most natural way possible, but they were together in the Outback, which was short on people and big on isolation. Now James and Catherine would not have the worry of prying eyes or pushy matrimonial advice from the hierarchy of their own families' establishments. At that time in the Northern Territory no one gave a rat's arse who you were, what colour you were, or what title or handle you had to your name. This made Lonesome Downs Station a better proposition than Rosengarten Castle or Hamilton Hill Castle in England to allow a genuine courtship to develop between James and the Lady Catherine.

The Chinese taxi driver pulled up out front of the Victoria Hotel. He jumped out and quickly opened the back passenger door to allow the once again elegant Lady Catherine to climb out of his cab and onto the footpath – smack bang between two inebriated stockmen. "One pound fare...please," demanded the Chinese driver. Of course the one pound fare wasn't fair at all, in fact James now realised it was daylight robbery. James paid the driver, but wasn't at all happy with the driver's choice of a drop-off point at the hotel. Much to his surprise, Lady Catherine stood on the footpath between the two drunken stockmen and never batted an eyelid. Dressed in khaki trousers and a crisp white long-sleeve linen shirt with the sleeves rolled up Territory style, and her unruly strawberry blonde curls pinned high upon her head, she looked a picture of good health and total elegance. James gathered the two suitcases and whispered to Catherine to follow him into the hotel before they woke the two stockmen from their drunken stupor. As James led Catherine past the front bar of the hotel towards the reception office beyond, an unruly ruckus broke out among the drinkers. Loud wolf whistles, accompanied by toasts 'to the lady', and the 'best looking broad in the Territory', spilled out from the blue-singlet brigade as James hurriedly climbed a flight of wooden stairs to Catherine's suite of rooms where he neatly placed the two caramel coloured leather suitcases on the luggage stand near the window. Lady Catherine stood in the doorway silently taking it all in. She allowed her beautiful green eyes to drift about the room and over the furnishings before coming to a halt on James. "James, thank you…the room is old but clean, the linen is clean and the view across that deep blue bay is to die for…a lovely room to recuperate in for a day or two. Thank you…thank you, James." The room was warm and filled with a good dose of the Territory's high, and at times suffocating humidity. Its cooling system was a large vulgar and slow overhead fan that emitted a knock on each full turn. But none of this was about to deter the Lady Catherine from feeling that today she was reasonably well off here, in the Australian Outback. Turning to her friend with her long arms reaching out, both Catherine and James moved swiftly towards each other. James gathered Catherine gently into his arms and gazed down into her teary eyes while ever so gently running his pointer finger across her still healing and rather large pink facial scars. They were not and never would be visible to him. Catherine flinched and stiffened her torso, remembering her doctor had told her that 'She would carry these scars for many years to come, if not for the rest of her life'. James, tall and physically strong, held her firmly to him, allowing him time to search into the depths of her soul, while her movement and slight resistance against him only made him want her even more. While holding Catherine's undivided attention, James whispered to Catherine, "Catherine, do you realise you are truly more beautiful now than ever before?" Catherine immediately relaxed into

James's strong arms, and allowed her beautiful mischievous smile to return to her face once more. For now Lady Catherine felt warm, safe and comfortable in the arms of the man she loved, and always had loved from the time they were children and had competed in equestrian events on the moors back home in England. While still entwined in each other's warm embrace, James moved towards the bed, lifted her lightweight body into his arms and placed her gently upon the bright cotton bedcover. Bar for the constant knock of the overhead fan, James and Catherine lay holding each other tightly, fully dressed and totally silent, both consciously fearful of losing the beautiful secure feeling of the love they had now both found.

As the chartered light aircraft flew low over the corrugated iron roof of the homestead on Lonesome Downs, the experienced pilot pointed out certain landmarks and points he thought would be of interest to James and Catherine. James was somewhat surprised to see just how rugged the landscape of Lonesome Downs really was, a mixture of mountainous ranges and deep gorges which fed a large river not that far from the homestead. All this was separated by valleys and brown plains dotted with billabongs and freshwater springs. Their pilot offered the biggest surprise of all when he pointed out the deep blue ocean beyond. "As the crow flies, it is about ten mile from the homestead," he said. James was gobsmacked. His Grandfather had never mentioned the wild ruggedness of the landscape, or even that they had access to the sea. James sat back in his seat, took hold of Lady Catherine's hand and said, "This property excites me, the whole formation of the land, it's a frontier filled with unidentified challenges to be met face on...what do you think Catherine?" Up until this point Catherine hadn't taken her eyes from the aircraft's small window, for she was mesmerised by the landscape. Catherine squeezed James's hand and looked up into his eyes. "James I know this is something you need to attend to, for I can feel the ripples of excitement from you... and I am truly happy for you, but, the habitation is so like Africa. It really does frighten me. For this country is so vast and isolated too, and..." Lady Catherine stopped mid-sentence and drew a heart with her finger on the back of James's broad hand. She did care deeply for this man, and hoped James's love for this vast cattle station in Outback Australia wasn't going to come between their feelings for each other. With Lady Catherine's words fresh in his mind, James leaned towards Catherine, pulled her closer to him and gently placed a kiss on her forehead, for he fully understood her fear. "Catherine, for the moment let's concentrate on the here and now. We have another five days together before your long return flight to good old England. Let us enjoy it and really get to know each other." Catherine smiled, happy to again be in agreement with James.

Looking out of the aircraft's window, James noted the extremely sad state of the Lonesome Downs airstrip. He could see that Tom had attempted to drag a lump of old railway iron from one end of the dirt strip to the other behind the Land Rover, trying to flatten the tough grey ant beds and clumps of dead grass that had taken over the strip during the previous Wet Season. Then, taking hold of Catherine's hand to reassure her all would be fine with their landing at the station's strip, James silently prayed to the powers that be…for just that. The aircraft hit the uneven ground with one hell of a thud, bounced over tufts of dead grass, and manoeuvred around the low grey ant beds. The noise from the whirring propellers scattered a mob of black feral pigs feeding close by. Their capable pilot brought the aircraft to a halt right by Tom and the busted-arse Land Rover.

James sensed Lady Catherine's relief to be safely on the ground. He again took hold of her hand to offer her further encouragement, for James accepted that all this vast ruggedness of the Outback would no doubt be alien to her. Lady Catherine hardly acknowledged James's gesture, and had gone quiet. James understood the rough landing may have unsettled her ladyship, and now he worried she may wish to return to Darwin immediately, and promptly leave for England.

Tom was there with his mile-wide smile to greet both James and his lady friend to Lonesome Downs Station. "Welcome home James…yahoo…and to you too ma'am, you look a darned sight prettier now than you did the last time I saw you." Tom introduced Bones the old caretaker and his wife, Quartpot, Spanner and Ringer, and a bunch of snotty nose kids from the black's camp on the river. "They wanted to watch this big white bird land here," offered Tom. Lady Catherine stood silent, trying to unravel her future here in the middle of nowhere with James Wentworth. What of her ailing father back home in England, and his expectations of her? Catherine lifted her head and looked towards the distant horizon. There was nothing but dead brown tufts of grass and areas of scorched red dirt. Despite the warmth, Catherine still felt cold and afraid. "Ar...ma'am," Tom said noticing the lady seemed many miles away and 'probably on the bloody green moors of England,' "Penny's got the kettle on the boil, let's get over to the homestead for a cuppa." Tom then began loading Catherine's two heavy suitcases and James's swag and duffel bag onto the back of the Land Rover while James paid the pilot. But before James did he took Lady Catherine aside and had a quiet conversation with her. It had gone well, for Catherine cracked a smile and stayed on the station as the aircraft belted down the runway, lifted high into the clear blue sky and was gone.

The Lonesome Downs homestead wasn't large by any means, and probably rougher than most others in the district. It was short on doors, and hardly had a pane of glass in any of its window frames. The homestead consisted of two bedrooms, a large kitchen-cum-dining room with a rough looking wood stove as its feature, a shower that somehow emitted the odd electric shock to those who used it and a flush toilet. Out back of the corrugated homestead was a copper and a couple of cement troughs, plus a washboard. Further out on the flat was a long drop dunny and an outside shower. Tom, his partner Penny and baby Tommy had one bedroom which left the other bedroom with two single beds for James and Lady Catherine to share. In a little wooden cottage just off the river bank lived the same old caretaker couple who had looked after Lonesome Downs for the past twenty-five years, back in James's Grandfather's time. This was a blessing thought James, for he hoped they would remain with Tom and himself to point out the good and the bad of the property to them.

James and Catherine stood in the bedroom doorway. The room was vacant bar for one cupboard and a simple chest of draws. Catherine gave James's hand a gentle squeeze, turned towards him on tip-toe and planted a kiss right on his lips. "Dear James, I know I'm here with you for just this one week, and I'll admit, I'm afraid of the isolation. I want to help make you comfortable so you and Tom can make this station work." These were the few words that James had wanted to hear from Catherine, and he certainly didn't want her here with him if it wasn't her wish too. To be afraid was to be expected, but in time James hoped it was possible for Catherine to overcome her fears. James took Catherine into his arms, then looked over her head towards the two single beds and smiled. "I apologise I have nothing better to offer you at this time my lady," and they both laughed. James couldn't help but notice that this very room was at some time in the past his beloved Grandfather's bedroom. Framed on the far wall was the Wentworth family coat of arms.

Penny and the caretaker's wife had presented the bedroom as best they could with what they had, but it still turned out to be a reasonably rough night for Catherine. Even the protection of the white mosquito nets tucked tightly under each mattress wasn't sufficient to deter the mosquitoes, or prepare Catherine for what was to come. For the mosquitoes seemed larger than any spitfire bomber, and their irritating whine was twice as loud. When James had kissed Catherine a good night, he tried to reassure her that the humidity of the day would fade into the wee hours of the night, but it wasn't so. Just before midnight, a mopoke owl frightened the hell out of them both with its loud and unusual call from the window sill. This was followed only hours later by a pack of dingoes serenading the new owner and his terrified companion. Heaven forbid thought James, Grandfather hadn't mentioned any nighttime entertainment when reciting his travel tales to me back home in England. Then it hit James – his Grandfather was probably inebriated on good quality whiskey anyway.

At breakfast the following morning, James and Tom made plans for the next couple of days. Tom had planned on surveying the property with 'Bones', the old caretaker, and would be away all day, while James planned to spend some quality time with Lady Catherine down on Bullocka's Billabong, which had always been a favourite place of his Grandfather. Together James and Catherine made several rounds of corned beef and pickle sandwiches. James picked up a billycan made from a used Sunshine Milk tin and grabbed an old grey army blanket from the cupboard. Happiness filled the air as James and Catherine left the homestead following a well-used footpath towards what was James's Grandfather's favourite place on Lonesome Downs. Within half an hour of following the winding path through high spear grass they arrived at Bullocka's Billabong.

"James…I've never seen anything quite so beautiful. Look at the many large blue flowers floating across the water, all this surrounded by those huge ghost gum trees you spoke of earlier." Standing quietly together on the edge of the billabong James had to agree. Even while working on Campbell's Run Station he had never come across an abundance of blue water lilies such as this. A whoosh of wings followed by panicked honking broke the silence as hundreds of wild ducks lifted from among the water lilies to resettle at the far end of the billabong.

Lady Catherine screamed, spun around and very nearly flattened James as she tried to distance herself as far away as possible from the immediate terror. James, super fit and fast on his feet, grabbed hold of Catherine around the waist and pulled her securely into his arms offering words of comfort. Catherine, physically shaken and extremely fearful of the unknown, clung tightly to James, not ever wanting to let him go. James reciprocated by holding Catherine firmly in his arms until he felt she had allowed a sense of calm to return to her body. Lifting her up, James carried this beautiful and now vulnerable woman towards the grey blanket spread under the ghost gums on the banks of the billabong.

"James," whispered Lady Catherine in a voice that still wasn't quite her own, "I'm terribly sorry James, what a fool I must have looked to you." Tears had begun to well in Catherine's beautiful emerald eyes, for she had been truly frightened. James placed his finger gently against Catherine's rose lips for he couldn't bear to see her cry again. "It's alright my dear, please don't cry my love." On hearing James's soothing words, Catherine felt safe and secure, and allowed her body to relax. James placed Catherine on the blanket and lay beside her. He raised his body up on one elbow to be much closer to Catherine and brushed back those loose tentacles of wild blonde hair glued to her forehead by the Outback's warmth.

James was no fool; he had noticed Lady Catherine had gone from a strong individual before her cliff accident on Campbell's Run Station to a more vulnerable person in the aftermath. But what had left James completely puzzled in the aftermath of Catherine's cliff accident was that she had never spoken a word, or even asked a question regarding it. James would bet his much loved Akruba hat on Catherine's strength and confidence returning, for time was a marvellous healer he believed. Yes, thought James, time had certainly been a healer. It suddenly dawned on him that he was no longer angry with his older brother Morgan, who before his sudden death had planned to wed the Lady Catherine of Hamilton Hill while James was far away in the Australian Outback. When the time was right, two of England's wealthiest families had acknowledged an unspoken agreement that James and Lady Catherine would one day wed and unite two of the country's largest farming empires. For some reason unknown to James, older brother Morgan was tempted to throw a spanner in the family's belief.

James leaned towards Catherine, meeting her lips halfway, kissing her lightly at first, then deeply and more passionately as his want for this beautiful lady swelled into wild hunger. Catherine's love and desire for James was as deep as his for her, for the ache in her own lower region had become an unbearable need. Both started breathing heavily and Catherine could feel the dampness in her womanhood build as her need for James grew. This was all new to her, for she had never experienced or wanted another man as she now desperately wanted to have James. James moved across on top of Catherine, lightly brushing her virginal womanhood with his hardened penis. Catherine reciprocated by raising her body towards James, electrifying both. Still both fully clothed, the gentleman in James came rushing forward, reminding him that there was a time and place for them to unleash their powerful love and hunger for each other, but not right now. With these thoughts in mind, James moved ever so gently from above Catherine, which slowly brought their highly intensified emotions back to normal. "Not right now my love, we must give you time to fully recuperate from your accident." Still on the picnic blanket, Lady Catherine lay shaken and emotional as she tried to gather herself and understand the depth of her own feelings for James – she had never before experienced such great love for any other. After the intenseness of the moment faded, James rose to his feet, shaken as he'd realised just how close they had both come to consummating their love for each other. With their hearts still racing, James locked eyes with Catherine as he assisted his beautiful lady to her feet. Still unable to let her loving gaze go, James pulled Lady Catherine firmly into his arms without losing contact with her eyes and asked, "My Lady Catherine of Hamilton Hill...would you consider marrying me?" Lady Catherine stood on her tiptoes, placed a hand either side of James's face and brought it down to meet her own. "Yes...yes, James Wentworth, I love you more than you would ever know." James whispered in Catherine's ear, "When the time is right my lady, I now make a promise to you...that I will more than show you just how much I do really love you."

CHAPTER 34

Love and Pain

Back at the Lonesome Downs homestead, James and Catherine were greeted by Tom. "Found your way to the billabong alright? Excuse the language ma'am, but you've both got bloody big grins on your dials." Tom was unable to wipe his mile-wide smile from his own face. "We did Tom," answered Catherine. "It is one of the most beautiful vistas I have ever seen, and now it will forever hold a very special place in my heart." Catherine smiled and looked at James. "Please James, you tell Tom and Penny." James broke their good news to both Tom and Penny, with Tom suggesting an immediate need for them all to celebrate this special occasion. But before any celebrations could begin James needed to immediately prepare a telegram to Catherine's father, the Lord Hamilton of Hamilton Hill Estate, asking for his lordship's permission to take the hand of his daughter, the Lady Catherine, to unite in marriage on his return to England in the near future. "Well, I suppose that's the right thing to do…pardon me again ma'am, but isn't it a tad old fashioned? I mean look at Penny and me and our son Tommy here, we got stuck right into it…with or without a wedding ring." James turned to Tom and said, "Tom as soon as we receive blessings from Lord Hamilton, I promise you we will all celebrate his blessings together."

James went into the dusty storeroom, flicked some cobwebs out of the way and pulled up a Sunlight Soap box to sit on. Holding his telegram, he tuned in to the station's two-way radio base, but before he was able to make the outgoing call, James heard the station's call sign followed by 'please come in'.

"Better answer that radio James, got an incoming call," yelled Tom from the kitchen. James promptly answered in his cultured English accent, "Eight-kilo-x-ray to base, reading you loud and clear, go ahead please." Tom got up from the kitchen table and moved closer to James in the radio room.

"Base to eight-kilo-x-ray, we have a telegram for a Mr James Alexander Wentworth. Reading:

'It is with much sadness that we must deliver this terrible news to you via telegram stop Your father, the Lord Alexander Wentworth III of Rosengarten Castle England, is now deceased stop It is with much regret that I inform you he died from a horse-riding accident during yesterday's Championship Equestrian event stop It is imperative you return home to England immediately stop My deepest condolences Lady Elizabeth Wentworth stop'"

The telegram was from Grand-mama.

Stunned, James sat at the radio unable to reply to base. He tried to digest this shocking news from home relayed to him via his Grand-mama. Tom jumped in and took over the radio, asking the operator to repeat the telegram. This time Tom would write it down word for word. Tom got the gist of the telegram immediately, while James wondered why the Wentworth family was still on the merry-go-round of awful tragedies which had all ended in death. Tom wrote the telegram into the appropriate diary and put his arm around his mate's shoulders. "Bloody hell James…can't bloody believe it…another tragedy in your family." Tom began to wonder if James had run over a bloody Chinaman. James looked up at Tom saying, "Thanks for taking that telegram down Tom…I had meant to but…"

At that moment the two-way radio crackled again with another telegram, this time for the Lady Catherine. Tom took immediate control. It was from Lady Catherine's father of Hamilton Hill England requesting she return to England immediately for Lord Alexander had met with tragedy and was deceased. Lord Hamilton had also sent a separate telegram to James, only this time addressing it to;

'The Lord James Alexander Wentworth IV of Lonesome Downs Station sending my sincere condolences upon hearing of the tragic death of your father, the Lord Alexander Wentworth III.' It was signed Lord Hamilton, England.

Later that morning Tom arranged a charter flight to collect James and Catherine from Lonesome Downs Station and deliver them directly to Darwin Airport where tickets had been arranged for the couple's return flight to England the following day.

In the privacy of the couple's bedroom, James broke the news of his father's sudden death to Lady Catherine. Standing in deep silence, each holding and taking comfort from the other, James and Catherine both realised that Lord Alexander's death had brought with it not only sadness to his family and friends, but also the prospect of massive changes for James.

James had been the sickly second son, born to Lord Alexander III and Lady Gabrielle Wentworth of Rosengarten Castle. As a child, James had been the weaker of the two until he reached maturity, when the tables turned. While growing up James believed he would be forever free of the realm and restrictions attached to it, and Australia would be his destiny. James hadn't forgotten how the establishment's staff had treated him as a child, always made to play second fiddle to his older brother Morgan, for it was well known Morgan would be the future Lord Wentworth IV of Rosengarten Castle. Even his Grandfather had said he believed young James was more suited to the freedom of Australia than England. Now, shocked by the sudden loss of his own father and the realisation of his responsibilities to family in England, James wished he could wipe from his mind forever the feeling of being cheated of his Australian dream.

After an early dinner that evening Catherine and Penny played with baby Tommy on a blanket on the dining room floor. James and his Aussie friend had a heck of a lot to talk about. James discussed managing the station with Tom, and suggested that after twelve months assessing the situation James would like to cut Tom in on a share of the cattle property. In the meantime Tom would have access to a bank account in Darwin for wages, improvements and living expenses. James would see to that.

To arrive back in England during the middle of a white winter wasn't the welcome back James had wanted. Lady Catherine handled the cold much better than James, although her time away in Australia had gone from her planned one week to six weeks. Lady Catherine had loved her time in the Australian Outback, its beauty and birdlife. Sadly it was marred by her terrible accident –something she never spoke of or asked questions about since – at Mitchell Gorge on Campbell's Run Station in the Northern Territory.

James rode with the Lady Catherine in Rosengarten's chauffeur driven Bentley to Hamilton Hill Estate. James wished to speak with Lord Hamilton himself. "James, you have a lot to attend to at Rosengarten Castle, your poor mother and Grand-mama, they must be distraught," offered an understanding Lady Catherine. "My dear lady, I wish to deliver you home safely to your father first…it is my duty. It is also imperative I speak with Lord Hamilton, for I shall ask him for your hand in marriage my lady." James was feeling extremely proud and content to be in the company of the Lady Catherine, and found it difficult to hide that mischievous twinkle in his eyes when taking in her striking beauty. Catherine took hold of James's work-hardened hand and looked into his deep blue eyes, where he now carried a few 'worry lines of wisdom'. "I do love you James…very much so," she offered before surprising him with a kiss on the lips.

On arrival at Hamilton Hill Castle they were met by Duncan, the family's head butler and manservant to Lord Hamilton. Duncan promptly delivered both Lady Catherine and James to Lord Hamilton's private rooms in the far right wing of the castle. Here they found Lord Hamilton dressed in an elaborate black and maroon silk dressing gown. His manservant made sure of his lordship's comfort, tucking a small pillow and woollen blanket around his now frail frame in the wheelchair. James noted the bright colours of his lordship's dressing gown did nothing to hide the obvious – Lord Hamilton's health had deteriorated considerably.

The furnishings were elegant and extremely expensive, James noted. There was no doubt that Lord Hamilton was more than pleased to have his daughter home from the wilds of the Australian Outback, for he greeted Lady Catherine with tears of absolute joy. His lordship then reached out to James with a frail hand dominated by an oversized emerald ring. He took hold of James's hand in his own, held on to it and then thanked James sincerely for taking care of his adventurous daughter.

Lady Catherine sat quietly close by, unable to hide her deep admiration of James and for what seemed her father's acceptance of him. Lord Hamilton then reached for his daughter's hand as well. Holding both, he sat in deep silence, as if studying James's suntanned and work-hardened hands, before lifting his gaze to James and telling him just how sorry he was to hear of Lord Wentworth's sudden death. "James, have no doubt in your own abilities son, you are more than capable of managing your family's farming estate and much more," his lordship offered. James was stunned but pleased by Lord Hamilton's words of encouragement. For he was well known in their circle of society for being a hard-nosed banker and a grumpy old bugger, certainly not one to hand out praise freely, and he had never suffered a fool lightly. Lord Hamilton continued. "I may be speaking out of turn here James…and please forgive me if I am, but your Grandfather and father have both spoken highly of your previous achievements here and in Australia. James was overwhelmed, and believed he should take this very opportunity to ask Lord Hamilton for his daughter's hand in marriage.

Both Lady Catherine and James were seated on the carpeted floor by the ailing Lord Hamilton. Each still had hold of his lordship's hand as James asked his lordship for Lady Catherine's hand in marriage. Lord Hamilton looked to Catherine. "Do you really love this gentleman Catherine?" "Yes…yes, father…more than you would ever know," cried Lady Catherine. James leant towards Catherine and kissed her gently on the forehead. "This union between the two of you…I know is the one made in heaven." Tears of joy rolled down the old man's heavily lined face as he again and again gave both Catherine and James his total blessings, adding, "If I should die this very day, I would die an extremely happy and content man." Shortly the manservant arrived to an overjoyed Lord Hamilton who was promptly reminded that "It is now time for your afternoon rest Sir." Agreeable and now a happy man, and without any form of protest, his lordship allowed his manservant to return him to his suite of rooms in the far right wing of the castle. Lady Catherine accompanied James to his waiting Bentley.

CHAPTER 35

End of an Era

To be overflowing with great happiness one minute, and the turmoil of draining sadness the next, was how James felt on leaving Lady Catherine behind with her father at their Hamilton Hill Castle. James's heart missed a beat as his driver delivered him past the huge granite lions at the gated entrance of his family's property of Rosengarten Castle. James felt queasy in his stomach on his arrival, for now the realisation of the whole situation really hit home. James understood there was a whole lot expected of him now as he was the only surviving male of the entire Wentworth lineage.

But before his wandering mind delved too deeply into his future responsibilities, James needed to greet his mother Lady Gabrielle and Grand-mama Lady Elizabeth, for the shock of another death in the family would surely take its toll on them both. Lady Elizabeth was as sharp as a tack, a spritely and immaculately groomed ninety-year-old woman. Lady Gabrielle on the other hand was the complete opposite, thought James. Her beauty had never ceased to fail her, but that terrible depression sickness had taken its toll.

Alone in the Bentley, and quite comfortable in his leather seat, James allowed his mind to drift back over his earlier years at Rosengarten Castle. He remembered how he was of slighter build and blonder than his older brother Morgan's more robust Spanish appearance. But his slight build never took from James the happy memories associated with his childhood. Sadly, older brother Morgan had tragically passed away in mysterious but unspeakable circumstances, and while he would be missed, his theatrical performances wouldn't be.

Then there were his much loved grandparents, and although his Grandfather was now deceased, Lord Wentworth II had left behind a Pandora's box of stories and colourful tales from his much loved travels abroad. On the other hand, the strength behind the Wentworth men in past years was dear Grand-mama, the woman a young James had always admired. Grand-mama was still here with her many strands of pearls and wisdom. James hoped Lady Elizabeth would remain with the family for some time yet, for deep down he knew he needed her strength.

His mother Lady Gabrielle, who James loved very much, was often envied by other women in their circle of society for her classical French beauty, for she had an abundance of cascading chestnut curls and a feminine figure to match, even now in her later years, thought James. However, he couldn't help but worry over Gabrielle's health, and believed at times she was away with the fairies when that terribly depression sickness had a hold on her. Now father was gone too, a horse accident they say, which didn't quite make sense to James given that Lord Alexander Wentworth III had always been so particular when he took to the jumps. In the past, he had always made a point of tightening the girth on his own saddle prior to competing in any type of horse event. Then again, James felt he never did understand what happened to his father's loyalties when it came to his marriage to his mother Gabrielle. It was common knowledge that Lord Wentworth III had wedded the most beautiful woman in all England, but still entertained a carriage of mistresses.

The Bentley stopped at the front entrance of Rosengarten Castle. Head butler Muldoon stepped up to greet James with open arms. After James had shaken Muldoon's hand, he held onto to it a little longer than was necessary, for both men respected each other, and James had noted tears well in the old butler's eyes. Muldoon had attended to, and buried, three generations of Wentworth males. All three generations of men were similar in many ways, for they had been tarnished by the Wentworth family curse of being unfaithful to wives – and even mistresses. The three, with their love of whiskey, wild orgies and the occasional dabble in narcotics, had died well before their time. Yes, a terrible shame, thought James.

"Lord James Alexander Wentworth IV, welcome home to Rosengarten Castle Sir," the ageing Muldoon offered as the pair stood at the front entrance of Rosengarten Castle. "Thank you Muldoon...I will always be simply James to you Sir." Muldoon arranged for a valet to carry James's suitcase to his rooms before he himself would inform both Grand-mama, Lady Elizabeth, and his mother, Lady Gabrielle, of James's homecoming.

James decided there was no real need for formalities. He would tidy himself up, collect both his Grand-mama and mother from their own suite of rooms, and have them join him by the log fire that Muldoon had warming the family's green and gold lounge room. James had arranged for Muldoon to bring out the fine crystal glasses, for not only was there sadness in their lives, but James was determined to announce his and Lady Catherine's engagement to his remaining family members this very night.

"James," cried out Grand-mama, who was visibly shaken from all that had gone on at Rosengarten since James was last at home. "I'm so sorry to have had to telegram you of your father's sudden death, please forgive me dear." James comforted and assured Grand-mama that there was no other way he could possibly have received the news any sooner in the Outback of Australia. Grand-mama delved into her beaded handbag and pulled out a fine cotton handkerchief and began to hurriedly pat at her tears. Her face was that of an elderly person who struggled to accept the death of her only child, Lord Alexander Wentworth III, James's father. Grand-mama gathered herself and sat upright, her back as straight as a rod in her favourite lounge chair, but her face was tired and swollen, and her eyes red and bloodshot from crying. Dear God, thought a now travel-weary James, I should have been here... father's death has really taken its toll on Grand-mama. This worried James because Grand-mama had always been the strength behind the Wentworth males. Shocked, James silently pledged to himself that from this night on he would take on all responsibility for Rosengarten Castle and the family owned farming estates. Yes, he would lift all worry from his loved ones' tired shoulders. During James's conversation with his Grand-mama, he noticed his mother moving slowly about the green and gold lounge room gathering up one photo frame after another and piling them on the ornate coffee table in the far corner of the room.

James made a mental note to speak with his mother of her intentions for the photos at some other time. Then it dawned on him. Dear Lord, thought James, I believe mother is disposing of father's photos already... and what if Grand-mama found out?'

"Mother," called James, "won't you come and join us now...I wish to pour the tea before it becomes cold?" While James waited patiently for Gabrielle's answer, Lady Elizabeth leaned closer to James. "James, did you hear that on the night of Morgan's terrible death, our lovely kitchen maid had also received an awful gash to her hand while cleaning up the broken glass left behind by the rowdy bunch in the ballroom? Muldoon told me that while everyone ran around in a flap over the gun shots, it was your dear friend Lady Catherine who had kindly taken it upon herself to administer first aid to the girl." "No Grand-mama...I never heard, I left for Australia the following week." James felt himself burning with shame; of course that was the answer to the spray of blood on Lady Catherine's powder-blue ball gown and matching evening slipper he told himself.

Gabrielle floated towards her youngest and only surviving son with open arms, and then she too broke down crying. Gabrielle's chestnut hair was pulled into curls high upon her head, while her deep amethyst gown only helped emphasise the clean lines of her neck and shoulders. Mother, thought James, was still very beautiful considering the sudden death of father. Somehow James felt that his father's death may have brought some form of relief to his mother's life. And it did, for Gabrielle would no longer have to carry on with that awful charade of a blissfully happy marriage to Lord Alexander Wentworth III now that she could be at peace with herself and the world.

Lord Alexander Wentworth III's burial was held three days after James had arrived home to Rosengarten Castle. His father was buried among his ancestors under the old oak tree in the family cemetery. The three remaining Wentworth family members chose not to turn Lord Alexander Wentworth's funeral into a rip-roaring party event, as would have happened in the past.

Three months later, James and Lady Catherine's elaborate wedding ceremony was held in the chapel on her father's Hamilton Hill Castle. The event hit the front pages of all the worthy newspapers throughout England and Europe. It was described as the 'most spectacular society wedding of the year.'

Acknowledgements

Thank you, Michael, for your support and availability
as a sounding board.

Big hugs to Tara. Your patience and support of all things technical
while having three little girls to contend with.

For you Rob, Brock and Cohen, Well …
I know this novel is a bit naughty.

Love you my beautiful Granddaughters. Lilah, Ella, Mia and
Annabelle – your joyfulness brightened my days.

For Leisha and Michaela, 'Naughty, Sexy and Outback'
I know you girls understand.

An extra big thank you to Pickawoowoo Publishing team and
Julie-Ann Harper. Your positive support and guidance
wrapped in a tonne of patience was second to none.

To my editor (Eddie Albrecht), whom I haven't yet met – a very big hug and thank you. Hopefully, I haven't embarrassed you with my written thoughts.

Love Sheryl xxx

About the Author

Sheryl McCorry grew up in the rugged Outback of the Northern Territory, Australia, where she spent her childhood running barefoot and free. Fishing and hunting in crocodile infested billabongs and waterways, her only companions were the local Aboriginal women.

At 18, Broome beckoned and so did a fast-talking Yank. Within an hour of this marriage it ended, when Sheryl locked eyes with Bob McCorry – a well-seasoned and hardened Kimberly cattleman, drover and buffalo shooter – the beginning of a romance with a man twice her age.

Bob supported her in a tough apprenticeship which took Sheryl to the Kimberley's harshest frontiers, where she learnt to catch rogue bulls and muster wild cattle, the only woman in a team of Aboriginal stockmen.

But Sheryl needed more than the stock camp in her life, and at 32 she became the first woman in the Kimberley to manage two million-acre cattle stations. So, began a lifetime of wild adventure of love, loss and excruciating heartbreak.

Three bestselling autobiographies have been written from a lifetime of diaries.

Gathering of the Realm is Sheryl's first novel, a blend of fact and fiction born from hiring a member of the realm to work on the McCorry's isolated cattle station in the West Kimberley. It is also, of course, a loving tribute to Sheryl's great love of the Outback and the rugged beauty of Australia's last frontier.

Today Sheryl lives on a farm north of Albany, Western Australia, and is still involved with cattle.